I got back to the parking lot just in time to see Susan's silver BMW flash away into the night. I ran to my car and followed. It was a hell of a long shot that she would be going any place interesting, but the rest of the evening had been a total loss, so I thought I might as well roll the dice.

They came up craps. She was going home. Her driveway wound around the outside of the development, past the garages attached to each unit. I drove down it. Perhaps a half-block from what I thought was Susan's garage I parked and got out of the car, intending to walk past her garage to see if any other cars were parked nearby. As I stepped out of the car I heard the flat *crack* of a long barreled pistol and the windshield of my car starred with a hundred tiny cracks.

I dropped flat on the pavement and inched my way back behind the car. . . .

JUDGMENT BY FIRE

Fredrick D. Huebner

FAWCETT GOLD MEDAL • NEW YORK

With Special Thanks To—

Robert Walton Sargeant, for sharing his knowledge of the King County Courthouse, and for a dozen years of friendship,

And

Harry E. Jennings, Jr., mentor and friend

Sometimes I feel like a hitchhiker
caught in a hailstorm
on a Texas highway.
I can't run
I can't hide
and I can't make it stop.

—Attributed to Lyndon Baines Johnson

CHAPTER 1

Somehow, this all started with a football game.

There is a football game played on the morning of every New Year's day in Seattle. It is a small game, played to empty concrete stands at the municipal stadium in Seattle Center. The field isn't covered, and the Northwest climate can usually be counted on to provide gray skies and bone-chilling rain. The game is supposed to be touch football, but the rules are freely interpreted. The touch can be anything from a hand slap to a full cross-body block. Broken bones are not uncommon.

The game started in the late 1960s as a match between two men's dormitories at the University of Washington. The teams are still called the Capitalist Pigs and the Running Dogs, but the names have stuck for purely sentimental reasons. The players now are mostly stockbrokers and salesmen of this and that, with the odd doctor and teacher and lawyer thrown in. It is a middle-class or better group. The players are all in their late thirties or early forties, the age when aches and pains start to linger, reminders that no one escapes the passage of time. The game is one small way the players have to give time a kick in the teeth.

This New Year's Day was my first game playing for the Running Dogs. My friend Hugh Prokop had recruited me to fill in for the Dogs' linebacker and tight end, a dentist sidelined by a broken ankle. Despite a massive collective

1

hangover, the Dogs took it, 28–21. The Pigs provided the party that came afterward.

The post-game party was held in Bellevue, at the house of a man named Greg Van Zandt. Van Zandt was the quarterback of the Pigs, a big solid man with a square Dutch face and white-blond hair. He was supposed to be some kind of financial genius, owning an investment company with offices in Bellevue, Seattle's high-tech business suburb across Lake Washington. I hadn't met Van Zandt before the game. I didn't know about the genius part, but the man had my respect. He could throw a mud-slick football thirty-five yards in the rain.

Unsure of my directions, I had driven straight to the party from the game, following Van Zandt's gunmetal Jaguar Van den Plas across the Lake Washington floating bridge and into Bellevue's curving, wooded streets.

Van Zandt's house was in the upscale Clyde Hill section of Bellevue, on the slope above Lake Washington. It was new, built of cedar and glass in a sort of modernized Victorian style, with big eaves and bay windows on the upper story. Stained gray, with blue trim, the house stood on over an acre of prime suburban property, with extensive gardens set around a tiered, gray-stained redwood deck overlooking the lake. A walkway wound down the hill from the main deck to a small Japanese-style bathhouse with showers and a large Jacuzzi pool. Van Zandt had given me a cigar and a bottle of beer, then loaned me his bathhouse to shower off the mud, grass, and sweat of the game.

After the shower, I tried the Jacuzzi. The water in the pool was boiling hot, and I soaked in it until the soreness in my legs and back began to go away. Given the water, a cold Heineken, and one of Van Zandt's little Cuban cigars, I was as close to heaven as I was ever going to get.

I soaked for twenty minutes or so, then turned off the Jacuzzi pump and floated in the silent water, eyes closed, drifting, not asleep and yet not fully conscious. After what seemed like a long time I heard the silver sound of women laughing. I opened my eyes.

Two women stood at the entrance to the bathhouse. One

was tall and blond, with high thin features and warm brown—rather than ice-blue—eyes, as though the Scandinavian had mixed with the Slav somewhere in her genes. The other woman was short and busty, with dark, Semitic good looks and long black hair. They wore swimsuits and carried towels. As I looked at them the thought passed through my mind that I had gone directly from shower to pool. And that I wasn't wearing any clothes.

Sometimes you just have to smile. I did. "Hello," I said.

Both women laughed again, this time at my discomfort. Anyone who thinks the nakedness taboo is just so much silly social conditioning ought to try it with a couple of total strangers.

The tall blond woman spoke first. "Hello, Matthew Riordan," she said. "Remember me? I'm Susan Haight. I've been dating Hugh Prokop for the last couple of months."

"Of course," I answered, lying politely while trying to conjure up the memory of where and how we had met. "Where's Hugh?"

"He's still up at the main house, with the rest of the party. What brings you out here?"

"I needed a place to shower, and the Jacuzzi was just too tempting to resist."

"It is nice. By the way, this is my friend, Sandra Kessler. I don't know if you've met her; her husband works at Van Zandt & Company with me. Sandy, this is Matthew Riordan. He's a friend of Hugh's, and his lawyer."

"Very pleased to meet you," I said to Sandy Kessler. "You'll forgive me if I don't get up."

Sandy Kessler laughed again. Her laugh was low and throaty and might have made me wonder about her plans for later on if she hadn't been married. "Don't sweat it, Matthew," she said, reaching down to pat my shoulder. "We'll just jump right in with you."

They dropped their towels and stepped into the water. When they were settled in, Susan Haight said, "Sandy's husband Walter is here, somewhere. Do you know him?"

"I think so. Isn't he Hugh's accountant?"

"He is," Susan replied, "but last year he joined Van Zandt & Company as our chief financial officer. That's not my area; I'm a broker and financial planner."

"I've heard that your company is doing very well," I said politely. "Every time I pick up the business page of the newspaper I see another story about you. You guys must be hot."

"Us and the market, which is warming up to crack 2500 on the Dow. It really has been exciting. At the risk of sounding crass, you should talk to us about your investments sometime. We've been doing a great job for our clients. Some of our partnerships and currency investments are yielding better than thirty percent a year."

"I would if you loaned me the money," I said, laughing. "Seriously, I really don't do much stock investing or anything like that. A bank account is about as daring as I get."

"I understand," Susan said, somehow taking this seriously. "Many successful people need advice in handling their finances. But putting money in a bank is just like standing still." She grinned. "Call me if you want to swing a little."

"Or me," Sandy added. Her thigh nudged mine under the water. I let that pass in a moment of awkward silence.

Their talk drifted around to Bellevue social doings, parties and gallery openings and business receptions at the new and booming computer-software and real estate companies headquartered in Bellevue and Redmond. I listened with half an ear, drifting in and out, nodding politely when the moment came. "Jennifer's winter formal was *wonderful*," Sandy Kessler was saying as I came back to attention. "Jenny's my daughter, sixteen and beautiful," she added for my benefit. "The boy she went with is a real hunk, a junior but starting on the football and basketball teams. His family isn't too well-off, though, so we pitched in and paid for the limousine for the night. I wanted to get them a helicopter to fly them to the dance, like our neighbors did last year, but you know Walter, he just refused to pay for it."

I didn't know Walter, but I murmured something sympathetically. A helicopter? I had gone to my senior prom in a 1957 Dodge pickup.

I was still listening to the women's conversation when a voice at the open arched entrance to the bathhouse boomed, "I knew we'd find Riordan out here! And look, he's got the women."

Greg Van Zandt and Hugh Prokop walked in wearing swimsuits, white towels draped around their shoulders. Van Zandt stood an inch over six feet, tan and well muscled in the arms and shoulders, with only a hint of a roll around his waist. Hugh Prokop was shorter and stocky, with big shoulders and thick, muscular arms. He had dark curly hair and a wide laughing smile.

"We caught Matthew out here, Greg," Susan said. "No clothes on, either. Shameful."

"Fine by me," Van Zandt said. He threw his white towel on a cedarwood bench and peeled off his black swimsuit before stepping into the water. "Ah. Advances the schedule of the party by four or five hours. Good job, Matt."

Hugh followed him into the pool, putting an arm around Susan Haight but leaning over to talk to me. "I wondered where you had disappeared to," he said. "I thought you must have left. Be sure to come back up to the house with me. There are a lot of good people here you should meet."

"I will," I promised. "But I'm getting old, and these bones require hot water after a game like that."

"Old, my ass," Van Zandt said. He slapped me on the shoulder. "When I tried that end around in the second half, old Riordan here just flat fucking ran over me. If I'd known about you, pal, I'd have never let Hugh and the Dogs recruit you. They say there'll be an east-side football league over here this spring. I want you on my team for that, fella."

"Sounds like fun."

"I'll call you. Say, Hugh tells me you haven't invested with us yet. You really should talk to me or Susan, Matt. If this market holds, we're going to make Hugh a rich man again, despite all those bad deals he used to be into."

"Thanks for the offer, Greg. But as I was telling Susan,

I just learned about banks last week. Maybe if I come into a big fee, I'll give you a call."

"Do that. Say, does anybody want another drink? Or some food? I'll call up to the house and get the caterer to send somebody down here."

Before Van Zandt could get to the phone a tall slender man with a stoop in his shoulders and a worried look behind his thick glasses stepped into the bathhouse. His hair was graying, and his skin had the white pallor of a man who stays indoors too much. In his arms he cradled a thick sheaf of computer printouts on the standard green-and-white paper.

"Greg . . ." he began.

"Walter," Van Zandt said, cutting him off, "get out of those clothes and into this Jacuzzi. You know Matt Riordan, don't you? Matt, Walter Kessler. Walt, your wife looks like she needs some attention. But first run up to the house and get us a six-pack of beer and maybe a bottle or two of champagne."

"Greg, I can't. You know we've got year-end reports to file. They're due in five days."

"Walter, it's New Year's Day. Don't be a drip."

"Greg," Kessler said like a teacher, patiently but with an edge in his voice, "if these reports aren't turned in, the SEC could be on our doorstep on the morning of January tenth. I don't think any of us want that, Greg. Now we have to go over these account printouts and get the books into shape. I need you to do that."

Van Zandt glared at him silently, then got out of the pool and stomped across the tile floor of the bathhouse, dripping wet. He snatched a towel from a low table and wrapped it around himself. "Your job," he said to Kessler angrily, "is to take care of these fucking things and not mess up my life with them. I trust that one of these days you're going to learn that. Or I'll have to get somebody else who can handle the job." He stormed out of the bathhouse, Kessler trailing behind him.

The room was filled with the awkward silence that follows an angry display like Van Zandt's explosion. After a moment, Susan Haight said quietly, "I'd better go see if

I can help." She stepped out of the tub, wrapped herself in a towel, slipped into her sandals, and walked back to the main house.

I caught Hugh Prokop's eye and looked a question at him. He shrugged. Van Zandt's outburst had surprised both of us.

Sandy Kessler stood up and got out of the tub. "I knew he'd do something stupid like this," she said bitterly. It seemed clear from her tone that she meant her husband, not Greg Van Zandt. She wrapped herself in a towel and started to head back to the house. "Come on, guys," she sighed, calling back to us over her shoulder. "Take me to the party."

After she left I got dressed down in the bathhouse and walked up the hill to join the party. It was a good-sized crowd of perhaps a hundred people.

Hugh took me around and introduced me to his friends in the mostly new-money crowd, like a fraternity brother with a slightly awkward new pledge. After the eighth or ninth introduction I took Hugh over to the caterer's bar and had the bartender pour us new drinks.

"Hey, what gives here?" I asked Hugh, kidding him a little. "You trying to find me some new clients? I'll have to get more cards printed up."

"No, it's not that," he said, reddening slightly. "It's just—look, I haven't seen you in months. And you're a good guy. So I thought I'd try to introduce you to some of my friends. They're all successful people. If you ever want your practice to expand, you're going to have to get out more. Besides, the past few months, you've been in hiding. Come on out and have some fun, for god's sake."

I hesitated before I spoke, genuinely touched by Hugh's thoughtfulness, yet mildly irritated by the intrusion into my life. I am prone to bouts of depression but do not like to admit it. I finally smiled. "That is awfully decent of you, Hugh, and I really do appreciate it. I guess I have been kind of closed up the past few months. But I'm going to have to come out of hiding a little bit at a time. Okay?"

"Sure. I just . . . never mind."

"To the New Year," I said, grinning, and he smiled and we touched glasses and drank. When we had refills I turned around and saw Susan coming back into the room.

"Susan looks like she's out of the countinghouse," I said. "Very pretty lady. You're lucky."

"I guess I am," he said, a little woodenly. "I'd better go rescue her from all the pick-up artists. See you later," he added, as he moved off.

I stayed at the party through a late lunch and finally left a little after four that afternoon. The winter sky was already dark, and the dark suited me, in a way. I was tired and oddly discouraged. The thought of the new year did not help.

Most of the people I had met at the party were friendly and prosperous, successes in their fields, good to their spouses and their families. Some of the women were single and very attractive, with lean exercised bodies and carefully made-up faces and hair. Few of the people smoked, and with one or two exceptions, they didn't get drunk or silly or start to paw somebody else's wife. In most times and places that is enough, or more than enough.

But all of the talk I heard was about money and stocks, German cars and Japanese stereos, houses that seemed to be built for display rather than for comfort and taste of the owner. Nothing had been said about the toxic wastes beginning to poison Puget Sound, or the homeless and mentally ill people clustered on the downtown steam grates or living in cardboard and plastic shanties underneath the bridges. When politics had been raised at all, it was to applaud a genial, mindless president who had made the world a safer place for real estate developers and munitions salesmen.

These were nice people. They didn't want to force gay people out of their jobs or rewrite schoolbooks to fit every dark prejudice and ignorant fear of the new religious right. They did not personally do cruel things, like evicting families from apartments going condo, cutting welfare payments to single mothers, or squeezing down farm workers' wages. But I feared that they had taken money and turned it into a yardstick to measure themselves and other people. Lifestyle, not virtue, had become their primary public good.

I kept these dark thoughts to myself. I went home to my hair shirt and my books, as you would expect, alone.

CHAPTER 2

A month or so of wet gray winter rolled by, as cold and bleak as an old man's hopes. The new-money folk, the brokers and bankers and real estate princes who made their wealth swapping dubious pieces of paper back and forth, all left the city for Maui or Mexico, returning to flash their winter tans as one more symbol of success. I felt small flashes of envy for their ease and checked my bank balances a couple of times, thinking I would follow. Eventually, with the fear of banks that only those who grew up on farms develop, I decided to pay down some debts and stick it out with the people who stayed in the city and walked to work each day in the rain.

January passed slowly. Choices were made. After much talk, an old girlfriend named Patricia Miller and I decided not to marry. We feared that the memory of her brother's death, an event we had watched as powerless, horrified spectators to a much larger crime, would stay between us for a long time, like an unwelcome guest at the wedding. Within days of our decision Pats left her job as a *Seattle Post* reporter to become an assistant city editor of the *Miami Herald*, a leave-taking that would turn out to be an inevitable, final good-bye.

After she was gone my moods began to drift up and down like the rise and fall of tides, sometimes black, other times climbing to an aching, sweet nostalgic high that made me want to call old friends in the middle of the night to ask if they had, just maybe, puzzled out something about this business of life. In self-defense I took to living life in cautious half steps, starting work at six every morning, running and lifting weights each night, ducking friends who called with offers of dinner or blind dates, avoiding all but the simplest of human contact. On Sunday afternoons I would take small, careful measures of Irish whiskey before the fire, rereading Russian novelists like Dostoyevsky and Turgenev, their characters being the only people I knew who just possibly were more bummed out than I was.

The telephone drummed me from sleep a little after three-thirty on a Tuesday morning in early February, the bleakest month of the year. Even before I was awake enough to talk I knew that it was not good news. At three-thirty in the morning it never is.

"Matthew," the caller said twice, repeating my name as I swam toward consciousness. "Matthew, wake up. It's Hugh Prokop."

"Hugh," I croaked, sitting up and swinging around so that my feet could find the floor. "What is it, man?"

"Bad news, Matthew. My building burned. The entire Marine Supply warehouse. It's still burning. They're telling me it's a total loss."

I groped for a notepad and pen on the bedside table. "Hugh, when did the fire start?"

"Around nine or ten tonight, I guess. I mean last night. The fire alarm was turned in around ten. They've just gotten it under control."

"Do they know what caused it?"

"They say not. But that's why I'm calling. I'm talking to a cop and an investigator from the Seattle Fire Department. They think it might be arson."

I came fully awake in a rush and sat straight up on the edge of the bed. "Where are you, Hugh?"

"At the fire station, downtown on Second South."

"What have you talked about so far?"

"Not so much, I guess. Mostly they've been asking

about some of the chemicals we stock at Marine Supply, the solvents and paints and other stuff that is flammable. The fire department wants to know what they're up against."

"Anything else?"

"They asked me where I was tonight."

"Where was that?"

"Out for dinner, then home. I went out for a little while to pick up some beer."

"If they ask you anything more than that, you say nothing, okay?"

"You coming down here?" It was less a question than a demand.

"Yes. As soon as I can."

"Okay," he said grimly, and hung up. I showered and dressed quickly and drove through the silent, rain-wet streets from my house on the northwest shore of Lake Washington, cruising down Bothell to Lake City Way and over to the Interstate. As I crossed the freeway bridge, high above Portage Bay, I could see the bright orange glow of the fire across Lake Union and the rolling, oily black smoke that rose into the cloud-whitened night sky. And I passed through my mind the surprisingly few things I knew about Hugh Prokop.

Hugh was the classic nice guy, solid, steady, a little shy but with an open heart for his friends and his young daughter from a previous, college-age marriage. I had met him when we both used to work out at the downtown Seattle YMCA, down in the weight room, standing in line to use the lat pulley machine. We got to talking that night and a couple of others, and after a while it became a sort of Wednesday-night ritual, the running track and the weights and maybe shooting a few hoops before going out for some beers and then home.

I had been Hugh's lawyer through the fairly bitter divorce and had pulled him out of more than a few late-night bars after that. The friendship had not been all one-way. There had been dozens of rainy winter nights when Hugh had shown up at my office door with basketball tickets, an offer of a blind date, or even just a six-pack of beer and a funny story. In a lot of ways it was accidental friendship, but it was no less real.

A year or so back Hugh had joined one of the expensive new health clubs and I didn't. I saw less of him then, and the friendship slowed a little. On the few nights I saw him it was usually just a quick drink with Hugh and one new woman or another. He seemed to be groping for a new way to put his life together after his divorce and the aimless time that followed.

Hugh was in the wholesale business, marine supplies and hardware. He inherited the business from his father but he ran it well, making some money even in the bad years after the Alaskan crabs were fished out and you could buy fishing boats for ten cents on the dollar down at the Ballard docks. I had handled a couple of bad debt cases for him, but I didn't know much about the business side of Hugh's life.

I got to the fire station a little after four-thirty. The desk officer told me Hugh Prokop was being talked to by Inspector Swenson in fire investigation, up on the mezzanine floor.

The fire investigation office was cramped and stuffy, a warren of dingy cubicles jammed to the limit with impersonal looking gray steel desks and brown vinyl chairs. The offices seemed empty. I stuck my head into the small office marked "Swenson." It was square and precisely organized. Commendations for good work and awards for physical fitness and marksmanship nearly covered the walls.

I finally found Hugh in a small windowless conference room with dingy green walls. He was sitting at one end of a scarred old dark-wood conference table, silent and pensive, his arms folded across his chest. He nodded silently as I walked in. There were two men sitting across the table from him. They gave me their names. Edwards and Swenson.

I remembered vaguely that Carling Edwards was a cop, not a fireman, a plainclothes detective from the Seattle Police fraud unit. He was in his early forties, a heavyset black man dressed in a rumpled gray tweed suit. Edwards's jacket was off, and his sleeves rolled up for a long night's work. He had dark, sleepy eyes beneath heavy lids, and a look of slow power in his wide shoulders and thick, meaty forearms. He needed a shave. Somebody had rousted him out of bed for this conversation. I began to wonder why.

David Swenson was a fire department investigator, almost surely from the arson unit. At first he didn't say. He was white, in his mid-thirties, tall, and built on angular Scandinavian lines. He was dressed in a crisp starched blue shirt, blue knit tie, and tan slacks. His eyes were hard, bright blue.

"Nice of you to come down here, Mr. Riordan," Swenson said with heavy irony. His voice was high-pitched and raspy. It bit at my nerves like the sound of squeaking chalk on a blackboard. "You've only slowed things up by an hour or more."

I did not like him worth a damn, but I let the comment pass. There would be plenty of time to get nasty later on.

"Is the fire under control yet?" I asked.

"We think so," Swenson replied. "When chemicals are present in the fire you never know. You keep waiting for the next time bomb to go off."

"I hope none of your people have been hurt," I said.

"Not so far, counselor," Swenson said coolly. "Suppose we get down to business."

"Fine. Suppose you start by telling me why my client is being questioned here at four-thirty in the morning in the presence of a police officer."

"We're just asking Mr. Prokop a few questions to help us fight the fire," Swenson replied blandly. "The fact that Edwards is here doesn't mean anything special, since as an arson investigator I've been through police training and have the power to arrest."

"Sure. My client tells me he's already told you everything he knows about the chemicals involved. If there's nothing else on that subject we can tell you, we're leaving."

"Just a minute, Mr. Riordan," Edwards interrupted. He spoke in a rambling baritone that suited his size, with a distinct New Jersey accent. "I've got a few things I want to ask. So far, your client hasn't been willing to talk to me.''

"So ask, Detective. But give me a couple of details. Just what is Mr. Prokop being accused of?''

"Nothing at all. This is routine.''

"Somehow I don't think you got out of bed for routine questioning, Detective. Have you informed my client of his rights?''

Edwards looked at me with his sleepy brown eyes. "Is that the way you want to play it, counselor?''

"If I have to, Detective. Suppose you tell me why you suspect arson. Then we'll see.''

"Nobody said anything . . .'' Edwards started to say. Swenson cut him off.

"It's all right, Carl,'' he said heavily. He looked at me. "The fire appears to have broken out at two distinct places in Mr. Prokop's building. The flames were seen at about the same time. They spread very, very quickly. That often means the arsonist is using some kind of accelerant. As you know, we've had a lot of arson-related fires lately. Detective Edwards is the SPD representative on a joint task force looking at the problem and giving us some extra help. We're not yet accusing Mr. Prokop. These questions are strictly preliminary, and as you know, he's not in custody. But just to be on the safe side, I am going to read him his rights.'' He took out a small card and read the famous words written by Justice Warren in the *Miranda v. Arizona* decision. When he was done he carefully put the card back in his wallet.

He looked at Hugh. "Do you understand your rights, Mr. Prokop?''

"I . . . think so. Yes.'' Hugh was clearly shaken.

"And Mr. Riordan here is your attorney, present at your request?''

"Yes.''

"Fine. Would you please describe your whereabouts last night beginning at six o'clock?''

Hugh closed his eyes to concentrate. "I left work at quarter to five, slow day. I went downtown to the Seattle Club to work out. I rode the bicycle and lifted weights for an hour, then showered, so I must have left the club a little after six.'' He paused, then went on, ''I had a date with Susan, that's Susan Haight, for dinner. We went to Daniel's Broiler, a place on Lake Washington.''

Edwards cut in. ''Did you pick her up or meet her at the restaurant?''

''Met her there. I was early and I had a beer and some oysters in the bar while I was waiting for her. Our reservations were at seven. We ate dinner and left around eight. No, maybe eight-thirty. Susan had work to do, so she went back to her place, in Bellevue. We had planned to see a movie. A French movie. I don't remember the title. Something Susan wanted to see.''

''What did you do then?'' Edwards asked. He had taken over the questioning, probably because he had more experience.

''I drove home.''

''Where do you live?''

''On Northwest Sixth, up in Broadview.''

''Did you go out again?''

''No. Wait a minute, yes, I did. I looked at the TV listings and saw that a hockey game was starting on the Vancouver cable channel at ten o'clock. I went out to get some beer at around quarter to ten, I suppose.''

''Where did you go?''

''A convenience store on Greenwood Avenue. A RapidMart, I think. There's one at 125th Street. If I drove by there I could tell you for sure.''

''How long were you out?''

''Fifteen or twenty minutes. The game was just starting when I got back.''

''Who was playing?''

Hugh almost laughed. He rolled his eyes at me, his initial shock giving way to exasperation. ''It beats the hell out of me, Detective. The Maple Leafs? I don't remember. I watched the first period or two, then the beer got me and I fell asleep.''

''Was there anyone at home with you?''

''No. I'm divorced, I live alone.''

''And nobody saw you at this grocery store?''

"Nobody I knew, if that's what you mean. I didn't talk to the clerk, I just paid for my beer. He was a scrawny little guy in his early twenties with big glasses and bad skin."

"Maybe we can locate him. Now, Mr. Prokop, I want to start talking about your business. Was Prokop Marine . . ."

"No," I cut in sharply.

Edwards turned his heavy-lidded eyes to me. "No, what, Mr. Riordan?"

"I mean we're not going to go into that, Detective. Not at five in the morning, before I've had a chance to talk with my client, and with both of us half-asleep. Mr. Prokop has cooperated. He's told you about the stuff that's in the warehouse and he's told you where he was all night. That's enough. Everything else can wait. Come on, Hugh. We're going."

"Who the hell said you could go?" Swenson rasped.

I returned his stare, holding his hard blue eyes with my own. "If you think you've got probable cause for an arrest, Swenson," I said, "you make the arrest." I looked at my watch. "It's getting close to five o'clock. The courts open at nine. My client will be out of custody five minutes after that."

I stood up and took Hugh by the elbow, pulling him up after me. I took a business card out of my wallet and placed it on the table. "If you want to reach either of us, call me at my office. Mr. Prokop will decline to talk to you directly when I am not present."

We turned and started to walk away. Behind me I heard Swenson say, "You think this is very cute, don't you guys? I hate fires and I hate the people who start them." I turned back to look at him. His face was rigid with anger. "You guys in your businesses, you get into trouble, hell, have a little fire to clear out the inventory. We lost two fire fighters in the last two years, both in arson fires. Guys with families. But you'd never think about that." He lowered his voice. "This isn't over, Prokop. I'm going to hang this fire over your head until I get ready to drop it on you."

I walked back to the table, staring at Swenson. He

glared back at me, his mouth working as if he wanted to say something more but had thought better of it. I turned to Edwards and spoke quietly, "I hear you're a good cop. Vince Ahlberg says you're the best. You and I both know just how stupid a biased investigator can be."

He smiled slightly and shook his head.

"Forget it," I said. Hugh and I took the elevators to the main floor and went out into the clean, rainwashed morning air.

CHAPTER 3

Hugh and I had breakfast at the Thirteen Coins restaurant, in the Furniture Mart building on Boren Street. The Thirteen Coins is open all night and serves breakfast at any hour. The crowd is a mixture of cops and crooks and users and juicers, a constant collision between the people who have gotten up too early and the people who have stayed out way too late.

As we settled into one of the dark, high-backed leather booths, Hugh said, "I'm really lost, man. I just don't know what to do. First my building burns, then the cops treat me like I'm the public enemy instead of a victim. Just what the hell did I do?"

"First things first," I said reassuringly. "Breakfast and the newspaper before any business. Then we'll hang out here and talk everything through, so we know where we're going."

Hugh picked at his food and sipped at his coffee while I demolished a three-egg Spanish omelet and two orders of toast. The papers came and I got a morning *Post* from the news rack in front of the restaurant. The fire at Prokop Marine had made the *Post*'s front page—not the headline, which screamed, "White House Sells Iran Arms To Get Money For Contras," but down below the fold, with a four-color night photograph of flames dancing from the roof of the warehouse. The public statements from the fire department spokeswoman were consistent with what the comedy team of Edwards and Swenson had told me. According to the *Post*, the first flames had been sighted and an alarm called in shortly after 10:00 P.M. The building was fully engaged by midnight, with recurring explosions from the hundreds of gallons of marine varnish and paint stored on the third floor. The fire department never even tried to save the building; they were more concerned that the fire would spread to the wood superstructure of the old ferry, the M/V *Santa Clara,* being restored as a museum at a Lake Union dry dock next door. The most ominous note in the *Post*'s story concerned the prospect of arson. When asked, the spokeswoman had said that arson was being "actively considered."

"What does it say?" Hugh asked, as I finished reading the story.

"What you'd expect," I replied casually. "The building is a total loss, Hugh. But I think you already know that."

"Yeah," he said sourly. "That's one reason my insurance has been so high. With chemicals and fuels stored around the place, any fire was likely to be a disaster."

"I think we should give the press a simple statement about the fire, cause unknown, and let it go at that," I said. "The press will want something from you. Hey," I added, seeing the blank stare of depression on his face, "the worst happened and it's no worse than you thought it could be." I forced a smile. "That's more than most people can anticipate from life."

He looked at me with angry amazement. Finally, he broke a strange sort of grin. "You know, Riordan," he said, "you've got a shitty crisis-side manner."

"I know," I said, "but it's all I've got. At my rates you're not gonna get Perry Mason."

Hugh sighed and took another stab at eating. He gave up after a few bites and pushed his plate away. He reached for the front section of the paper. Folding it back to the front page, he read the story about the destruction of his business slowly, wincing from time to time, as though he felt the damage inside himself. When he had read the story twice, he put the paper down carefully, closing it to hide the article, like closing a door on a chapter of his life.

"Okay," he said finally. "Where do we go from here?"

"We should review your insurance today and get claims filed as soon as possible. I've got a real estate guy, a broker and appraiser, coming down here to meet us. I called him when I went for the papers. He won't cost you anything; he owes me a favor and I'm collecting. He can tell you something about what the land under your building was worth, maybe help you decide how to rebuild, if that's what you decide you want."

Hugh nodded. "Might as well get started. And Matthew, thanks. I appreciate your coming down in the middle of the night to help. Forget that crack I made before."

"Don't sweat it. I'm doing it for a reason."

"What's that?"

"I know you didn't torch your own building, Hugh. At least that's what I think. Don't disappoint me, okay?"

I expected him to look shocked. He didn't. He lowered his eyes like a small boy accused of stealing. "I didn't burn it. I don't know why the fire department and the cops are on my case. All I know is that I wasn't anywhere near the building last night."

I reached across the table and tapped his arm. "Hey, relax. I know that. Don't worry about the cops and the firemen. The owner of a business is a natural suspect when the business burns. They're just doing their jobs. They'll drop this within a day or two."

Hugh looked up at me, his eyes red-rimmed and tired. "I hope so," he said quietly.

I was still mulling over the way Hugh had responded to the questions about arson when Warren Soames walked in. Warren is a lanky Yalie of about thirty-five, the scion of a wealthy Seattle family that had lost most of its money in an oil fraud and left Warren with the unexpected problem of making a living. After considerable research into how he could make the most and work the least, Warren settled on real estate, reasoning that there was no heavy lifting and little supervision, and that having enough charm to sell shoes to a snake, which he has, was a distinct asset. He does well enough at it to provide himself a measure of the luxuries, like Porsches and London-tailored clothes, that he regards as his by divine right.

I stood up and waved Warren over to our table, then introduced him to Hugh. As they were shaking hands, I offered Warren breakfast.

"No thank you, Matthew," he replied. "Just coffee. I can't eat at this ungodly hour." He turned to Hugh. "I'm sorry about the loss of your business, Mr. Prokop. When Matthew called me I pulled the county tax information about your building out of my home computer. If you wouldn't mind answering a couple of questions, I think I could offer some preliminary advice."

"Go ahead," Hugh replied.

"Fine. Your place had about 12,000 square feet, right?"

"Yes."

"On two floors?"

"Four. We had only one freight elevator, which made moving stuff around a serious problem."

"Right. The building was built sometime in the 1920s, right?"

"Yes. I'm not sure when. My father bought it in 1949."

"So it's paid for?"

"Yes. Thank God."

"Had you spent a lot of money on upgrading it?"

"Not a lot," Hugh replied. "Electrical was up to code, but that's about it. I get fined every time Occupational Safety and Health comes through because they always have some new requirement. We thought about trying to convert the place to offices a while back, but the building's pretty plain and we couldn't get the historic-preservation tax credits. So I didn't want to spend too much on it."

"That's probably wise." Warren looked up and smiled at the waitress as his coffee was placed on the table. She was a lovely Irish redhead with sea-green eyes who looked amazingly composed for six o'clock in the morning. Warren watched longingly as she swayed away.

"Someone you know?" I asked politely.

"Not yet," he replied. "Anyway, I think I've heard

enough. Hugh, the property you've got is fairly valuable. It's next to the waterfront promenade the city is planning to build as part of the new South Lake Union redevelopment. It still has industrial zoning, which means a developer could put up anything he wants on it. Office, commercial, condo, maybe a mix of all three. A lowball guess on the land alone, properly marketed, would be a million-point-five. I could get you a million-point-three tomorrow. Hell, I'd buy it for that.''

''What about the building?''

Warren shrugged. ''Take the insurance money and run with it, 'cause the building wasn't worth a dime. No good for warehouse anymore with all those floors, and it was too ugly to convert to offices. The way I see it, the fire not only got you the insurance money, it saved you demolition costs.'' He laughed and added, ''If you find the guy who burned it, you should buy him a beer.''

Hugh's face turned ashen. He stood up and slid out of the booth, turned and headed for the door.

Silently I watched him go. He would be back when he'd cooled off. Warren turned to me. ''What,'' he said, looking puzzled, ''did I say? Or do I want to know?''

''The fire department called Hugh in at three o'clock this morning,'' I explained. ''They started asking him a lot of questions about arson. Hugh's just a little spooked right now.''

''I'm sorry. Stupid thing to say. How can I make amends?''

I handed him a dollar. ''Take this. You've just been retained by me as an expert consultant in anticipation of a lawsuit. This conversation is privileged, as attorney work product. If anybody comes sniffing around you asking questions, you close up. Tight. And you call me. Okay?''

''Agreed. Does this mean I don't get to bid on the land? I'm thinking I might want to buy it.''

''Later, vulture. Right now I think I'd better get my client calmed down. I mean it about any cops.''

''All right. Sorry again.''

He left, stopping to chat up the waitress who had moved so elegantly down the aisles. I paid the bill and went out to cool Hugh down, hoping that it was just shock and the heavy-handed questions that had him climbing the walls.

I found him standing by his car, leaning against the roof on his forearms, fists clenched.

"You okay?" I asked.

"Fine," he said bitterly. "Perfect. Tell me something. Am I going to have to put up with this sort of crap forever?"

"What sort of crap?"

"You know. The knowing little looks, the jokes, the question in the back of everybody's eyes. 'Did he torch it? Couldn't make it in the business, could he?' That crap."

"Yes. You're going to have to take it, for a while, anyway. When a building goes up in a fire, people are always going to look at the person who benefits. They're going to wonder."

"And there's nothing I can do about it."

"That's right. So just shove that thought to the back of your mind. We've got things to do."

"What's next?"

"The fire's probably out. Let's go look at your building."

CHAPTER 4

The Prokop Marine building looked like a relic of 1945 Berlin. The blackened brick walls were still standing, but the fire had burned through the roof and collapsed the main timbers onto the floors below. Thousands of gallons of water had been pumped onto the fire, and the stench of smoke and water and chemicals assaulted us before we ever got into the building. A half-dozen city and county cars were still parked in the lot in front of the building. We stood around for a moment and wondered where to go. A young fireman dressed in a lime-yellow fire suit emerged from the front of the building, carrying a shovel. He started walking toward a fire truck at the far end of the lot before I stopped him.

"Excuse me," I said. "I'm Matthew Riordan, an attorney representing the owner of the building. My client's here and would like to look at his property. Can we do that?"

He nodded. "Check with Captain Wallace or Inspector Swenson first. Let me drop this shovel off, then I'll go back in and tell them you're here."

I went back to the car and waited with Hugh. The young fireman returned to the building, disappearing into it like an explorer entering a dark cave. A few minutes later Swenson came out and walked over to the car. He was wearing yellow coveralls smeared with soot and dirt. When he reached the car he took off his fire helmet and rested it on the hood. He wiped the sweat on his forehead with his hand, leaving gray sooty streaks on his skin. Weariness was embedded in his face like grit.

"What is it you're after here, Riordan? You looking for something?" he rasped.

"Mr. Prokop wants to see how badly the building is damaged, and whether anything can be salvaged," I replied evenly.

"All right, all right. The fire is out and I can't keep Prokop off his own property. But as far as I'm concerned this is a crime scene." He shoved a finger into my chest for emphasis. "You look, no touch. Understand?"

I have a temper that holds just so long and then lets go. "Look, Swenson, why don't you save the scary stuff for when you do the 'Bad Mr. Fire' programs in the grade schools, okay? It is not going to work on me, and you probably need to save the strength for something really important, like looking in the mirror and showing yourself how tough you really are."

Instead of snarling back, he smiled a little to himself. He looked pleased. The one thing I knew about guys like Swenson was that you could always get them angry. Yet Swenson wasn't biting. A small, cold finger of doubt began to run up and down my spine. We followed him into the building.

The foul stench of wet smoke and soot became overpowering as we entered. The front portion of the first floor was still easily recognizable as the order desk and waiting area for Prokop Marine's customers, since the second floor had not collapsed down into it. The carpeting was ruined by the water and soot, but the counters were intact, as were the file cabinets behind them.

"This doesn't seem that bad," Hugh marveled. He went behind the counter and opened up a file drawer. The orders and records inside were soaked and swollen into a mass of gray pulp. Hugh tried to pull out a file and watched in dismay as the soggy mess fell apart in his hands.

"We were just starting to put in computers," he said

sadly. "Most of the receivables and inventory files are on paper. We'll never get them reconstructed."

"Don't worry about what you can't fix," I said. "There are a lot of ways to reconstruct billing. Insurance companies do it all the time to cut their losses. Come on."

Swenson led us back down a hallway to the rear of the building. The light from the few small windows grew faint. The damage got much worse. The interior walls were broken down or missing completely, leaving the ceiling supported only by heavy charred timbers.

"We're not too sure of the layout of the building," Swenson said as he led the way back. "We think most of the flammable stuff was up on the third floor. Everything above this ceiling is rubble. We're not too sure how long it's going to hold up, either. Prokop, when we're done you'd better arrange for the site to be cleaned up, because there's a lot of stuff up above that'll come crashing down on anybody inside."

"I will," Hugh said. "The way you're describing the damage fits the layout of the building. The first floor was mostly offices in front and on this side, loading dock on the south side. Second floor was hardware, tools, and some marine parts. Paints and varnishes were up on the third floor, in the back. Fourth floor was mostly dead storage.

"Here's my office, off to the right," Hugh continued. The remnants of a waist-high wall with what had been big windows defined the edge of the hallway we were walking through. Shards of broken glass were scattered around the floor. The interior of the office was heavily charred. The chair was burned down to its metal base. Hugh's desk looked like a huge lump of coal dumped in the center of the room. Hugh paused for a moment to survey the wreckage.

"I had a pretty decent bottle of bourbon in that desk," he sighed. "Oh, well. Let's keep going."

Swenson led us on through the darkened corridor, saying nothing. There was rubble on the floor here, and we stumbled over it. In other places our feet slipped on the slimy paste of wet soot and ash accumulated on the floor.

"What's back here, Hugh?" I asked.

"Bookkeeping. Some files and the safe." He seemed as unsure as I was why Swenson was leading us back there.

The file room was a jumble of desks and file cabinets, some scarred and twisted by the heat of the flames. The room was lit by lights set up on stands. A piece of floor had been set off by poles with yellow police crime-scene ribbons wrapped around them. Two men, one dressed in coveralls, the other in a suit ruined beyond the ability of drycleaning to repair, stood in the corner, outside the pools of light cast by the electric lamps. The man in the suit was stocky, with broad shoulders. Then he turned and I recognized Captain Vince Ahlberg, the head of the Seattle Police homicide unit.

"Riordan," he said, coming over and shaking hands, "what brings you down here?"

"I represent Hugh Prokop, the owner of this building. He's right here with me. What the hell is going on here, Vince? The last time I looked the cops had to have a warrant before searching a fire scene. I haven't seen one yet."

"Didn't Swenson tell you?"

"No." I turned to look at Swenson. A malicious little smile played across his lips.

"We found a body in this room, Riordan," Swenson said. "While checking for hot spots, part of our legitimate fire work under the *Clifford* rule. The stiff apparently died in the fire. That makes this a homicide investigation."

"Jesus Christ," Hugh said. He whispered in a strained little voice, "Who was it? Do you know?"

"No," Ahlberg replied. "The body was too badly charred. The medical examiner will have to find out, either from teeth or subcutaneous prints." Ahlberg stopped talking and eyed Hugh in silent appraisal. "You're Hugh Prokop?" he asked.

"That's right."

"I'm going to want to talk with you later."

"I'll be there," I said to Ahlberg.

"Of course," he said reassuringly. "Right now we

don't know very much. We're hoping Mr. Prokop can fill in a few missing details, that's all.''

"All right," Hugh said. His eyes were distracted, his voice deadened with shock. "Jesus," he said again. "It must have been one of my people." His voice rose with emotion. "I've got to get out of here, start calling and checking up on them."

"Mr. Prokop, did you have a night warehouseman working here, or somebody who came in at night?"

"No. All the security was electrical."

"Then why do you think that it was one of your employees?"

"Who else could it be? The alarms never went off, did they?"

I saw the danger signs and changed the subject. "Has the fire department come up with anything new on the cause of the fire?" I asked.

Swenson spoke up before Ahlberg could get back on track. "We think we've found two different points of ignition, judging from the flame spread and the direction the fire moved. One was in this room, over in the corner. Somebody used a can of paint thinner, splashing it on the heater and over some of the paper from the files. There's definite scorching and a flame-spread pattern up the walls.''

"How do you know that thinner was used?"

He picked up a large plastic bag. Inside the bag I could see a charred black box. Swenson said, "This is a two-gallon tin of paint thinner, Riordan. Or it was. And it's got two holes punched into the top, probably from a screwdriver. You're not going to be able to kid anyone about this. It was arson. And murder."

The words hung heavy on the air. I could feel Hugh standing behind me, trembling. He was about to speak, maybe saying something that might hurt his case if it came to that. I took his arm and squeezed it, hard. "You want to see anything else?" I asked him calmly. "If not, I'd like to get out of here and shower this crappy smell off me. And you've got those calls to make."

"I'd like to check the safe before I go," Hugh said.

"There are two file drawers of records inside. I need to know whether they made it through the fire."

"Where's the safe?"

"It's in a little room behind us, through that door. What used to be a door." He led us through a burned-out archway into what apparently had been a bookkeeper's office. The air and light were better in here; the room had an outside window that had been knocked out. I went straight to the window. The clean, cold air was heaven. I drank it in.

The safe stood in the corner, an old Prescott & Walter floor safe that had been built back in the 1920s. The fire had chipped and eaten the grand gilt lettering on the safe's door, but the name was still visible in outline on the blackened steel. Hugh stepped up to the door and tried the combination lock. "It still turns," he said. "I think it's all right. I'll just be a minute."

"Hold it," I said, turning to Ahlberg and Swenson, who had followed us from the file room. "Gentlemen, please leave. We'll be done shortly."

"I want to see what's in the safe," Swenson said. His rasping voice grated on my nerves. I swallowed some anger before answering.

"I'll bet you would," I said dryly. "But you're not going to. Not without a search warrant. Leave."

Ahlberg turned and started out of the room. Hugh said, "Oh, for Christ's sake, let them stay. There's nothing exciting in here, anyway."

I said tightly, "Hugh, just do as I say on this, please."

"The man says we can stay, Riordan," Swenson said heavily. "I'm not going anywhere."

I turned back to Hugh. He was already dialing the combination. I bit my lip and tried not to look upset. What I should have done was walk out of the room and quit as his lawyer then and there. When the client doesn't take your advice, you're through. Like a damned fool, I stayed and watched as Hugh opened the safe.

The safe door was about five feet high and three feet wide and must have weighed five hundred pounds, but despite the heat from the fire it swung open easily, without a sound. On the inside there were a few open shelves, a row of pigeonholes and two file drawers. Hugh opened one of the drawers and let out a low sigh of relief. "Thank God for small favors, anyway," he muttered.

"What'd you find?" I asked.

"The master inventory and the company books are here. They're still dry. And only a little singed around the edges." He pushed the drawer closed. He looked around the rest of the safe, checking a petty-cash box, pulling out a couple of red bound ledgers. On the top shelf there was a big, cheap attaché-type case of molded plastic. It had been partially melted by the heat of the fire and was stuck to the shelf of the safe. Hugh jerked it loose and pulled it out, a puzzled frown on his face.

"What's that?" I asked.

He shook his head but said nothing. The case was held shut by two metal clasps. Hugh tried to open them, but they were stuck closed. He set the case on the floor and took out a bone-handle pocketknife. He selected a short stubby blade and began to pry the clasps open. The first one popped easily. The second took him three tries. Eventually it snapped open. Hugh lifted the lid of the case.

It was full of money. Used twenties and fifties had been bound in rubber bands and marked with brown paper slips bearing penciled notations. The bills on top were a bit browned by the heat, but eminently spendable.

We stared. Hugh stared the hardest of all, his mouth open in amazement. Vincent Ahlberg finally broke the silence.

"Mr. Prokop," he said, his voice a polite, deadpan drawl, "is that your money?"

Hugh said nothing. He shook his head, slowly, and closed the attaché case. He turned and looked up at me, his eyes blank.

"Put it back in the safe, Hugh," I said, "and lock it." He did. I turned to Ahlberg. "If you want anything else, Captain, get a search warrant."

"Don't worry, counselor," he replied. "We will. You can go now." We left, stumbling out through the blackened building, two people looking for any way out they could find.

When we got to my car, I stopped to catch my breath and get the fire stench out of my lungs. I looked at Hugh. He was leaning against the car, his hands pressed flat against the door.

"Hey," I said, "tell me what's going on. Where did that money come from? And why was the dead man in your place?"

"I don't know," he said slowly. His eyes were red-rimmed, full of shock and fear.

"What?"

"Take me home, Matthew. Now. I can't take any more right now."

I stared at him for a long minute as he crawled into my car and sat in the passenger seat, huddled against the door. I started to say something, then thought the better of it and drove him home.

CHAPTER 5

The next day was busy. As I half expected, the SPD and the fire investigation unit of the fire department served search warrants on Hugh for his business and personal financial records. The warrants were served at Hugh's home by Carling Edwards, the fraud unit detective who had questioned Hugh on the night of the fire, and a young fire investigator who worked with Swenson at the FIU. After a panicky phone call from Hugh I drove up to his house in the quiet Broadview neighborhood to monitor the search. I read the warrants over carefully. They were broadly, but correctly, phrased, and there wasn't much I could do except stand and watch. Edwards was quietly methodical and searched every room, even though all the business records that could be salvaged from the fire had already been picked up and were carefully laid out to dry on the Ping-Pong table in Hugh's basement. When Edwards had finished his search and gathered all the records, he sat down in the basement and wrote out a longhand manifest of the documents that were going to be seized. During the search Hugh paced silently around his house, nervous as a cat. The search was rubbing something raw inside him. The sanctity of the home is etched far deeper into the American mind than most people think.

Edwards and his helper from the FIU were still working up the manifest when there was a ring from the front doorbell. Hugh moved to answer it, but I cut him off with a gesture and went to get the door myself.

It was Vince Ahlberg. He stood on the stoop, looking over the front yard and squinting into the pale winter sunlight, wearing his trademark black suit.

"Well," I said. "We're honored. It's not often that we get a captain of detectives coming around to toss the house. Come on in."

"Morning, Matthew," he replied, almost cheerily. He stepped into the front entryway and glanced around the house. "Nice place. I'm just checking up on my guys. They do the search right?"

"I'm afraid so," I replied, "But I'll think of something rotten to say about you later. Not that it matters. You're not here about the search. What's up?"

"I've got a few things to tell you and Prokop. Where is he?"

"Down in the basement with Edwards and the kid from FIU."

"Bring him up. Let's talk in the living room."

"Okay," I said, nodding. "I'll get him. He's not answering any questions."

"We'll see. Bring him, please."

I went down the steps into the basement and got Hugh. "Captain Ahlberg from homicide is here. He's got things to tell us, he says. Don't say anything without my permission, okay?"

Hugh nodded gravely. "Not a word," he said. "Not after what happened last time." We walked up the basement stairs and into the living room.

Ahlberg had taken a seat on one of the two oatmeal-colored sofas that formed an L in front the rock fireplace. He was leafing through a magazine on the glass coffee table in front of him. He stood up when we walked into the room and nodded at Hugh Prokop. He did not offer to shake hands.

"Mr. Prokop," he said softly, "please take a seat." Hugh sat down on the other sofa, facing Ahlberg. I sat down next to him.

"The reason I came here today," Ahlberg said, "was to

tell you who the victim burned in the fire was. The medical examiner has identified the body. I think you knew him. His name was Kessler. Walter Kessler.''

"My God," Hugh said. The color drained out of his face and he shook nervously. "Walter was my accountant. His wife is a friend of the woman I've been dating. Poor Walter. What a goddamn awful thing.''

I decided to jump into the conversation before Hugh could say anything else. "Has his wife been told?" I asked.

"She has," Ahlberg replied. "This morning. One of the less pleasant parts of my job.''

"How is she doing?" Hugh asked.

"Not well. She's been sedated and taken to a hospital over in Bellevue. They live there. Mr. Prokop, how well did you know Mr. Kessler?" he continued.

"No way," I cut in. "Hugh, don't answer.''

Ahlberg turned his pale grey eyes at me. "Why, Matthew? It's a perfectly innocuous question.''

"Not after a search warrant has been served, Captain. After that, no question is innocuous.''

"Matthew, I can't look at any other possibilities without decent information. You know that.''

"Horseshit. If you were going to look at other suspects for this crime you would be someplace else right now. Whatever my client has to say he'll say in court, if at all. Hugh, why don't you hang out someplace else for a minute? I want to chat with Captain Ahlberg. Okay?''

Hugh seemed puzzled, but he agreed and left the room. When he was gone I turned to Ahlberg and said, "What the hell is going on here, Vince? This is about the weakest homicide case I've seen your office try to push since I came out here in 1980. You haven't got an eyewitness who can place Prokop at the scene of the fire. You haven't got any motive for him to kill this guy Kessler. Why are you putting my guy through this?''

Ahlberg seemed untroubled by my outburst. "We've had four good-sized burnings for profit in the past six months," he replied. "All businesses burned by their owners for the insurance. We haven't been able to take one of them down. Not one. This looks to me like the best case we're going to get. We're going to see if we can make it.''

"Jesus, that's wonderful. You can't make your cases, so you've decided to take your best shot and hassle some guy as a warning to others. I have always hated selective prosecution. It is nothing but fraud, an attempt to scare the crooked or the desperate by taking somebody out every once in a while and hanging him out to dry. It never works.''

"Prokop has means and motive and opportunity.'' Ahlberg replied. "He had a troubled business and a fat insurance policy. And somebody died in this one, Matthew. That makes it special.'' He paused and added. "What's the matter with you, anyway? You used to be able to maintain your objectivity.''

"Yeah,'' I said sourly, "and you used to be a good cop, Vince. Even by my standards. I think your guys downstairs are nearly through. I want copies of everything seized. And don't hold anything back, Captain. This time we go by the book.''

After all the cops had left, Hugh and I stayed in his living room, kicking around the things that had developed so far. Hugh was tense, both angered and saddened by the sudden intrusion of cops and fire investigators into his home and his life.

"I don't understand why they've accused me,'' he kept saying. "I thought they had to investigate and really be certain before they could barge into someone's home.''

"That's not exactly how it works,'' I told him. "Especially in a case of arson. All the cops need for a search warrant or an arrest is probable cause, which they have here. The fire was clearly intentional, and you are one of a limited number of people who had access to the building. You're a very logical suspect.''

"Why? Why would they think I'd want to kill Walter?'' He shifted uneasily on the sofa.

"I don't know. Let's go back to the basics. How much

do you know about Walter? And why would he have been at the warehouse?''

"Walter's been my accountant for five or six years. When he joined up with Greg Van Zandt's company he said he'd like to keep doing my books at night, so I gave him a key to get in after hours. I guess that's why he was there.''

"Did Kessler have anything to do with that quarter-million bucks that was sitting in your safe?''

He looked away. "Maybe Walter brought it.''

"Brought it? Why? I've been going easy on you, Hugh, until the cops were gone, but now you've got to level with me. Who owns that cash? What's it for?''

"I really don't want to go into it.''

"Damn you, you have to. I'm your lawyer, Hugh. Anything you tell me is privileged. If I disclose it to anyone else, I'd get disbarred. Now talk to me.''

He sighed. "The money's part of a deal I'm doing with Greg Van Zandt and my girlfriend Susan. We're going to buy some real estate in Hawaii.''

"From who? And why all the cash?''

"It's supposed to be an all-cash deal. Greg or Susan can give you the details. It's mostly their money.''

"Why would Kessler be bringing it to you?''

"I'm the courier. Walter was bringing it because I was going to keep it in my safe. I was expecting the call at any time.''

"What happened to the deal?''

"It's lost, I guess. The police are holding the money.''

"Why didn't you tell me any of this before? Is the deal dirty?''

"No,'' he said. "And things have been kind of busy.'' He got up and paced the room, irritated. "What's all this got to do with the fire anyway?''

"Maybe nothing. Maybe a lot. Look, if they bring the case against you, they're going to try to establish financial gain as your motive, which means evidence of insurance, business losses, your personal finances, the value of the land under the building. Based on that plus what Warren Soames said yesterday, their theory will probably be that you burned it to get the insurance for the building and contents, then planned to sell the land for the new Lake Union development. As far as Kessler is concerned, I think they would concede that was an accident. I would, if I were prosecuting you. Under the felony murder rule they don't need to prove a specific intent to kill. As long as the victim dies in commission of the primary crime, you can be stuck for first degree murder. Which means twenty to thirty years in prison.''

"My god.'' He shuddered. "All I can say is I didn't do it.''

"I know. We don't know whether they'll even try to indict you. If they do, there are a lot of ways to defend this case. But first we need to talk about who's going to be your lawyer.''

"Why?'' Hugh asked, puzzled. "I thought you would defend me.''

"I will, if that's what you want. But Hugh, listen to me carefully. I have a general practice. I do some criminal work, and I used to be a Justice Department strike-force prosecutor in Boston and New York. But, murder trials are the World Series of criminal cases. You've got money. Let me hire one of the guys who specializes in major criminal defense, like Tony Brown or Lanny Kelleher. They really are the best.''

"I'd rather have you. I know you and the fact that you're my friend makes it easier for me to expose my . . . life and my problems.''

"I can appreciate that, Hugh, but you must understand that if I stay on this I am your lawyer, not your friend. There is a large and dedicated group of people down at the courthouse hard at work right now, trying to find the best way to lock you in a five-by-seven-foot room for the rest of your life. This is not something you can work out with them. This is not something that will go away.''

"I don't know what to do. I'm going to have to think about it.''

"That's okay,'' I replied. "In the meantime, I am going to tell you what I tell every other client. First, and most important, you must tell me everything you can that has any possible relevance to this case, and you must tell me the truth, no matter how unpleasant. If you lie to me, I will make mistakes that can cost you your freedom. Do you understand that?''

Hugh nodded, tapping his fingers together nervously.

"Second, this is going to be expensive. Clients usually expect lawyers to go easy on them because they are in trouble, but they forget that lawyers are in business to take care of people's troubles. I will charge you by the hour, as I have in the past, but I require a retainer for a criminal case. A fair guess right now is that this case will cost a minimum of thirty thousand dollars. It could easily be more, but that is what I would need as a retainer.''

Hugh looked shocked. He placed his coffee cup carefully on the table in front of him. "I'll have to raise it,'' he said. "I haven't got it in the bank anymore.''

"What happened? You've been one of my few rich friends.''

"The usual stuff. Before I met Susan I had one of my old college buddies as my stockbroker. He put me into a lot of small stocks, metals and mining and stuff. They went to hell just as the market took off in the blue chips. When I tried to play catch-up, I lost some more money. Five years back I had a lot of income from the business, and he got me into some tax shelter deals that have been disallowed by the IRS. I've been hit with back taxes and penalty interest the last two years running, over two hundred thousand dollars' worth.'' He shrugged ruefully. "He wasn't smart as a kid. I don't know why I thought he'd turn into a financial genius.''

"Why didn't you tell me any of this before this whole mess came up?''

"It's not the kind of thing you like to admit to your friends, Matthew. I mean, you don't feel too smart standing around at a party and saying, 'You know that Open Trails stock? Hell, I bought it at twenty and now it's all the way down to four.' '' He ran a hand through his thick brown hair and gave a tired sigh. "Anyway, the tax payments are behind me and I've got the rest of my money invested over at Van Zandt. They really know what they're doing with their currency trading partnerships and stock selection. I thought that in a couple of years I'd be back to even. Now, with the business gone, I don't know. I really need the insurance on the building to pay off, I guess.''

He really did say it. I leaned back and tasted the words and shuddered at how they would sound to a jury. Eventually I said, ''The insurance won't be paid unless you win this case. Hugh, we're going to have to run through the financials on the business and on you. The cops are already doing that, trying to prove your motive to burn the building. We have to prove the opposite.''

''I understand. Susan made copies of all my personal financial stuff very early this morning, before the cops got here. She's doing a financial statement and will have everything ready for you tomorrow.''

''Good. Let's get started on the business stuff.''

Hugh got up from the sofa and led me down to the basement where his corporate records had been drying. Those that weren't seized by Carling Edwards remained on the dark green table, laid out like the pieces of a jigsaw puzzle. Hugh surveyed them sadly. ''What a mess,'' he sighed. ''Okay. What do you want to know?''

We worked at it for three hours, until I had a better sense of the history and management of Hugh's company. Porkop Marine had been started by Hugh's father in the early 1930s. It was a classic old-style business, a warehouse wholesaler of marine parts and supplies to the fishing fleets in Ballard and Anacortes and to the small shipyards that once had surrounded Lake Union. Hugh's business had fallen on tough times with the rest of the fishing industry. Gross profits had fallen from over half-a-million dollars a year in 1980 to a small loss in the past year.

Prokop Marine was a corporation. Hugh owned eighty percent of the stock, inherited from his father. The other twenty percent were owned, ten percent each, by Hugh's sister, Mary Alice Theirrault, and his nephew Howard Gaines, the son of Hugh's oldest sister, who had died in 1982.

''I've always tried to pay Mary Alice and Howard a dividend, but I couldn't last year,'' Hugh said, ''I've taken only salary for the last three years in order to protect the working capital.''

''Did you think about just selling the company? Before the fire, I mean.''

''Oh, sure. I didn't talk to anybody about it, if that's what you're getting at. But I thought about it. I've been working twelve, fourteen hours a day for a long time, and I don't seem to be getting anywhere. Sometimes I think we would all be doing better if we just sold out.''

I frowned. That was not the sort of story I wanted the jury to hear. I wanted to paint a portrait of a man who had devoted his life to the running of the family business, not someone who'd just as soon sell out and move to a condo in Hawaii.

''Tell me about the other owners,'' I said. ''Would either of them have a motive to burn down the place?''

Hugh stared at me as if I'd suddenly become insane. ''They're family,'' he said finally. ''Mary Alice has her own business, graphic design, but she's always helped by doing our catalogs and advertisements. And Howard's not a bad kid, exactly. He's a biker, runs with a motorcycle bunch out of the Rainier Valley, but he has his own motorcycle shop and makes his own way. No. I can't see it.''

''How about disgruntled employees? Or somebody that you've fired?''

''Nobody comes right to mind, but I've always had union trouble. Let me try and get a list together.'' A doorbell rang upstairs. Hugh said, ''I'll get it. It's probably Mary Alice. I don't think you've ever met her. She and Susan were coming over to have dinner. Why don't you stay? You'll probably need to get to know both of them better.''

''Okay,'' I replied. ''I will. Thanks.''

Hugh returned with a short, thickset woman in her middle thirties. She wasn't fat, but solid and strong, as if made for a harsher life than the one she was living. She was casually dressed in blue jeans and a heavy sweater. Her long brown hair was plaited into a single thick braid that fell down the center of her back. She shared Hugh's broad plain face, wide brown eyes, and shy smile.

"Mary Alice Theirrault," she said, extending a hand.

I took it. "Matthew Riordan. I'm Hugh's . . ."

"I know," she said anxiously. "The lawyer. Mr. Riordan, can't we get this thing straightened out? Hugh is so obviously innocent I don't see how they can be thinking that he did it. It's ridiculous. I mean—"

"Wait a minute," I said, putting up a hand. "I think you're right, but Hugh is a logical target. I'm not saying he's guilty," I added hastily, seeing the storm warnings in her expression.

She was about to argue the point further when Susan Haight came down the stairs. She walked up to Hugh and they embraced.

"Hugh," she said, "are you okay? You look tired, sweetheart. I was so worried about you. I wanted to come by yesterday, but I got tied up at work."

"Hey," Hugh said smiling, taking her by the shoulders and moving her six inches away, "I'm okay. Really."

She nodded. Hugh stroked her cheek and brushed her long, straight blond hair away from her face. "Say hello to Mary, and to Matthew. We've been working and I haven't had a chance to make dinner. Sorry."

"That's all right. I stopped at an Italian take-out and bought some things for dinner." She turned toward Mary Alice and me. "Hi, you guys. I'm sorry for ignoring you. But I've been worried about him."

"It's been tough on him," I agreed.

Susan nodded. "I'm going to start dinner. And we should all have a drink. Mary, want to help?"

Mary Alice followed her upstairs to the kitchen, a curious lack of expression on her face. She had said nothing, yet I sensed that Susan was not on her list of favorite people.

Hugh seemed happier after Susan had arrived. "Come on, counselor," he said. "Let's go get ourselves a drink."

We went up to the living room. I made a fire in Hugh's handsome rock fireplace while he poured the liquor. He took drinks into the kitchen for the women, then came back and poured solid slugs of bourbon on ice into heavy glass tumblers. In the forty minutes before dinner he poured himself two more while I switched to club soda.

Susan served lasagna and salad for dinner along with a dry red wine. Hugh didn't eat very much, but he drank wine steadily, working through two liters almost by himself. The conversation lapsed into pensive silences as we all tried to stay away from any topic touching on the business or the fire.

After an hour at the table Hugh's words were slurred and he wavered unsteadily in his chair. Finally, mercifully, he fell asleep, slumped back with his chin falling against his chest like a tired child.

I couldn't avoid Mary Alice's eyes. She shook her head. Susan said, "I'll just put him to bed. Poor guy. He's going through so much."

She left her chair and went to his, taking his arm. "Come on, baby," she said softly, gently shaking him awake. "Come on. You've got to get to bed."

Hugh came half-awake and wobbled up from his chair. Susan put one arm around him and nearly carried him into the bedroom. I was surprised at her strength as she guided him away.

I looked back at Mary Alice. "Has Hugh been drinking a lot lately? Before the fire, I mean."

She shrugged. "Some. He's been under a lot of stress because of the business. And he wants badly to be successful, because he thinks it's important to her." There was no mistaking who the *her* referred to.

"Money is a way of keeping score," I said. "Hugh's done well in past, and these kind of problems can hurt."

"But that's just the point. She does keep score." Mary Alice's voice was flat.

"So do a lot of people," I replied. "Susan was pretty good with him just now."

Mary Alice's face softened into a small smile. "You're right. And it is not my place to intrude."

"Whether it is or not, he needs both of you now. Perhaps more than he's needed you before."

Mary Alice nodded. We were silent until Susan came

back. I thanked her for dinner, found my coat, and headed for the door.

Susan came with me. "I'm glad you're here with us. I know you can get Hugh out of this."

Her choice of words was no better than Hugh's. I didn't answer her directly, keeping my budding fears about Hugh to myself. "Take care of him," I said. "He's going to need it."

"I will," she promised, and I went out to my car and a slow, thoughtful drive home.

CHAPTER 6

The SPD arrested Hugh Prokop at five o'clock the next
afternoon, taking him from his home to King County Jail.
I got the call a little after six, too late to bail him out that
night.

He was arraigned at 11:00 A.M. the following morning, a
Friday. The County Prosecutor's Office had filed the information directly in the Superior Court—King County almost never uses grand juries—so there was no district
court preliminary hearing to decide whether the case should
be bound over for trial. The purpose of arraignment is to
read the defendant the information charging him, take his
plea, set bail, and schedule the omnibus hearing and trial
date. Arraignment is a matter of form, a ritual of droning
clerks, bored judges, overworked prosecutors, and cynical
public defenders. For those who love the stately myths of
Anglo-American jurisprudence, it is a process best not
watched.

Felony arraignment is done in the small, glassed-in
courtroom on the first floor of the new King County Jail.
The prosecutor, the public defender, and the private lawyers, called "retained counsel," cluster in front of the low
blond-oak railing. The judge's clerks sit immediately behind the rail, with the judge sitting at a desk above them.
The families of the accused sit on pews behind a glass
wall, struggling to make out what is going on in the court,

45

aided fitfully by a microphone system that never really seems to work. After their husband or daughter or son appears and is led back into the jail, they must tap timidly on the locked glass door to get the attention of the bored Court Services guard who will relay the result like a radio reporter reading a box score. "He got PR'd, out in an hour," he says when the news is good and the court has granted a personal recognizance release. When the news is not good, bail revoked or set impossibly high, the guard just shakes his head, and the families walk away.

On this Friday morning the jail seemed to be working under the influence of a minor curse or a major hangover. The prosecutor's office didn't have a copy of the information charging Prokop, and nobody seemed to know which deputy was handling the arraignment. The new electric doors to Felony Holding had jammed in the locked position, so I was unable to get to Hugh to prepare him for the hearing. I shouted about Constitutional rights for a while at a couple of jail guards, middle-aged men with large, hard guts and indifferent expressions. Then I gave it the hell up and waited on a bench in the arraignment courtroom, feeling like a minor character in a Fellini film that the critics were going to love.

Prokop was the third man in the shuffling chain of prisoners clad in washed-out red and blue coveralls with KING COUNTY JAIL stenciled on the chest and back. The prisoners' hands were cuffed together to a waist belt in front of their bodies, so that each prisoner was forced to stand in a manner that suggested penance before the bench. Half the prisoners this morning were black, one Filipino, the remainder white. Before the prisoners were brought in I had expected Hugh to look visibly different from the others. But with two days' beard growing black along his jaws, his hair skewed and cowlicked, and his red tired eyes, he looked as bad as the rest.

The cases were called in order, Hugh's third. "*State v. Prokop, Hugh Robert*, Case Number 86-1-44322-9," the prosecutor droned. Her voice carried more respect when she read the charge. "First degree arson. First degree murder."

The judge on criminal arraignment that morning was Edgar Chung, an elderly Chinese with a broad placid face and large head that, with his robes, made him seem much bigger than he really was. I had never had a case in front of him. The book on Judge Chung was that what he lacked in legal scholarship he more than made up in his understanding of human frailty. We could do far worse.

Hugh and I stood by ourselves in front of the court. Judge Chung leaned over the bench and looked down at Hugh. "Is that your attorney with you?" he asked, his voice polite but cold.

I could see Hugh's mouth working, as if he were trying to work up enough spit to speak. "Yes," he said finally, croaking out the word.

"I'm Matthew Riordan, Your Honor," I said cutting in. "I am representing Mr. Prokop."

Chung nodded. "Your appearance is noted. Will you waive reading of the information?" the Judge asked.

"No, Your Honor," I said. "The State has not yet provided a copy of the information."

Judge Chung's face took on a frown of surprise. The formal reading of the information is almost always waived when a defendant is represented by an attorney, but the charge of first degree arson and first degree felony murder was unexpected. The first degree allegation could mean that the State thought it had evidence of premeditation, that Hugh knew that someone was in the building and burned it anyway. I wanted to hear the specific charge, and I wanted time to think.

Judge Chung turned to the prosecutor and sighed. "Do you have an extra copy? No? Then go ahead, Ms. Kleinfeldt. Get started."

The deputy prosecuting attorney who conducts the arraignment is called the "Talking Head." The Head is usually a deputy with some experience, able to cut plea bargains on the spot if necessary. This morning the Head was a slender woman of thirty-two or so, with a long thin face, strong jaw, dark eyes and black hair. Talking Head duty is rotated every couple of weeks. I had been to arraignment on Monday of that week, and Gary Wilhelm had been pulling the duty. This woman was new. I began to wonder why she was there. Something was going on.

The prosecutor looked down at her file and began to read. Her voice was low-pitched but clear. She spoke with the accentless precision that you can hear in upper-class neighborhoods from the Main Line to Marin County.

"Mr. Prokop, you are charged with arson in the first degree," she began. "The State must prove that you knowingly and maliciously caused a fire or explosion which is manifestly dangerous to any human life, including firemen; caused a fire or explosion which damages a dwelling, or caused a fire or explosion in any building in which there was at the time a human being who was not a participant in the crime; or caused a fire or explosion on property valued at ten thousand dollars or more with interest to collect the insurance proceeds. Arson in the first degree is a class A felony.

"Mr. Prokop, you are also charged with murder in the first degree, charged here as felony murder. The state must prove that you committed the crime of arson in the first degree, and in the course of, and in furtherance of this crime, or in immediate flight therefrom, you or another participant caused the death of a person other than one of the participants in the crime. Murder in the first degree is a class A felony."

The words from the Washington statutes died away. The prosecutor paused to catch her breath. The courtroom was silent except for the muffled shuffling in the chain of prisoners. A gray-haired stocky courthouse reporter who had wandered into the spectator pews for lack of anything better to do suddenly began tapping the glass door, demanding information. The prosecutor started to read again.

"The State of Washington charges that Hugh Prokop did willfully and maliciously cause a fire manifestly dangerous to human life in a building at Westlake Avenue North on Tuesday, February 4, 1986, said building being a property valued at more than ten thousand dollars, with intent to collect insurance proceeds. At the time of the fire there was in the building a human being, Walter Kessler. Said fire caused the death of Walter Kessler."

Judge Chung looked down at Hugh. "Mr. Prokop, the State has charged you with first degree arson and first degree murder. Do you understand the nature of the charges against you?"

Hugh was silent. I prodded him gently. "Answer," I said.

"Yes, I do," he replied, his voice shaking.

"And how do you plead?"

"Not guilty, Your Honor."

Judge Chung nodded and marked something on a paper in front of him. "Application for bail?"

"Your Honor," I said, stepping forward a half step, "Defense requests bail. Mr. Prokop is a lifelong citizen of Seattle and a respected businessman. He presents no danger to the community. The State's case is very weak. The State will not be able to put on a witness placing Mr. Prokop at the scene of the fire because there isn't one. A reasonable bail would be twenty thousand dollars." I had considered asking for no bail but I didn't want to antagonize Judge Chung. If the prosecutor wanted to oppose bail I wanted her to be seen as unreasonable.

"Ms. Kleinfeldt?"

"The State does not oppose bail, Your Honor, but Mr. Prokop is accused of very serious charges and might well be tempted to flee. Bail should be high enough to discourage that. We propose two hundred thousand dollars."

"Mr. Riordan?"

"That's unreasonably high, Your Honor, given that the State apparently has no evidence to put on suggesting that Mr. Prokop is a threat to the community or is likely to flee. I haven't seen the Court Services report yet, but I'm sure it will bear me out."

Judge Chung nodded. He looked down and read from a document on his desk, then glanced up. "You're right about the report, counsel, but Ms. Kleinfeldt makes a good point, too. Let's say fifty thousand dollars."

"Thank you, Your Honor. We propose a property bail, secured by Mr. Prokop's house. He owns it free and clear, and it is worth twice that."

Judge Chung said, "Work it out with Ms. Kleinfeldt. If

the papers are okay with her I'll sign them. Are there any pre-trial issues?"

"I think there will be, Your Honor," I said. "A suppression and possibly a three-five hearing." A suppression hearing is a procedure for suppressing, or not allowing into evidence, facts or physical evidence that have been unlawfully seized. A Criminal Rule 3.5 motion seeks to exclude statements taken from the defendant while in custody. I thought Hugh was smart enough not to answer police questions while he was in county lockup, but he might have said things to a guard or a Court Services interviewer that I didn't know about. In criminal cases you argue every point you can.

"Any problem with waiving the speedy trial rule?" Judge Chung asked.

"Yes, Your Honor," I replied. "We will not waive." I wanted to put some pressure on the prosecutor and the arson squad. So far they had no evidence actually placing Hugh at the scene of the fire. If they couldn't come up with any, they were going to be in trouble, and I didn't want them to have a lot of time to dig up a witness.

"Very well," the judge said. "The omnibus hearing is set for Friday, February 21. The trial date is March 10. Mr. Prokop, subject to approval of the bail paperwork I am going to release you on bond. The conditions of that bond are simple. You must have no contact with the victim's family, if any; you are not to leave the jurisdiction, which is King County, Washington; and you are not to commit any crimes while on bail. Do you understand these conditions?"

"Yes, sir." Hugh's voice was less shaky but sounded very small.

"Next case."

As the next case was read, I gripped Hugh's arm to get his attention and said, "You'll be out in an hour. I'll get the papers signed and get your bail ticket. Go back and take it easy."

"I can't go with you now?"

"No. You've got to be processed out and get your stuff back. It won't take long. I'll see you then."

"All right." He still seemed dazed by what happened. I squeezed his arm again and took a seat on a bench against the side wall.

I waited while the rest of the arraignments were heard. When the hearing was over, I went up to the table where the prosecutor was shuffling her papers together and handing them to an assistant.

"Matthew Riordan," I said, extending a hand. "I have the property-bail paperwork here for *State v. Hugh Prokop*, if you'd like to look it over."

"Oh, hi. Liz Kleinfeldt." She shook hands briefly. Her hands were long and slender. She seemed shorter than she had appeared to be while reading the information. "Let me take a quick look at these," she said, gesturing to the papers. She read them with a studied intensity. When she was nearly through I said, "You can call WestAmerica Title and check the property's legal description if you want."

"No," she replied, putting the papers down on her table. "Your word is good. At least until I know otherwise."

"Okay. I'll just take them in and get them signed."

"Fine. Send me a copy, please."

"All right. You mind a question?"

"No. Depending on what it is, of course."

"I don't understand why you're here, being the Talking Head, today. I thought Gary Wilhelm had the duty."

"He does. To tell the truth, I came down here to look at Mr. Prokop. I've been assigned to the case for trial."

"That means you're thorough."

"Very. Nice meeting you, Mr. Riordan. I'll be in touch." She gathered up her briefcase and strode out of the courtroom. I watched her go. She had a nice walk. In another time and place I would have enjoyed watching her walk a great deal more.

I got the bail papers signed and went down into the processing area to collect Hugh Prokop. The court detail got him out quickly, and inside an hour we were walking back through the tunnel to the County Courthouse on the way to my car.

It was just after the lunchtime rush had returned to

work, and the courthouse was quiet. I had to stop off at the Court Clerk's office and check out a file, so I left Hugh sitting on a bench outside of the law library. When I came back five minutes later he had fallen asleep, leaning back against the wall with his chin resting on his chest. I woke him gently. He rubbed his face with his hands and said, "Can we stay here just a minute? I'm not feeling too hot."

"Anything serious?"

"I don't think so. Just stress and no sleep. If I can bathe and shave and get some sleep, I'll be okay."

"I'll take you straight home. Jail pretty rough?"

"I can't recommend it. They took me in and booked me and took my fingerprints. I had to get deloused and wear a jail uniform. After that I was interviewed about bail by somebody from Court Services who couldn't find my file and kept yawning and asking me what the hell my name was. Then a homicide detective and that fire investigator I talked to before came in to ask me questions. I told them I wouldn't say anything without you there."

"Did they stop bothering you?"

"After a while. I think they passed the word to the guard that I wasn't cooperating. They said they were running short on holding cells so they put me in the holding tank. The 'Hold 'Em Hilton,' one guard called it."

"I hear the tank is no fun," I said sympathetically. "Not even in the new jail."

Hugh grinned sourly. "Hearing about it does not quite do it justice. I was there five minutes when the first drunk came over to the bunk I had staked out as mine and pissed on my foot. A little later on a Spanish-looking guy, maybe a Cubano, swaggered over and told me I was going to be his woman for the night."

"Wonderful. What did you do?"

"Ignored him at first. The second time he came over, I kicked him in the balls as soon as he got close enough. After that everybody left me alone. But I stayed awake the rest of the night."

"You've had it rough. I'm glad to see you're still hanging in there."

Hugh smiled and then flushed with pride. He had been put through a test and passed it, and the rush of that victory was going to hold him together for a few days. In the long run he would need to find another way to keep his spirits up, some other reason to keep going. The sooner he found that support, in himself or someone else, the easier my job would be. But for now I would use his simple triumph in handling one night in jail to get Hugh through the first few days.

We talked a bit longer, sitting on the hallway bench like two strangers in an Edward Albee play, watching the courthouse people, criminals and ex-wives and children and bag ladies flowing down the dreary gray-marble corridors, until Hugh said he was feeling well enough to go on home.

CHAPTER 7

· Hugh picked me up at two o'clock the following Monday to drive over to the Van Zandt & Company offices in downtown Bellevue. The relationship of Seattle to Bellevue is akin to that of San Francisco and San Jose. Bellevue has become the office and residential center for the burgeoning computer-software and real estate industries sprawling into the green Cascade foothills east of Lake Washington. The business style is fast and loose but somehow curiously puritan, revolving around seven A.M. breakfast meetings and six-mile lunchtime runs through the adjacent residential neighborhoods. The obsession with work has not led to a vision for building the city. There are few parks and no sidewalks. The art museum is in a storefront. The city hall is in a shopping mall.

Van Zandt's offices were on a high floor of something called the Synsesis Tower, a thirty-story slab of pinkish-gray granite and bronze glass near the freeway. I remembered dimly that Synsesis used to be a company called Washington Radio, a manufacturer of marine radios and radars for the Navy. To spiff up their high-tech image they had spent vast sums hiring a public relations firm to come up with the new name. I guess they liked it. I thought it sounded vaguely like a new and as yet incurable disease.

Van Zandt and Susan Haight were still in a meeting when we got there. The receptionist, a pale cool blonde, told us to take a seat. Most brokerage firms try for a traditional look in their offices, but Van Zandt's lobby was done in the Darth Vader style of interior design, an overpowering combination of grays and blacks and stark whites, softened only by large watercolor paintings in cool greens and blues. Hugh and I sat down in low-slung chairs of black leather arranged around a black marble coffee table. Hugh leafed idly through an investment magazine. I drank coffee poured from an angular chrome-and-black pot and looked at my notes, feeling the minutes drag by reluctantly. By the time Van Zandt came through the door to greet us a half an hour later, I understood the decor. I was ready to buy anything.

Van Zandt bounded into the lobby with just the right combination of pleasure at our presence and concern for our problems. "Matthew," he said warmly, gripping my hand as I rose from my chair, "it's damned good to see you again." He turned to Hugh and shook Hugh's hand with both of his own. "God, Hugh, this is just terrible for you. I don't know how the police could have made such a stupid mistake. You look like you're holding your own, though. I know you're tough enough to get through this, and I'll do anything I can to help."

Hugh basked in the attention. He smiled widely and said, "Thanks, Greg. I knew I could count on you. Where's Susan?"

"Getting the stuff together for our meeting. She'll join us in my office. Come on back."

We followed him down a gray-blue corridor to his office. It took up most of the northwest corner of the building, with floor-to-ceiling windows on two sides that commanded a view over Lake Washington to Seattle, with Puget Sound a thin blue line on the horizon. The office was furnished in the same black-on-gray style as the lobby. As you entered there was a glass conference table atop a black marble base with four leather chairs around it. Van Zandt's desk was a black lacquer table, fitted with a phone and nothing else, that faced into the room. Against the far wall, behind the desk, a matching black credenza supported two large personal-computer set-ups and a second telephone console.

Van Zandt ushered us to seats around the table. When we were seated I pointed to the computer stations on the far wall and said, "So that's where all the money gets made. I'm impressed."

Van Zandt laughed heartily. "That's right," he said. "I do the currency trading and Susan runs the retail side of the brokerage. All the major currency markets—London, New York, Zurich, Hong Kong, Tokyo—have trading data on-line, so I can review price movements and trade directly, right from here. Hell, if I wanted to, I could do it from Tahiti. All I'd need would be a couple of computers and some dedicated phone lines."

"How do you keep up with all those markets? Do you ever sleep?"

"Well, the secret is to keep it simple. We zero out our balance at the end of each day, so we're back in dollars, no activity, when I go home for the night. Then everything stays steady until I come back in the next morning. If a day looks too bad, I may not trade at all. That doesn't happen very often. Traders love volatile markets. That's how we make our money."

Van Zandt could, I knew, talk about making money until sometime in the next century. I decided to change the subject. "Greg," I said, "how is Sandra Kessler holding up?"

"Not too well, I'm afraid. Sandy is the sort of woman who needs a lot of stability, a lot of structure. Losing her husband just rips that away."

"God," Hugh said, "I feel so awful. I've been so wrapped up in my own problems I've completely forgotten about her. I'll have to talk to her."

"Not if you want to stay out of jail," I said dryly. "One of the bail conditions is no contact with the victim's family, remember?"

"Oh," Hugh said in a small voice. "I didn't . . . never mind."

"Don't worry, Hugh," Van Zandt chimed in, "Susan and I will pass along your condolences and explain."

"Greg," I cut in, "while we're on the subject, what can you tell me about Walter Kessler? I only met him once, and I need more information about him if I'm going to try this case."

"Uh-huh. Well, the truthful answer is, not all that much. I can have somebody make a copy of his résumé and personnel file for you. I'll do that now." He strode to the desk telephone, whispered into its receiver, and hung up. "The file will be at the desk when you leave," he said, returning to his chair. "Not that it will be much help. Walter worked for me for thirteen months. The guy worked very hard, but not much personality, you know? I do remember being absolutely amazed when he fell for Sandra. She was working here then, as a trading assistant. They were really an unlikely match. I wondered if the guy had ever had a serious relationship with a woman before. When they started dating, he used to come shyly into my office to ask me for advice on how to do things, where to take her." He shook his head sadly at the memory. "And now he's gone. Poor bastard."

"Do you know why Kessler was in Hugh's building when the fire was started?"

"No. Why should I? I mean, he wasn't on company business or anything like that. I assume he was working on Hugh's books. I knew that he still had one or two private clients that he did accounting for."

"Is there anyone you can think of who would want to kill Kessler?"

"No. I mean, the man was an accountant, like every joke you've ever heard about accountants. Quiet, shy, hardworking. As far as I know he didn't have an enemy in the world."

"What about you?"

His eyes narrowed. "What do you mean by that?" he asked tightly.

"I mean I want you to think. The last time I saw you and Kessler together, it was New Year's Day and you very nearly took his head off. That's the kind of thing I'm looking for, Greg. Now please, think."

He nodded. "I see your point. I know I got mad that

day. It was a holiday, and I didn't want to be disturbed to fill out some forms for the damned government. I was pretty childish about it, as you saw. I apologized to Walter as soon as we got up to the house. We didn't have any other problems after that. I never saw Walter get into it with anybody else, even to the extent that he and I got into a snit at New Year's. As far as I know he did not have any enemies, did not gamble, was not being blackmailed.''

"Thank you for answering that so thoroughly, Greg. But, if you can think of anything else, anything at all, please call me right away.''

Van Zandt nodded, still less than happy about being put through the wringer, when Susan Haight walked into the room. She wore a tailored double-breasted suit in a light gray with a pale lavender silk blouse and a matching show handkerchief. Her hair was brushed out, long and gleaming against the suit, and her makeup highlighted her striking narrow face, high cheekbones and dark eyes. She looked like a *Vogue* image of the perfect working woman, businesslike but still very attractive.

She put a thin stack of manila folders on the conference table and went to greet Hugh.

"Hi, darling,'' she said, bending over to kiss him lightly on the cheek. "I'm sorry to slow things up but I wanted to get this material put together, and the phones just kept ringing.''

"How's the market doing?'' Greg asked.

"The Dow closed at 2340, up eleven points. Everyone is buying. If I keep writing orders at this rate I'm going to demand two weeks in Hawaii just to rest my fingers,'' she replied, grinning. "Sorry,'' she added, suddenly sobered by the purpose of the meeting. "Let's get down to work.''

She passed a folder to each of us. "This is Hugh's financial statement and a couple of recent account statements from us,'' she explained. "Basically, Hugh's now recovering from losses on stock, leveraged real estate, and oil tax-shelter investments. When you add in the tax penalties, the losses over the last two years total about a half a million dollars.''

Hugh glanced down at the papers sourly. "I think everybody knows that, Susan," he said shortly.

"Not me," I replied. "Susan, keep going."

"When the IRS was paid off," she continued, "Hugh retained his house, the business, which we value at just over two million dollars before the fire, and about a hundred and fifty thousand in cash and other stocks. We've reinvested the liquid assets, dividing them between stocks and our currency funds. Here are the current statements. We've got capital gains and income since last September of over forty thousand dollars."

"Great results," I said, skimming over the statements. "I don't see the money found in Hugh's safe listed. I thought some of it was his. Where does that fit in?"

Susan Haight hesitated before answering, then looked at Van Zandt. He picked up the cue and answered. "Matthew," he said slowly, "that's a very touchy deal. Is there any way you can keep that out of the trial?"

"No," I said tersely. "Hugh's books will be gone over by an expert accountant, working for the State. I have to be prepared to respond to everything."

Van Zandt chewed that one over, unhappily. "All right," he said, "but you're not going to like it. The cash was to be used to purchase a house on Oahu. It's a very good property, oceanfront. It belongs to a Filipino businessman who was tied to the Marcos regime. He thinks he's going to be a target in some lawsuits brought by the Aquino government. Or maybe it's worse, maybe he's on somebody's shit list. I don't know. He wanted to disappear for a while, and so he needed cash. One of his investment advisors had worked with us before, and he offered me the house for a quarter-million cash. It's worth twice that, or more. Hugh was going to go over and buy it. The deal was set to go down last week. By the time the call came, the police had impounded the money. The banks were closed, and we couldn't deal. Somebody else got it, I guess."

"Whose money is involved?" I asked.

"Susan and I each put up a hundred thousand; Hugh put up fifty."

"I don't see the fifty on Hugh's financials. Why?"

"I put up the extra fifty as a favor to Hugh," Van Zandt said. "This way he keeps his money working in the market while we have the house cleaned up and resold. The property appraised two years ago for nearly six hundred thousand, and with very little effort it could be worth more."

"Why isn't Hugh's note shown in the financials?" I persisted.

"Because he hasn't signed one yet. If the deal had gone through, we would have drawn up the papers."

"Isn't that kind of a risky deal for a guy who's had some serious losses, Greg?"

"A lot less risky than the stock market," he replied. He rolled his copy of Hugh's financial statements into a tube and tapped it lightly on the table. "We would have doubled our money in six months with almost no downside. I understand from Susan that you're not much of an investor, Matthew. That's true of a lot of lawyers and doctors. So take my word for it. Every once in a while you stumble across a deal like this caused by somebody else's need for quick cash. When you do it's free money. You make out because you can take the time to market the property properly."

"How did the money get into Hugh's safe, Greg? Hugh didn't know it was there when he opened the safe."

"I don't know. I was expecting the call from the seller at any time, so I told Walter to get the cash together and deliver it to Hugh. I assume he put it there the night of the fire."

"A quarter million's a hell of a lot. Why not take it yourself?"

"It was late in the day. Hugh was gone. And Walter would have had to go with me, anyway. I didn't know the combination to Hugh's safe. Walter did."

I stopped and thought. Van Zandt's story could at least account for the money and Kessler's presence in the building. Buying property from a Marcos crony with a suitcase of cash would not help build the honest, neighborhood businessman image I had in mind for Hugh, but that's the way lawsuits go. No case or client is perfect.

"I think I'm going to need both of you to testify about this at trial," I said slowly, looking at Haight and Van Zandt. "Both the real estate deal and the profits Hugh was making in the currency funds. It would be even more effective, Greg, if you could testify a little about how the trading is done."

"Jesus," he said, with sudden, surprising anger. "That's a really strange idea, Matthew. I mean, what's that got to do with the fire?"

"It helps reduce Hugh's motive to set the blaze," I replied. "A guy who's covering his losses, making it back, is less likely to do something desperate, like burning his own business."

"I suppose, but I really hate to spread my affairs all over the newspapers like that. God, this thing's going to get a lot of publicity."

"Some, Greg. But I'm going to need your testimony. If I have to, I'll subpoena both you and Susan, and your records." And would do it anyway, I added mentally, if only to make damn sure that they showed up at the trial.

"Damnit, you just try that. See how far you'd get," Van Zandt responded angrily.

"Hey, wait a minute," Hugh said, trying to smooth things over. "Let's not get carried away. Maybe the case won't even come to trial. Aren't there some motions you want to make, Matthew, to get it dismissed before trial?"

"We're going to try that," I said, "but it doesn't always work. I know you don't like it, Greg. I don't blame you. But right now I'm only concerned about my client's case. Anything else is just not my problem."

"I see." Van Zandt stood up abruptly and looked at his watch. "I've got to go, people. I've got some late meetings out of the office. We're trying to find new accountants to take over for Walter. Come on, Susan." He strode out of the room, Susan Haight trailing reluctantly behind him. She looked back at Hugh, just once, before she went out the door.

We drove back across the Evergreen Point Floating Bridge in silence. Hugh was wary and defensive after the tense scene in Van Zandt's office. Traffic was heavy and we inched along. Hugh glared angrily at the stalled drivers around him, as if the traffic was a personal affront.

He seemed to relax as the traffic cleared and we rolled up the curving on-ramp to Interstate 5.

"Where do you want to be dropped off?" he asked at last.

"My office, please. Just get off at 45th and go down Roosevelt to Northlake Way."

"Okay."

When we were off the freeway I said, "Did you have a chance to think about getting another lawyer? You should decide soon."

He didn't answer. The light in front of him turned red and he stopped. He turned to look at me.

"What the hell is going on here, Matthew?" he said angrily. "Why do you want to get out so bad? Do you think I'm guilty, too?"

"No," I said quietly. "But Hugh, I think you are in very bad trouble. All the financial losses you've had are not going to look good to a jury. You're going to need the best criminal-defense lawyer you can get. I am competent, but I'm not the best."

"Jesus. You really know how to build my confidence, don't you. I want you to defend me, but not if you've got doubts about me." He pulled his Porsche over to the side of the road, into a boat-broker's empty parking lot, and switched off the engine. "Look," he said, "it's obvious to me that you've got some doubts. Let's drag them out and look at them."

I didn't say anything right away. I opened the door and got out of the narrow bucket seat, standing and stretching out my legs, easing the ache in my football-racked right knee.

Hugh got out, too, and sat on the hood of the car, staring out through a tangle of masts and marine junk at the moody waters of Lake Union. I walked around to his side of the car and parked my rear end against the driver's door.

"Okay," I finally said. "Suppose you start off by telling me where the money in the safe really came from."

"Jesus. We told you that. It came from the three of us. For the house in Hawaii."

"Yeah, I heard Greg tell me that. But I also saw your face when you opened that briefcase after the fire. You didn't know where the money came from then. And last Thursday you didn't know what Kessler was doing in your office."

"I was just surprised, that's all. I didn't expect the money to be in the safe yet. I didn't know Walter was bringing it over."

"If you knew that this real estate deal was in the works, why didn't you mention it on the night of the fire? You were looking at a quarter of a million dollars getting burned up. You should have been breaking down walls to get into the building."

"I didn't know the money was there yet, and I had other things on my mind. That business has been in the family for my whole life. It was like losing a brother, watching it burn."

That seemed reasonable but hardly complete. I pushed on.

"What about Walter, Hugh? Did you three really know him well enough to trust him with a quarter of a million bucks? In cash?"

"I didn't know him personally that well, but he'd been our accountant for years. If he was going to steal from me or Van Zandt, he would have done it a long time ago. You don't think he was involved in the fire, do you?"

"He's the one that wound up dead," I replied. "And unless somebody else turns up soon, that's what we're going to have to say. Look, what about the rest of them? Van Zandt and Susan, I mean. You've put a big chunk of the rest of your money in their hands."

"And they're doing great things with it. That's got to be part of my defense, just like you said. I didn't have a motive because I'm still not broke and they're helping me earn it back."

"What about Susan?" I persisted. "How much do you know about her?"

He turned away from me to stare again, past the lakefront buildings and into the distance. "Just that I love her, man." He said quietly. "Just that I love her. I didn't know how much until this happened."

"Yeah, but she had a key to the warehouse."

"That was so she could come in at night, if I was working late," he said angrily. "Leave Susan out of this. And don't subpoena her, or Greg. They'll get whatever records you need."

I didn't say anything. I rubbed the tired out of my face with both hands and thought hard. The explanations about the money sounded just far enough out to be true, but Hugh seemed just too dense on the subjects of Kessler and the Hawaiian real estate deal. I couldn't shake the feeling that something was missing, the small measure of fact that distinguishes truth from explanation. Or had I simply dealt with too many liars over too many years to be able to tell the difference?

Hugh nudged me. "So where do we stand, Matthew? You going to stick it out with me?"

"It's not a question of that, Hugh. It never was. I can't make you decide to get another lawyer. If you want me to stay with it, I have to, under the code of ethics. And because I'm your friend."

"Good, man. Good." He smiled like a child, big and wide, yet somehow shy. "So where do we go from here?"

"Let's get started back to my office. In the meantime you can tell me more about anyone else who might have had a motive to burn you out."

We got back in the car and Hugh put the Porsche into gear and pulled back onto Northlake Way.

"I've been thinking about that ever since I got out of jail," he said slowly, "and I can only come up with two. One is my nephew, Howard Gaines. I talked to Mary Alice about him this morning, and I guess he could have done it. You see, he wants the company to liquidate. That would give him a quick two or three hundred thousand, which he wants pretty bad."

"Why doesn't he just sell his stock?"

"You know how it is with closely held companies. There's no real market for the stock and you have to sell at a big discount, maybe as much as half the book value. Mary or I would have bought him out, except I didn't have the money last year."

"How's your personal relationship with him?"

Hugh grinned sourly. "Just lovely. The kid hates my guts. He'd probably be willing to burn me out for fun."

"Anything behind it?"

"I think it goes back to his mother's death, four years back. He wanted to come live with me, but I was just finished with my divorce and going through the usual binge, drinking a lot and seeing how often I could get laid. I didn't want the responsibility, so after a month or two I enrolled him in the boarding division at Seaside School. He hated it and dropped out a couple of years later."

I nodded. Children, right or wrong, have very long memories.

"Who else could have a motive, Hugh?"

"The only other person I can think of would be Ray Bowen."

"The labor leader?"

"Uh-huh. His union has represented our workers since the late 1930s. The union struck me and a couple other companies two years ago and it was nasty. A lot of threats got made. My house had rocks and bottles tossed at it, even a Molotov cocktail–type thing that burned up on the front sidewalk."

"Why would Bowen burn you out? Wouldn't his people lose their jobs?"

"Yes. In the short run, anyway. We've got contract talks next month if I'm still in business. I've told him that if he demands too much I'm going to go nonunion. Maybe he wanted to send me a message that got out of hand. Maybe I'm supposed to be the example for the other companies."

"How about one of your employees? Did you make that

list? It's not unheard of for a pissed-off employee to set a fire. Kessler could have been caught by accident.''

"I've been through it. We only have about forty people working for the company, and I like to think I know them all pretty well. I couldn't come up with anybody.''

"Yes, but this was such an amateurish job that it fits the pattern. Can I look at the personnel files?''

He looked at me ruefully. "Burned up, remember?''

"Right. I forgot. I'm going to want a list of every employee—names, addresses, what they do for the company. I'll give you a dictation machine, since yours is burned up, and you can just talk it out. Make a note of any employee you think might have a grudge against you or the company. I'll have them checked out.''

"Okay. Anything else?''

"Not that I can think of.''

He pulled into the parking lot of my building and stopped the car. "Listen,'' he said as I got out, "I really appreciate you sticking with me on this. I know it'll work out fine.''

I smiled at him and said, "It's going to be tough, but if you stay put-together, it'll be okay. Keep loose, and go easy on the drinking, okay? Think of it as staying in training. And when the trial is over, we'll go out and throw the damndest party you ever saw.''

He grinned. "Sounds good. I'll stop by and get that machine from you sometime tomorrow.''

"Good night.''

Hugh's car pulled away. I went up the outside wooden stairs to my second-story office. I put a new Dire Straits tape on the small stereo and listened while I cleaned up the files in cases I had neglected since Hugh's problems had started dominating my life. As I worked the momentary rush of good feeling brought on by Hugh's faith in himself and his innocence began to fade away. The nagging doubts I had about the real source of the money in the safe and Hugh's shaky financial position chewed away at me. When I finished with the other work it was nearly eight o'clock. I thought about going down to the YMCA gym to work out but decided it was too late and drove home.

The house I live in is on the northwest shore of Lake

Washington, sheltered beneath tall pines and alders planted nearly thirty years ago by my aunt, a painter and teacher who had built the house as a summer cottage. The other cottages that once stood nearby had been pulled down years ago to make way for more expensive glass-and-cedar boxes that sprawled down the hill to the lakeshore. I could probably borrow enough against the value of the land to put up something fancy, but the house suits me well enough. It is squarish and plain, but then again, so am I.

I built a fire to take the night chill off the house and reheated some leftover Chinese carry-out, then found I couldn't eat it. I threw it away, poured myself some Irish whiskey, and carried the glass around with me as I paced the house.

Finally I went to the desk in the living room, set down the glass, and reached for the phone. My friend Bernstein, a private investigator, was supposed to be in Seattle, working on a case. He had left a Seattle number at my office a couple of days before.

I dialed the number he had given me. The phone was answered by a woman's deep, warm voice, a great voice with just enough of a growl in it to make me think of warm September afternoons. In Paris. In bed.

I spoke to her briefly and waited. A few seconds later Bernstein came on the phone.

"I want to meet that woman," I said. "Soon. Preferably tonight."

"Not on your life, Matthew. And no, she has no sisters. Or equals. What's on your mind?"

"You got any free time? Or any you can spare? I need some things checked out."

"Some. Do I get paid?"

"Yes. Is forty bucks an hour okay, considering you're probably going to be charging the time to someone else, too?"

He laughed. His laugh sounds harsh, even when he is in good humor. "When you do good work nobody checks the bill. What's this about?"

I filled him in quickly on the fire and Hugh's background. "I want you to check on the victim. Walter E.

Kessler. He's an accountant." I gave Bernstein the rest of the facts I knew about Kessler, including his address and employment. "I'll have his personnel file for you tomorrow."

"Anything else?" he asked, when I was finished.

I hesitated. "I want you to see if you can find me a professional torch who might know something about the fire. It looks like an amateur job, but it could have been made to look that way."

"That's a little out of my field, but I can try. What gives? I thought you said you were defending this guy."

"I am, but I've got to know. Give me a call if you find anything."

"I will." He rang off and I put the phone down on the desk.

I knew at that moment that I should never have taken Hugh's case. A good criminal-defense lawyer cares nothing about whether the client is guilty or innocent. Guilt and innocence are labels; outcomes, not states of truth. The good criminal-defense lawyer cares only about his or her performance and the result. Winning is the only good. To care about anything else wrongs the client. I had always been able to work like that. Always. But now I felt I was losing my perspective. I wanted to know the truth of what had happened here. Winning or losing no longer seemed to be enough.

CHAPTER 8

The International Warehouse Workers of the World, the I-Triple-W, had once been a union to reckon with, one of the three unions, along with the Teamsters and the Longshoremen, that could shut down ports all the way down the West Coast to San Diego. First organized in the 1930s, the IWWW had been the most left-wing union and the toughest, willing to take on everyone from Governor Arthur Langlie's National Guard to the Teamsters under Dave Beck and Jimmy Hoffa. In the old days they fought with their wits as much as their fists. In 1939, when the Teamsters tried to muscle in on their brewery workers, the IWWW retaliated by shutting down the beer supply to the roadhouses along old U.S. Highways 2 and 99, the main routes in or out of Seattle. The truck drivers drove dry until they nearly lynched their own leaders. The Teamsters had to sue for peace.

Like other unions the IWWW was a victim of time, union busting, the Japanese, and its own success. From 1945 to 1980 IWWW members made top wages in a union town with the highest average wage in the country. Union workers moved out of the Rainier Valley and Fremont and Wallingford into the new suburbs, buying homes right beside those of doctors and dentists and company managers. They bought boats and Buicks and summer cabins on the Hood Canal and then retired happily, even as the union was becoming more Black and Asian in membership. Union jobs grew scarce, and wages were cut back in the face of company threats to go bankrupt and break the union contracts.

The IWWW hiring hall was north of downtown on Elliott Avenue, a ramshackle, three-story brick-and-frame structure looking unhappily aged between two newer, midrise office buildings made of white concrete and black mirrored glass. I found a parking place on Elliott and walked into the hiring hall, looking for the union offices.

It was still early morning and big copper coffee urns steamed at the entrance to the hiring hall. The floor was cracked vinyl tile, scarred by a million cigarette burns. Uneven rows of straight-back chairs had been set up in front of the dispatcher's window at the head of the room. The stained brown walls might once have been beige. They were covered with union posters and announcements of union and political meetings.

There was a sign marked OFFICE at the stairs beside the dispatcher's glass box. I went up the steps to a second-floor landing and started to walk down the gloomy hall, when a black man the size and shape of an NFL tackle stepped out of a doorway and blocked my path.

"Hey there, friend," he said easily, "where you headed?" His voice was polite, neither threatening nor servile. His eyes and face were dispassionate.

"To see Ray Bowen," I said. "His office down this way?"

"Does Ray know you're coming?"

"I guess so. I talked to him yesterday. My name's Riordan."

"Wait here." He turned around and walked to the end of the hallway and into an office.

I waited in the hall and reviewed what I knew about Ray Bowen. He had been the first and only real leader the IWWW had ever had, a red-haired kid still in his twenties when he became head of the Seattle local in 1934, the year before the warehousemen had pulled out of the American Federation of Labor. The Seattle local had been the home office of the union even after it had organized into San

Francisco, Portland, and Los Angeles. Bowen had become known as Ray the Red during the late 1930s, when his united front with the Communist party led to six month's jail time on a bogus Smith Act conviction. In 1950 Bowen and Harry Bridges of the Longshoremen had gotten on the wrong side of Harry Truman when they shut down West Coast shipping during the Korean War. Bowen had pulled more jail time in 1953 when he'd told Joe McCarthy's committee to go to hell. He was equally tough when it came to keeping control of his union. There had been a rebellion in the union ranks in 1974, but it had stopped cold when one of the leaders of the rebellion had a swimming accident in his own bathtub. Nothing was ever proved, but a new generation of people learned that it was healthier to stay clear of Ray Bowen.

The tall black man returned. There was a gently amused smile on his face. "Ray say he don't know what the fuck you want to talk to him about," the man said, "but he'll give you five minutes." He started to walk toward Bowen's office.

"I hope I don't go overtime," I replied as I followed. "What happens if I do?"

The man turned and smiled over his shoulder. "We got a tradition in this union," he said. "First I throw you down the stairs. Then I buy you a beer to show you there's no hard feelings."

"That's nice. If I buy, can I throw you down the stairs?"

The man's booming laughter accompanied me all the way down the hall into Ray Bowen's office. "Have a seat. Ray'll be right back."

The office was big but hardly palatial. There was a scarred oak desk with a padded leather chair facing the door, turned away from the picture window view of Puget Sound. Visitors got their choice of two straight-back wood chairs or an ancient, sagging sofa in cracked black leather. The walls were grimy and needed fresh paint. They were covered with framed pictures of Bowen at union picnics, Bowen with assorted politicians, Bowen standing up and screaming obscenities at Senator Joe McCarthy and his much-despised aide, Roy Cohn. The photographer had caught McCarthy with his mouth open, slack-jawed with amazement that anyone would dare to tell him where to go.

I sat down on one of the chairs and continued to study the parade of history on Bowen's office walls. I was still lost in them when Bowen came in.

"You're Riordan?" he demanded, his voice raspy and worn from what sounded like decades of bourbon and cigarettes. "I'm Ray Bowen." He walked past me and sat down behind his desk. He was in his mid-seventies now, gray and balding, a bantam rooster of a man with wide, strong shoulders and long arms. He was wearing brown cotton-twill work clothes, the kind they sell in the back of the Sears catalog. The sleeves of his shirt were rolled up to the elbow. His arms were heavy from years of warehouse work, his wrists thick as fence posts, veins bulging in his forearms. His fingers were stained yellow from nicotine.

"So what the fuck you want with me?" Bowen asked irritably, idly picking up a sheaf of papers and tossing it on the far corner of his desk.

"It's like I told you over the phone," I replied. "I'm a lawyer, representing Hugh Prokop. His warehouse burned down."

"So I heard. I got a couple dozen guys out of work because of it, and I've got nothing coming in to feed them. The word is Prokop torched it himself."

"The word's wrong. Prokop didn't burn it. I'm trying to find out who did."

He gave me a stare that could have flash-frozen a side of beef. His eyes were gray-green and watery with age but still nasty. "So why are you coming around here?" he croaked. "You think maybe I had something to do with it?"

"The Prokop Marine strike two years ago was a nasty one. There were pickets, and threats got made when the temporary workers crossed the lines. Personal threats, of the I-Know-Where-Your-Kids-Go-To-School type. You've got another negotiation coming up in less than two months, if Prokop is still in business. Maybe somebody tried to send Prokop a message. Maybe the message got out of hand.''

Bowen let his breath out in a long whistle of disbelief. "Brother," he said slowly, "you might be a lawyer but you're sitting on your brains. I'm trying to keep little guys like Prokop in business. If guys like him get pushed to the wall, it'll be just me and the big companies, with their goddamn union-breaking consultants and their squad of lawyers. I'm not getting younger. Those are fights I'm starting to lose.''

I stayed with it. "I'm not saying you'd want to burn him out. Just wake him up a little before the contract expires. Little fires sometimes turn into big ones.''

He picked up a pack of Luckies and shook one out. He lit it and exhaled, then picked a piece of tobacco off his tongue. "You're fishing," he said calmly. "None of my guys had anything to do with it.''

"Come off it, Bowen. You've never been afraid to mix it up in a strike or any other time. Guys cross you, they get hurt. Want me to make a circus of this? Subpoena your records, call you as a witness, throw up a cloud of smoke about the IWWW? You can't afford that.''

He leaned forward in his chair. He held his cigarette between his index and middle fingers and pointed it at me as though it were a poker. "You try that, you shithead, just try it. You think I'd back off from a fight like that? I go back a long way in this town. There's things I can do that'd stop you dead.''

"Like what? Break my legs?''

"No." A sweet, crafty smile spread over his face. He coughed once, a deep rumbling hack, and stubbed out the cigarette. "I'd let you put on your circus. And then I'd show up with the governor and a couple of other people willing to testify to my upstanding character. I'd paint Prokop as the sort of union-busting creep that'd do anything for money. I'd tell that jury, and I'd swear it on a stack of Bibles, that I'd never do anything like that. Not me, a doddering relic of the thirties with six months left from lung cancer, which happens to be true.'' The sweet smile reappeared. "I been in court a time or two. That jury would convict Prokop in five minutes."

I let his words hang on the air for a minute. Bowen was right and we both knew it. He went on.

"Let me tell you something else, for what it's worth. When we went into contract this time we were going to give Prokop a sweetheart deal. All he had to do was show us his books, demonstrate how thin his margins were. I know times have been hard for his company. We always fought him hard, but I would never put a guy like that out of business. He's pretty honest. Not like these fucking conglomerates."

"What about the guys that work there?" I asked. "Could one of them have a grudge against Prokop or the company, something the union wasn't backing him on?"

"I haven't heard anything like that. None of the guys out there are hotheads. Most are in their forties or fifties, solid family guys. We haven't had a single work-related beef out of Prokop Marine for a year."

I paused and weighed what Bowen had said. It sounded right. Prokop had no evidence that the union was involved in the fire. Finally I said, "You need to understand. We've got to try every angle."

"No, I don't," he said angrily. "Christ, Prokop should know better. Sure, I fight him. That's my job. But I've got nothing against the guy. I knew his old man." His voice softened. "Look, if you want a character witness for Prokop, I'd be willing to do that. If I'm still alive. Give me a call."

I got up and thanked him for his time and walked out of the union hall and back down the street. In an ironic way Bowen and Prokop were a lot alike. Both of them could handle problems when they came straight on, when there was a card you could use to tell which players were good, which bad. Both of them seemed out of place in a world where nameless, faceless institutions made collective decisions that might be good or bad, but were never individual, in the sense that you could find the man or woman responsible and judge what they'd done. The old disappearing world they still lived in seemed better to me, but that was only nostalgia. What mattered was that another door for Hugh Prokop's escape had been shut firmly in my face.

By the time I got back to my office it was lunchtime and Bernstein was waiting for me, wearing a severely cut black business suit made of bulletproof banker's flannel and a scowl that I could see right through his heavy black beard. Bernstein is the best, and probably only, private detective in Kalispell, Montana. We share a history that seems to go back forever, to a dusty courtyard behind a third-rate Saigon hotel during the hell of a rocket barrage in April of 1970. After the war I had gone to learn and practice law in Boston and New York while Bernstein had stayed with the CIA. We dropped into each other's lives in those years like distant relatives on long vacations, but our friendship managed to hold together. And Bernstein was always the first person I would call if I was in trouble.

Bernstein had been in Seattle on and off for the past six weeks, working on a fraud case involving the sinking of a heavily insured fish-processing ship off the British Columbia coast. The insurance companies had denied coverage and Bernstein was working for Lloyd's of London, the primary insurer, trying to prove that the ship had been scuttled by her owners. The ship owner's attorney had been taking Bernstein's deposition for the last two days. His temper, never good, hadn't held up.

"About time," he growled as I came in. "Our lunch reservations won't hold much longer."

I went over to my desk and checked my phone messages as he put on his coat. "Where am I taking you?" I asked, looking up from my desk.

"Canlis," he replied. "I want a couple of drinks. And a steak."

"There goes the rest of the afternoon," I sighed. Lunch with Bernstein is a serious process. "Your deposition finally over?"

"That fucking lawyer," he growled, heading for the door, "is a *serious* pipsqueak. I should have strangled him."

"Well, the case isn't over yet. You'll get your chance. Hang on. I'm coming."

We drove around to Canlis, an old-style expense-account palace across Lake Union from my office. We walked in past the bar and were seated at a table overlooking the lake. Bernstein studied the lengthy menu and guzzled a double vodka martini while I fiddled with a weak whiskey and water. After considerable thought he finally signaled one of the kimono-clad waitresses over to our table and ordered a large, carefully selected lunch. A second martini arrived, and he tasted it thoughtfully, found it adequate, and looked me over.

"You look lousy, my friend. Case not going well?"

I nodded. "Not well at all. All of the evidence so far is circumstantial, but it all points right at Prokop. Christ, the guy can't even prove where he was at the time of the fire. I can try the case on the basis of the presumption of innocence, poking holes in the evidence and raising doubts, but a jury is always happier acquitting when there is another explanation of who did it. So far I haven't got one. My best guess just went out the window this morning."

"Hasn't Ahlberg got any other suspects?"

"If he does, he's not telling me. Did you have a chance to check out Kessler? I know you haven't had much time."

Bernstein sipped at his martini and put the glass down, nodding. "I've had some free time this week, before my deposition started. I've done a background on Kessler and wife. Jesus Christ, is he boring. The next time you ask me to check out an accountant, I'm going to charge you double."

"So?" I asked impatiently. Bernstein was on his second drink and in danger of becoming expensive.

"So not much. Kessler was forty-three years old, his wife is thirty-five. They were married less than a year. It was his first marriage, her second. She has a daughter, sixteen, from the first one.

"Kessler did a couple years in the army, a quartermaster's clerk. He has a B.A. in accounting from Ohio State and came out here to join one of the Big Eight accounting firms. He passed his CPA boards but he didn't cut it with his employers. Six years ago he was fired, so he opened his own accounting firm with a couple of other guys. They were in business for five years but didn't do too well. Prokop was one of his clients. The firm folded about a year and a half ago and Kessler went to work for Van Zandt a few months after that.''

"What about the wife?''

"Not my favorite sort of person. She was a trading assistant at Van Zandt; that's how she met Kessler. She quit after they got married. The gossip is that the marriage was plenty rocky.''

"How so?''

"He works all the time, she doesn't. I hit a couple of the bars where the stockbroker types hang out in Bellevue. Seems like she's in those places pretty often. She doesn't always go home alone.''

"That doesn't mean much. Not in this day and age.''

"Maybe not. You're about to say I'm just applying the infamous double standard, and you might be right. But being the all-Bellevue boffing champion is not going to win her a free subscription to *Family Circle*. And I suspect it would have bothered Kessler.''

"Possibly. How are their finances?''

"Not good at all. Kessler was well paid, but they lived a whole lot better. Two cars, one a Benz. Big house in a nice neighborhood, but it's got a second mortgage right up to the hilt and they've got more credit cards on fire than the average bankrupt. I looked at their credit file. The banks are starting to get anxious.''

Lunch arrived, cutting off serious conversation. Bernstein ate with his usual appetite. I picked at a small steak and a salad. The stuff about Kessler was interesting only in that it confirmed so many cliches I held dear: the not-too-bright, workaholic husband, the bored, neurotically sexual housewife, the financial strain of maintaining a lifestyle equal to their expectations about what life should be. It did not answer the central questions. Why was Kessler at the warehouse that night? True, Kessler was moonlighting as Hugh's accountant, with access to the offices and the safe.

He could have been there legitimately, working late on Prokop's books, only to have been accidentally caught by the fire. He could have been placing the money into the safe, preparing for the real estate deal in Hawaii. Or worse, had he been trying to steal the money, only to have Hugh find him and kill him, then set the fire in a moment of panic? Once again, all the evidence could be made to point at Hugh.

I was still trying to figure out what the information that Bernstein had dug up meant when he reached across the table and speared my almost-untouched steak with a fork.

"I know you're not going to eat this," he announced, slicing away the corner that I had nibbled on, "so I will." He poured the last of the big, heady cabernet he'd ordered into his wineglass to go with the steak. After a while he said, "So where do we go from here?"

"I need you to do three things, I think. First, retrace Hugh's steps that night. He says he left his health club sometime after six, then went to dinner at Daniel's Broiler on Lake Washington until eight-thirty. Try to get the driving times. And check on his alibi. He says he stopped at an all-night grocery on Greenwood Avenue around ten. I've got the name of the clerk who was working that night. See if the clerk, or anybody else, remembers Prokop. I'll get you a picture.

"Second, like I said before, check around and see if you can find an active arsonist who might have taken on this kind of job."

"I didn't find anybody, but I'll try again. I thought it looked like an amateur job."

"It does. Too amateur. Third, check out Howard Gaines. He's Prokop's biker nephew. I'm going to question him tomorrow, but see what you can find out. The kid owns ten percent of the business. Maybe Gaines set Hugh up by making it look like an amateur job. Run it into the ground."

"I think it's a mistake, to look for a torch. Nine chances in ten anything I turn up will be incriminating. But you pay the money, you call the tune. Anything else?"

"I don't know," I replied. "I can't think of anything else we can do today." I rubbed my temples with both hands to ease the ache that had been building there since my talk with Ray Bowen that morning.

Bernstein smiled. "Good. That means the afternoon is free for drinking and other indoor sports."

"I don't think I should. I've kind of been in training since this case started. It's going to take all I've got."

He fixed me with his dark eyes. "The most important thing about training," he said severely, "is breaking it. Hemingway said that, I think. Come on."

Bernstein led me into the bar and selected a table near the fireplace, already stoked and roaring on this cold, dim, rainy afternoon. We stayed there drinking coffee and cognac as the rest of the lunchtime crowd filed out and returned reluctantly to their offices. In mid-afternoon we switched to beer, congratulating ourselves for avoiding those dreaded coffee jitters. Bernstein told war stories from his days with the CIA and other, even less savory outfits until five o'clock, when a smiling but firm maître d' expressed his appreciation for our business with a bill for two hundred dollars and a free cab ride home.

CHAPTER 9

The motorcycle shop was on Rainier Avenue South, taking up half of a low brick storefront building on a mixed Black-and-Asian block about half a mile south of Interstate 90. I missed the shop the first time I drove by, and had to turn around and come back. I parked in front of a soul-food shack a block past the shop and walked back up the street, holding my raincoat closed against the swirling gusts of wind and rain. It was not quite nine o'clock in the morning and I felt lousy already.

The motorcycle shop I was looking for had no sign, just a hand-lettered card in the window that said "Howard's Bikes and Parts." The card was taped in the window next to a poster for something called Ronco Cams. The poster featured a woman bodybuilder wearing a fair amount of oil and an extremely small bikini. The woman had very strong shoulders and arms. Her breasts were nothing more than pectoral muscle, flexed into a bulging mass. The top of her bikini seemed superfluous. Had she, I wondered, once been a ninety-eight-pound weakling, with scrawny arms and little nubbins of breasts, determined to build herself into an object of desire? It seemed like a good question for a stormy morning made hazy by a mild hangover.

I knocked on the front door to the shop. It was open, so I pushed my way in. The door opened into a front room used to sell bike parts. There was a counter made out of wood and covered with formica and cheap pressed paneling. A big loose-leaf catalogue of parts lay open on top. Hundreds of boxes were stacked on floor-to-ceiling metal shelves behind the counter. A couple of grimy molded-plastic chairs stood against a side wall. The walls were dingy off-yellow and covered with motorcycle posters from Honda and Kawasaki and Harley-Davidson. The floor was concrete and had been used as an ashtray. The whole place smelled of dust and motor oil and neglect.

To the left of the parts counter was a long hallway that led to the back room. I walked down the hallway and called out, "Hey, anybody here?"

A voice from the back answered. "In the back, man. Come on through." The voice was tired and gravelly sounding, as though its owner had had a much tougher night than Bernstein and I had. The hallway opened into a large back room that had been turned into a repair shop. A little grimy light leaked in through multi-paned skylights gray with dirt. The garage door at the back of the room was open a couple of feet to let in air.

The voice belonged to a gangly kid of twenty or so. He was sitting on a big early post-war Harley older than he was. The bike had been chopped and the kid sat on the saddle, his feet up against the handlebars and his back leaning against the high rear sissy bar. He had long stringy brown hair that flopped in his face, a long straight nose, and a sharp chin. His eyes were large and gray, but they looked bruised around the edges, as though he had lost a lot early in his life. Or maybe he was just hung over.

He had a beer in one hand and a cigarette in the other. He gestured with both of them toward a greasy chair next to a tool bench. "Sit," he said grandly, "I'm still finishing breakfast. You want a beer?"

I thought it over a little more than I would most mornings. "No thanks," I said, "I got things to do later today. You're Howard Gaines, right?"

"Correct. And if I were to take a wild-ass guess, I'd say that you would be my Uncle Hugh's lawyer, considering that you got a suit on and don't much look like a biker."

I took a good look at the proffered chair and decided to stay standing. "Good guess." I said. "I'll bet you know why I'm here, too."

"You're here because my dear uncle got caught holding a gas can and a book of matches when the old family business went up in smoke. Serves the cheap bastard right. Well, I own ten percent of the fucking business and I want my money out of it, man. I want it now."

"Then you'd better hope he didn't torch it. If he did the insurance won't be any good and you will be out two-thirds of the money you're expecting."

"Even if all I get's a piece of the land, man, that'd be more than I've got so far. My dear uncle paid exactly nothing to me last year in dividends. He could have paid fifty K but he wanted to buy himself a new computer or something. The prick."

I smiled. He might think he was tough, but he was still a boy, whining about what he thought was his. I was not in the best mood myself. I decided to stick a needle in him and see if it drew blood.

"Nice to see families stick together." I said sweetly. "You're what, his sister's son?"

"My mother was his oldest sister, older than Mary Alice. She got killed in a car crash when I was sixteen. My daddy was long gone, so Hugh put me in the boarding prison at Seaside School to be rid of me. But as you can see, man, I'm not exactly the prep-school type." He spread his arms, took in the grimy machine shop, and laughed.

"Yeah, well, you didn't have to be too bright to punch a couple of holes in a can of thinner and light a match, Howard. Where were you when the place burned?"

"What was that, the fourth? Probably out riding with the Warriors, man, drinking some beer and checking out the foxes. Usual stuff."

The Warriors were a local motorcycle club, an offshoot of the much larger Bandidos gang that had spread up and down the West Coast. The club was mostly Anglo but used the profile of a cigar-store Indian embroidered inside a black circle patch as its symbol, sewn to the backs of their leather jackets. So far as I knew they weren't into the heavy trades—cocaine and arms sales—like the larger gangs. That didn't mean I wanted a social chat with a couple members. I'm fond of my face, such as it is. I went on.

"You got anybody that can place you, Howard? Place you exactly for the time of the fire?"

"What for, man? I haven't been near that place in a couple of years. I used to work there but I didn't like the management. And I didn't torch it."

"No, maybe you hired it done. Punching a hole in a can of thinner and slopping it over the body of a guy in the warehouse would be a nice change of pace for some of your friends in the Warriors. It'd be just about their speed."

"Hey, look, man," he said nastily, his voice rising and becoming nasal with anger, "You don't run down the Warriors, okay? Now I had nothing to do with burning the business. I didn't do it and I didn't ask any of the brothers to have it done. You tell my uncle he's off on his own. But if I don't get my money out of the business, he's going to regret it."

I laughed. I decided to push him harder while he was angry, hoping he'd say or do something stupid. "Tough talk from a scrawny teenager," I scoffed. "Listen up, kid. Maybe your uncle wouldn't want to have you get caught up in this thing, but I don't give a shit. I'm out to win, and if that means hanging the fire on your sorry ass, that's fine with me. You're a biker, a punk. You've got all kinds of motive to torch Prokop Marine because liquidation would mean a quick two, three hundred thousand for you. You've got access to those subhuman freaks you ride with. They'd love to start fires for you. You're perfect. Pretty as a picture. All I need now is the frame."

He was smart. He didn't say a thing. He sat for a minute, face screwed up in thought. I decided it was best to leave him hanging. I was turning to go when two bikers came in the same way I had. They were both in their late twenties or early thirties, both about six feet tall, both overweight, burdened with lardy rolls around the gut. They wore heavy, bushy beards and long hair that almost, but not quite, hid their small hard eyes.

"What's the suit doing here, Howie?" one of them

said. "We heard a little conversation. He don't sound friendly at all. Want us to get rid of him?"

I watched them very carefully. Their weight would make them slow, but it would take nothing away from their thick arms, big, hard-knuckled fists, and heavy boots. I took one or two very careful steps back and thought. There was a breaker bar on the tool bench about five feet to my right. If things got nasty, I would go for it. Bikers fight in packs, and their style is to get you down and stomp on you. If it came to a fight, I would take the bar and do my best to knock them both out as quickly as I could.

"Go ahead," I said to Gaines. "Tell them to take their shot. Forty-eight hours from now you'll be in county lockup. All you need to do is give the cops an excuse. They'll absolutely love you for it."

I waited and watched the two bikers carefully. They started to come for me, spreading out and walking toward me in careful half steps. After a long five minutes Gaines said, "Hold it. If we take him it'll just mean heat on me. Let him out of here, guys. Then he can't do a thing." There was the edge of a laugh in his voice. He was right and he knew it. I started to go.

"And don't forget my fucking money, man," he said to my back. "I love it. Even if Hugh burns, I still win."

I walked out listening to him laugh.

Elizabeth Kleinfeldt, the county prosecutor assigned to Hugh's case, had left a telephone message at my office that she wanted to talk about the case. After I called in and got the message, I drove over to the courthouse and killed an hour doing some research in the law library on a motion in another case that was to be heard the next morning, then went down to the prosecutor's office on the fourth floor. I found her there, talking on the phone, but as I moved to back away from her office door, out of earshot, she motioned me back in. I looked around her office as I waited. It was furnished with the standard-issue desk and chair in pale wood, but she had brightened it with a couple of carefully tended plants and framed dance posters from the San Francisco and Pacific Northwest ballet companies.

Her degrees and honors certificates had been framed and hung on the wall nearest the door. Unlike most of the lawyers I knew hers were worth framing. University of California at Los Angeles with honors. Columbia Law School. Law Review. Order of the Coif. Maybe I should have felt intimidated. Maybe not.

Eventually she rang off. "Sorry," she said, turning in her chair to greet me. "I'm supposed to do a seminar in a couple of weeks and I'm trying to get out of it because of our trial. They aren't too happy with me. Anyway, I thought we should talk. Is it too early for lunch? I skipped breakfast this morning and I'm starved."

"Lunch is fine. Any particular place?"

"There's a hot dog take-out place in the lobby of Columbia Center on Fourth Avenue. Would that be all right? I don't have much time. I'm running behind the world today."

"Fine with me," I replied. "Let's go."

She put on a tan raincoat and we took the elevators down to the courthouse lobby. As we walked out of the building I said, "You must have been a dancer."

She frowned slightly and said, "That's right. What made you think that?"

"You walk like you might have danced. And the posters in your office. I'm sorry. I'm not trying to pry, I just don't feel like talking about law at the moment. And I'm not much good at making polite conversation."

She turned and looked at me in frank appraisal, her hands thrust deep into the pockets of her raincoat. "You're a strange guy, Riordan, you know that? I've talked to a lot of people in the office about you and nobody seems able to put you in a category. Most of them are surprised to see you handling this case."

"I'm surprised, too. I've advised my client to get somebody else, one of the big-time criminal-defense lawyers like Kelleher, or Tony Brown. He won't listen."

"Why would you do that?" she asked, her voice puzzled. This case could do a lot for your career, if you get Prokop off."

"I don't care who gets Prokop off, me or somebody

else. Just as long as he gets off. I'm really not that concerned about my career. I eat and the bills get paid."

She let that one go. I knew as soon as I had said it that I was handling this wrong, that I should be tough and cold and sarcastic, jousting for every psychological advantage I could get. Most trials are skirmishes. Murder trials are wars, and most lawyers handle them as wars, bitter and personal combat. After a while it becomes second nature, which is why lawyers lead most other professions in alcoholism, divorce and stress-induced heart attacks.

The shopping plaza lobby of Columbia Center was the architectural equivalent of a salad bar, a jumble of forms and elements arranged so that you could pick what you wanted. The floors were rough brick, the walls a mixture of pale paint and mirrors. The shop spaces were arranged around a central courtyard and set off with glowing neon signs. The center of the joint was taken up by a still-unfinished fountain, dry as the Mojave and littered with construction dust and cigarette butts.

We found the upscale hot dog counter a little ahead of the lunch rush. I looked over their selection of Yuppie dogs without enthusiasm, finally settling for a veal wurst and a lukewarm seltzer. We found a table in the courtyard and sat down. I took a bite of my dog, thought about it, and set it back down on my plate.

Elizabeth Kleinfeldt said, "Is this all right? Hot dogs are my major vice. But you don't look enthusiastic."

"It's fine," I assured her, "I was just thinking that I missed the hot dog vendor I used to go to on Wall Street. You can't get a decent hot dog on the West Coast. Not a New York Italian sausage with peppers, anyway."

"I know. You used to work in New York?"

"Yes," I said, a little more shortly than I intended. She was sizing me up and I was getting a little tired of it. "Look, Ms. Kleinfeldt, if you are short of time, we'd better get down to cases."

"Call me Liz. You're right. I'm going to offer a plea of arson two and manslaughter one. This is a major case and I'm not going to dicker. That's what I can do."

"I understand. If we were guilty it would be a good

offer, and I'd tell Hugh to take it. He's not guilty, so the answer is no."

"I don't expect you to admit his guilt, but you have to look at this reasonably, Riordan. The guy can't demonstrate where he was when the fire occurred. He's got big financial problems. The fire is without question an arson."

"The last time I checked there was a presumption of innocence," I replied. "You haven't got an eyewitness that can place him anywhere near the scene. You can't prove that he paid anybody; there isn't any paper trail or any suspicious changes in his bank accounts. You're barely going to get to the jury."

"He had a quarter of a million dollars in cash in his office safe. Given Prokop's financial troubles, there are only two possible explanations for that. First, I think Prokop was skimming from his business by cashing in his inventory. That would increase the amount he'd get from his insurance—a double fraud. Second, and it's not inconsistent with the first point, was that Prokop was going to use the money in the safe to pay off Kessler or somebody else for setting the fire. Kessler doesn't have any criminal record, but he needed money, badly. A quarter of a million dollars would be more than enough to pay off an arsonist."

"But it is not proof that something was paid. Even if Prokop paid Kessler to start the fire, why would he want to kill him?"

"I think it goes back to the skimming. Kessler's an accountant—he either set it up, or he finds out about it. He's got a key to Prokop's place. His wife told us that. Kessler is about to set the fire. Prokop stops by. He kills Kessler and burns the place to cover up, figuring that Kessler will be blamed for the fire."

"It still doesn't connect," I said stubbornly. "Suppose, for the sake of argument, you're right about the money. Prokop wouldn't pay off somebody who could be tied to him so closely, and Kessler doesn't know to make the fire look accidental. Maybe Kessler was trying to steal some money and set the fire to cover his own tracks. He got caught in it before he could get out."

"Then why was the money still in the safe?" she asked. "Kessler had the safe's combination. We found it written in his file on Prokop's business. You've seen it, we turned it over in discovery. If Kessler had set the fire himself, he would have had the money out of the safe, in his hands, ready to run. No, Mr. Riordan. Somebody hit Kessler. The M.E. found evidence of a blow in the autopsy. Prokop either killed him to get rid of him, or he caught him trying to steal. Either way, Prokop is the only one with a motive."

I took a deep breath and held it before answering. "You've got too many theories in there, counsel. If you can't decide which one's right, this close to trial, you're in deep shit. Why are the police focusing solely on Prokop? There are other people who had a motive to burn that place."

"Like who?"

"Like a biker punk named Howard Gaines. He's Prokop's nephew, owns ten percent of the stock and wants to get his money out of the business. He couldn't before, but he can now."

"That doesn't give him any more motive than Prokop."

"It gives him enough. Slugging Kessler and dumping a bunch of thinner to start a fire is just about the level of planning I'd expect from a motorcycle gang." I shook my head in frustration. "Look, I'm not going to argue it any further. You're wrong. Prokop's had some financial troubles, but he could just shut down or sell the company and come out of it with over a million bucks. He's got no real motive. And Kessler wasn't stealing. Too obvious. The guy was Prokop's accountant, for Christ's sake. If he wanted to steal from Prokop, he'd do it with a ledger book. Accountants don't do black-bag jobs in the middle of the night. Not even CPAs do that."

It wasn't a very good joke and she refused to smile. "We're not dropping this one, Riordan, even if we look bad at trial. Arson for profit has gotten too far out of control. When somebody dies, we prosecute."

"I'm not arguing with that. All I'm saying is find the right guy."

She nodded and stood up to go. "Thanks for taking time out to talk. I guess we know where we stand."

"Sounds like it. I'll see you at the omnibus hearing. I'll walk back to the courthouse with you, if you don't mind. I've got some work to do in the library."

We walked back down Fourth Avenue to the courthouse in mutually agreeable silence. When we reached the gloomy gray-marble lobby, Liz Kleinfeldt nodded a curt good-bye and disappeared through a door into the stairwell winding up the south side of the courthouse. I punched the elevator buttons for an up car and waited, thinking. There was no doubt in my mind that Kleinfeldt would be good. She was smart and tough and thorough. She had made it clear that she saw Prokop's case in clear, hard lines and would give no quarter. I was distracted by the fact that I had liked her. She seemed honest and carried herself with a sense of grace that I envied. But for all of that there was not one chance in a hundred that we would ever become friends.

The elevator came. The hell with it. I had work to do.

CHAPTER 10

The omnibus hearing was held on the twenty-first of February. I brought four evidence motions and batted only one for four, losing on the motions to exclude evidence of Prokop's finances and business practices, and to suppress the evidence found at the scene of the fire, since Swenson and Ahlberg had been there without a warrant. The only winner was a motion to exclude testimony about a fire that had occurred some years before at Hugh's Tacoma branch warehouse, just before the branch had been shut down. The insurance company that had covered Hugh previously had suspected arson in that fire, also, but had never been able to prove the source of ignition. Hugh had insisted that the fire had accidentally started, and eventually won a settlement of the claim and a letter of apology from the insurer. The evidence cut both ways, but I decided that I didn't want the jurors trying to figure it out on their own.

When the hearing was over I went down one flight of stairs to the law library, on the sixth floor of the court-house. I wanted to bone up on the law of arson and start rough drafts of special jury instructions I hoped I could get the judge to use.

The library was quiet. Rain spattered against the wide, wood-framed windows and splashed in the gray streets below. I had been twitchy all day but my nerves began to settle down as I moved through the silent library stacks of treatises and case reporters, tracing the development of Washington law on the elements of criminal arson. The librarians, almost all of them old men, moved through the library silently, shelving books or answering questions in low whispers, like monks in a medieval cloister.

By six o'clock I still hadn't gotten a message from Bernstein, who was out trying once again to turn up an arsonist who might know something about the warehouse fire. I went out to a pay phone in the gray marble hallway, silent except for the distant humming of a floor polisher. My answering service said that I should meet him in Chinatown at seven o'clock. He would either have something solid or he wouldn't, in which case he would be grumpy and need beer and a Szechuan dinner to appease him. I was so tired that either one was fine with me. The strain of trying to defend a murder case when I was unsure whether I had all the facts was starting to build up in my bones.

At quarter to seven I left the courthouse and drove the ten blocks over to Chinatown. The rain had slowed down to a light mist. I found a parking spot on Main, up the hill past Seventh, near the freeway overpass that looms over the neighborhood and rumbles like a distant thunderstorm in the night. I pulled over and sat for a moment in my car, looking down the hill.

Chinatown always looks to me like a movie set. It is just a small fragment of the city, perhaps six blocks square, cut off from the more modern parts of town by the freeway and the railyards that emerge from the tunnel below Fourth Avenue South. The streets are brick and cobblestone. On that night they gleamed black and wet in the rain. The streetlamps glowed like old moons beneath metal shades of oriental bronze. The buildings are brick, of three and four stories, dating from the turn of the century. Most are cut up into small shops and restaurants. Here and there the benevolent associations had dressed up their buildings with false-front pagodas and the Chinese characters spelling out their proper names. And always there are the lights, the neon pagodas and rice bowls and dragons, lights like living creatures in the soft velvet night.

I was snapped out of my reverie by the sound of tapping on the windshield glass. I rolled down the window.

"You okay, Matthew?" Bernstein asked.

"Yeah. What time is it?"

"Half past seven. You're late."

"I'm sorry. I must have dozed." I got out of the car and shut and locked it, then stood up and stretched, feeling the fatigue like grit in my joints. "I'm okay," I said as we walked down Main to Sixth. "What have you got for me?"

"I'm not sure. The best arsonist for hire in the city right now is a Vietnamese guy named Tran Loc Minh. He doesn't bother with little stuff, like house burnings in the Rainier Valley, or retail shops that want to have an inventory clearance sale at four in the morning. He's strictly commercial—warehouses, offices, shopping malls."

"Where'd you get this stuff?"

"I was getting nowhere by myself so I hit up an insurance company. Not the one that insures Prokop. I did some work for them on the fire at Anna Kelly's in Great Falls last year. I made a few friends."

"What in hell is Anna Kelly's?" I asked, still groggy.

"Let me," Bernstein said, severely hardening his eyes in mock anger, "hear you speak with respect for the finest topless poker parlor in the history of the State of Montana."

I rolled my eyes. "Only when love and need are one," I said.

"It was a tragedy," Bernstein replied primly.

"Not to change the subject," I said, "but where do we find this torch you've told me about?"

"With any luck, straight ahead," Bernstein replied. "He keeps office hours most evenings in a booth at the Dragon Gate Bar and Restaurant."

"And this way we can eat while we're staking the place out, right?"

Bernstein patted himself on the stomach. "Right."

The Dragon Gate was on Sixth, up a long flight of stairs from the street-level door. The stairs led to a lobby with wine-red carpets and silvered mirror tiles on the walls. To the left, a large dining room, half-filled with a mixture of

Asian and Anglo families, stretched back to the street-side windows, one flight above the sidewalk. To the right there was a red-and-black enameled door marked BAR in English and Chinese characters.

We walked through the door and paused, letting our eyes adjust to the dim light. The walls of the barroom were lacquered red. There were red leatherette booths and black chairs. A six-foot-long black dragon had been enameled on the wall behind the bar. Cigarette smoke wafted in clouds from tables packed with young Chinese and Filipino men. A few of the men turned to look our way as we paused. The din of rapid English and Chinese subsided.

"Kind of quiet," Bernstein said.

"That's because we look like heat," I replied.

Bernstein fingered the lapel of his new Burberry trench coat. "Very well-dressed heat," he said.

"Heat all the same. Let's get a beer." We stepped over to the bar. The pretty Chinese bartender glided over. "You guys want something?" she said in a husky, pissed-off barmaid's voice.

"A couple of beers. Rainier would be fine." She turned away and reached into a low cooler. She brought out two long-necked bottles.

"Glasses?" she asked.

I shook my head. She brought the bottles and set them on the bar. I gave her a twenty. When she brought back the change, holding the bills in one hand, I reached out and closed my hand over hers. "We're looking for somebody," I said. "A Vietnamese guy who hangs out here. Named Tran Loc Minh."

"I don't know anybody like that," she rasped, pulling back her hand and dropping the change from the twenty on the bar. "Try someplace else."

Bernstein stepped in to negotiate. He picked up the loose bills and straightened them on the bar. "You don't understand," he said cheerfully, smiling and nodding his head. "If you don't tell us, we're just going to keep asking. We'll ask everybody here. Some of them we won't ask as nicely as we just asked you. But we'll keep asking, every night, even if everybody here decides to hang out somewhere else. Understand?"

"No trouble," the barmaid said, sullenly. "He's in the back, near the back door." She sighed and shook her head. We probably weren't the first people in history to threaten to bust the joint up.

We walked to the back room of the crowded bar, feeling rather than seeing the silent sidelong glances from the men at the crowded tables that lined the walls of the place. For a moment I worried that some signal had been passed, that Minh would be long gone through the back door to the alley below. But it wasn't that sort of bar; the mixed Chinese and Filipino and Anglo crowd was tough, but had no particular loyalties to anyone. As long as we weren't there for them, they had no more than a spectator's interest in our presence.

Minh sat at a back corner booth, eating Peking ravioli with a pair of ivory chopsticks and reading a newspaper that he held in the other hand. He was about fifty, big and solidly built for a Vietnamese, perhaps five-ten and a hundred seventy pounds. His wide sallow face was calm as he looked up from his paper and saw me coming through the doorway from the main barroom. His eyes caught mine. They had the light of amused intelligence in them. Whatever else he might be, Minh looked like a man who loved a fight. He wasn't going to be easy to jerk around.

Bernstein and I walked quickly to the corner booth where Minh sat. We each took one side of the booth and slid in, leaving Minh caught in the middle. Minh smiled. He put down his paper and placed his chopsticks carefully on his plate, then pushed the plate away.

"Gentlemen," he said quietly, "what can I do for you?" His English was good but had the slightly French accent of the educated class in Vietnam. He took out a red box of Marlboros, offered it around, and got no takers. He shrugged and lit one for himself with a steel-cased Zippo lighter.

"Ah," he said, letting the smoke drift out of his nostrils. "One of America's finest products. Far better than the M-16s you used to send us during the war."

"You were in the war?" I asked. "Which side?"

"ARVN, of course. Only losers have to flee their country. I was a major, Second Division. A very long time ago." He paused, waiting for us to say something.

"I don't think we need names," I began. "I have an interest in a certain fire. The fire was at the Prokop Marine warehouse, on Westlake Avenue, at the south end of Lake Union."

"Yes, I know," Minh replied. "I heard about the fire. Why would you come to me about this?"

"I'm told you have a certain technical expertise in this area," I said dryly.

He looked amused, as though used to clumsy approaches. "That may be true," he said lightly. "But if I were involved, I would not tell you anything."

"I know that. I don't think you burned it. This job was too amateurish for you to have done it. Empty solvent cans lying around the body of a dead man isn't your style. But you're in the marketplace, offering your services. You see a lot, hear a lot. Maybe somebody made a pass at you to handle this one and couldn't meet your price. That's what I need to know."

"What would you offer me for this information? Money?"

"No. Peace of mind."

Minh laughed, exhaling little puffs of smoke with each laugh. He crushed his cigarette out in a cheap plastic ashtray. "Peace of mind I have, my friend. The peace of an exile. Exiles have already lost home and family and livelihood. They have peace of mind from knowing that nothing else can be taken from them."

I smiled back at him. "You don't understand," I said quietly. "If you don't tell me what I want to know, I'm going to put my friend here on your miserable sorry ass for the rest of your days, waiting until he can get you for one of your little professional barbecues. Or maybe he'll set you up for a burn he's made himself. Or maybe he'll get tired of the whole goddamned thing and just whack you out. That kind of peace of mind."

Minh grimaced and gave his head a little nod. "You make an interesting proposition. Most are not so direct."

"I try. Perhaps you have another office where we could discuss this."

"Through that door," Minh said, pointing to the fire door at the restaurant's back wall.

"Let's go."

We got up in unison and went through the back door into a narrow set of fire stairs. "Let me go first," Bernstein said. "I'll check out the street, see if it's clear. You watch our friend here."

Bernstein started down the dark stairs. I held Minh back at the first landing. Bernstein opened the street door and a bit of pale blue light leaked in from the street. "Okay," Bernstein said. "Send him down."

I prodded Minh. He took a few steps and seemed to stumble. Then a knife flashed from nowhere into his right hand, and Minh rushed for Bernstein standing at the door.

"Bernstein!" I hissed, but he had already seen it. He got his fist wrapped around the wrist that held the knife and pulled, sending Minh sprawling through the doorway. Minh rolled in the alley, then got into a crouch and lunged for Bernstein, the knife hand coming low and tight. Bernstein sidestepped and chopped the knife out of Minh's hand. He got Minh by the elbow of the same arm and whirled him around, smashing him against the tired old brick of the building so hard I thought Minh would lose consciousness. Bernstein slapped him into alertness and then pinned him against the building, one hand against Minh's throat.

"Listen to me, man," he said in a tight, throaty growl. "I did my time in Nam and if there was anybody I hated, it was you fucking ARVN officers, strutting around in the base camps in your starched fatigues and lavender scarves and stealing every fucking thing not chained down, while your soldiers and ours went out and did the dying. Now you tell us what we want to know or I'll kill you." The hand went to Minh's face and grasped him at the cheekbones. "Listen to me. You know I'll do you."

Bernstein let go and Minh sagged against the brick building like he'd been shot. He leaned over and grasped his knees while he breathed, ragged as a broken engine. Eventually he straightened up.

"One month ago," he began, "one of my people gets a call from a man I don't know, but he knows about me, says a friend told him about me. He wants to talk business, so she tells him a thousand dollars and we can talk. A few days after the call we meet at a tavern that my cousin owns. On the north side. It's a Tuesday, raining, nobody in the place. He wants to know how much it would cost to burn a warehouse. He tells me there's a lot of flammable things, like paint. I tell him I can use that, so it costs twenty-five thousand."

"Did you burn it?"

"No. The man wasn't sure he wanted it done. He says only if he has to. I checked out the building, but I never heard from him again."

"What did he look like?"

"White, Brown hair, curly. Shorter than you but wider, stronger."

Minh's description could have fit Hugh Prokop. Easily. It hit me like a blow to the belly. God, could he have been that stupid?

I turned back to Minh. "You sure about that description?" I asked, trying to keep my rising panic out of my voice.

He shrugged. "It was dark. I'm not sure I could know him if I saw him again." He looked up at me as he finished the statement, eyes searching hard for the main chance. I was sure that if I paid him he would forget that face. But then someone else could pay him or pressure him more. And bribing a witness to stay silent is the lawyer's shortest ticket from the courthouse to the jailhouse.

"Did you do anything else?" I demanded.

"One thing. A week, maybe two weeks later I went out to see the warehouse. I had the man checked out before I met him, of course, but I wanted to see the building. I drove by the building two or three times every day. I wanted to know the area, when the quiet times would be. On the last night I thought the man had decided to hire someone else. The building had just begun burning. I saw a man leaving.''

"Who was it? The same man?"

Minh shrugged, painfully. "Too dark. I stayed in my car and kept driving. I could not see."

I tried to bluff my way out. "It doesn't mean anything to me," I said nonchalantly. "But if I hear this conversation being repeated you're going to lose that peace of mind. Understood?''

He nodded. "Okay," he said, but he said it like a man who has drawn an ace on the last card and recognized that life has possibilities. He turned, and Bernstein and I watched him walk down the alley until he was out of sight. When he was gone I turned to look at Bernstein.

He read my face. "Bad news," was all he said.

I shook my head and we walked out of the alley, a whole lot worse off than when we had walked in.

CHAPTER 11

"Jesus Christ, Hugh, what in hell were you thinking? Did you think I wouldn't find out? This guy Minh is one of the best torches on the West Coast. If the cops or the fire investigation unit finds him, he won't protect you. He'll spill his guts. And he can identify you, man. He can put you in Shelton or Walla Walla for the next twenty years."

It was nine o'clock on a dreary Saturday morning and I was in my office yelling at Hugh Prokop. He sat on the couch along the far wall of my office holding his head in his hands, frightened and bewildered at the razor edge of hostility in my voice and the flush of anger on my face.

"But I didn't burn it, Matthew, honest to God, I didn't." He said it from behind his hands as they covered his face.

"Don't lie to me, Hugh. I saw Minh last night and had to bounce him off the walls to get him to talk. When he finally did talk, I believed him. The guy he's described couldn't be anyone else but you. Damn it, if you lie to me, you're dead. Facts will come out at the trial and I won't have a defense prepared. There will be nothing I can do to save you."

He raised his head and took his hands away, staring at them as if they belonged to someone else. "All right," he said hoarsely, "all right."

"Tell me."

"I went to see him. I was . . . thinking that my problems could be solved easily if I could get rid of the business. I don't know why I did it."

"Were you drinking?"

"A little. I was scared that night. I'd . . . well, I'd been drinking for a couple of days before I saw him. Not all day, but I was drinking quite a bit every night for a week of so. It was that damned oil thing, and the condo deal, and then we did the monthly books and we lost money again in December."

"Wait a minute." I got up from behind my desk and walked over to the coffee maker and poured him a fresh cup. I took it to him and put it on the low table in front of him.

"Slow down," I said. "Drink some coffee, clear your mind, and then tell me what you did. All of it, from the beginning."

He sipped at the coffee, then held his cup in both hands. "It was in early January," he said, his voice suddenly old and tired. "My oil-drilling investment had just gone bad. Tax write-offs disallowed. And I'd finally gotten out of that student condo deal in Eugene. Took a forty-thousand-dollar loss. Christ, I don't know how I got sucked into that thing. Lost forty grand, and I still had back taxes to pay, because that shelter was also disallowed by the IRS. Anyway, I took my beating and was getting the money together to pay the taxes when I got the December totals. Another loss, which means we took a loss for the whole year, a loss bad enough to kill the dividend and leave me with just the salary. After work I went down to Susan's athletic club, you know, North Sound Conditioning. I was working out and got to talking to one of the other guys there, a client of Susan's. He was in the carpet business until his place burned down last April. The insurance paid off, a million bucks free and clear. Hell, he didn't have a care in the world. After the work-out we went over to Maguire's on Shilshole Bay and had a few drinks and some dinner, and sometime after dinner when we're putting away the brandy he gives me this phone number and says that maybe what I need is a little fire to close out the business.''

"What's his name?"

"Bassingame. Ed Bassingame. He used to run a big carpet company over in Ballard.''

"What happened then?"

"A couple days later I called the number. A woman answers, a high-pitched, singsong kind of voice. I guess she was Vietnamese. She asks what I want. I say I've got a business problem, I might have to liquidate. She tells me she's interested. She tells me to go to this tavern on Aurora the next night. Nine o'clock. And to bring a thousand bucks.''

"What did you do?"

"I went. Damn it, I went. I took a thousand bucks out of the till and went. Christ, what a dive. The only people in there were a pimp and a hooker. The bartender was Vietnamese. I ordered a beer and waited. After a while this guy in the back of the room lights a cigarette and tells me to come back. I jumped about five feet. I didn't even know he was there.''

"Was there anybody else in the room?"

"I don't think so. The pimp and his girl walked out as I went in. The bartender left when the other man motioned me back.''

"What did you do? And say?"

"I gave him the thousand and said I just wanted to talk, you know, I wasn't sure about . . . what I wanted to do. He wanted to know what kind of business it was and I told him.'' Dismay spread over his face like a cloud. "Oh God," Hugh said slowly, "he must know who I am. He probably checked me out with Bassingame. Shit, how could I be so stupid?'' His face went back down into his hands as he began to weep.

"Hugh, knock it off," I said harshly. "I have to know exactly what you did or you really are done for. Did you give the man your name?''

"No, but I told him that Bassingame had told me about him. He would have checked me out, wouldn't he?''

"Probably, but that's not something we can cure. What did he tell you?"

"He said he wanted twenty-five thousand to do the job. I told him I'd have to think about it."

"Are you sure he understood that? Did he know he wasn't supposed to just go out and burn it?"

"He knew. He said he wanted ten thousand in advance. And he told me to make up my mind soon."

"Did you have any further contact with him?"

"No. I never went back. Honestly, I didn't. You've got to believe me."

"I do," I said dryly, "but I'm not quite sure why. Has he tried to shake you down? Have you had any oddball things happen since then that might be Minh trying to communicate with you? Any odd phone calls, unsigned letters, anything like that?"

"Nothing. I haven't . . . I've been trying to put it out of my mind. I'm sorry, Matthew, I just didn't want to tell you. I was afraid of what you'd think."

"Hugh, it's not what I think that matters. This game is for your life. You've got to remember that. And if there is anything, anything at all about this case that you haven't told me, tell me now."

He didn't answer. I poured myself another cup of coffee and went back to my desk and thought. If Hugh's meeting with Minh came out at trial it could be devastating, if the prosecution used it in the right way. It didn't seem likely that either Minh or Bassingame, the ex–carpet wholesaler, would come forward voluntarily. Either one of them might get busted and use the information to plea-bargain, but the prosecutor hadn't disclosed any information in discovery that could even remotely tie in testimony by Minh or Bassingame. If the meeting with Minh did come out, the legal effect might not be conclusive. Hugh had thought about having his building burned and had done one act, contacting Minh. That would be evidence to support an attempted arson rap, motive plus one overt act, but it wouldn't be enough to nail Hugh for conspiracy or for the arson itself. It could be lived with. Maybe. But if it got to the jury, they would roast Hugh on the spot.

He was silent. "Look," I said finally, "the prosecution's going to say that you were skimming cash by selling the inventory off, that Kessler tried to rip you off, and that you caught him at it and killed him. Is there anything in what's left of the company records that will support that? Anything at all?"

He shook his head. "I wasn't skimming anything. I went to Minh because I was . . . I don't know. It seemed like an easy way out." He shook his head, as if he could clear his thoughts, make them go away.

"Don't tell anyone else about this, not even Susan. What you've told me is protected by the attorney-client privilege. Bernstein, my investigator, can't be forced to testify, because he is working for me. The chances are these facts won't come out in court, because I don't think the prosecutor knows about Minh. But there's one more thing I have to know. Minh said he went to your building to check it out on the night the place burned down. He said he saw somebody leaving. He wasn't sure if it was you or not. So tell me honestly, were you anywhere near the building on the night of the fire? For any reason?"

"No. Everything I told the fire investigator right after the fire was true. I left at five, worked out, had dinner with Susan, and went home. The only time I went out after that was to the grocery store on Greenwood Avenue. I never went near the building."

"Okay." I looked at my watch. It was ten-thirty and I had a deposition in another case scheduled at eleven. "Listen, I've got to go downtown. I'll see you at one o'clock tomorrow to start working on your testimony. For God's sake, don't start drinking. Just hang loose and I'll see you tomorrow."

"All right," he said, smiling wanly and standing up to go. "Thanks, Matthew."

"For what?"

"For not judging me. For being a friend."

"Listen, I've heard lots worse. You forget that. Now take off. I'll see you tomorrow."

He nodded and left. He seemed oddly relieved. Perhaps confession really is good for the soul. I pulled the file and the exhibits I was going to cover in the deposition and put on my raincoat. As I turned to go I began thinking that Hugh's comment that I hadn't judged him was not quite right. I had heard much worse things admitted in ten years of practicing law. But I hadn't heard them from a friend. Or a former friend. For whatever was left of our friendship was still in the office when I left, broken in a thousand pieces and scattered like glass on the office floor.

The next week was busy. With the help of a paralegal hired from one of the temporary agencies I reread, sorted, and organized all of the documents concerning Hugh's finances and business practices that would be introduced at trial. In the afternoons I worked with Hugh on his testimony, using a borrowed videotape camera to show him how he looked to others. Hugh took to videotape like a frustrated actor. He learned to control his gestures and moderate his voice, in response to the questions I put to him. As we worked, I began to regain some confidence in his case. After all, he had merely talked about burning his building. Talk is not necessarily a crime. He had formed no agreements with Minh. Even if he had, conspiracy was not charged in the information and we could keep out a jury instruction about conspiracy as a lesser included offense. Liz Kleinfeldt still gave no sign that she even knew of Minh's existence.

Bernstein had gotten nowhere with Howard Gaines. Gaines appeared to have been telling the truth about where he was on the night of the fire. Bernstein found that Gaines had cruised the biker taverns on Pacific Highway South until closing, then had sex with an old girlfriend in the back of her van while parked in the Mount Baker district. It was still possible that Gaines had hired the job done, but if he had, he was smart enough to use out-of-towners, freelance talent that would have been on their bikes and down in Medford or Sacramento by noon the next day. There wasn't enough time or money to prove that theory even if it was true.

I kept trying. Sandra Kessler had refused to allow me to interview her, so I noted her deposition for Wednesday of that week. She came to my office with Liz Kleinfeldt and her own lawyer, a man named Waterston whom I had not known before.

Sandra Kessler was drawn and thinner, so subdued I thought she might still be taking tranquilizers, but her diction was clear and her answers were short and pointed. Yes, she knew her husband had been doing Hugh's accounting. He had liked the work and the extra money was nice. She knew he was going to Prokop's office on the night of the fire. Her daughter had a date, so Sandra had gone out with friends for a drink and dinner. The friends she named had no connection with Prokop or Van Zandt & Company. She returned at eleven, but had not called anyone about her husband until morning. Sometimes he worked all night. She knew nothing about Prokop or his business; she knew him only as Susan Haight's lover. Her husband had not acted strangely before his death. He had said nothing about changing jobs or leaving the area.

When the deposition was over and Sandra Kessler had left, I caught Liz Kleinfeldt's arm as she was packing up to go.

"Excuse me, counsel," I said, a trace of sarcasm coloring my words, "but am I missing something here? Kessler refused to be interviewed, but that deposition is as a big waste of paper as I've seen lately. What's going on?"

She shrugged. "Beats me, Riordan," she said. "She didn't say anything to me that you haven't heard." She picked up her briefcase and trenchcoat and walked to the door. When she reached it she turned and said, "Kind of odd, isn't it? Victims' families, if they have them, are usually all over me, right through trial. With this one it's been almost nothing. See you in court."

On Friday of that week I took Hugh and Susan out for an early dinner and a few hours of Irish music in the smoky back room behind Kell's restaurant on Post Alley. Hugh seemed to relax under the influence of the music and the ale, but Susan remained stiff and pensive. With her blond hair, high cheekbones, and dark somber eyes, she looked like Meryl Streep's portrayal of Sophie in *Sophie's*

Choice, and I wondered what it was she was thinking about, trouble behind or trouble yet to come.

The next morning was a Saturday. I woke up early, around six, but without a definite commitment to getting out of bed. For a brief moment I felt as I had as a child, not sick but perhaps able to fake it well enough to fool my mother, so I could lay in bed at home and read the paperback science-fiction novels that sold for thirty-five cents at the drugstore down in Great Falls. The feeling was so strong that I felt momentarily disoriented by this big bed in a plain white room, so different from my small, attic bedroom back home in Montana. Then the phone rang, a loud harsh sound that filled my room and chased the ghost of childhood memory away, back where it belonged. I picked up the receiver after a brief scramble. "Yeah," I snarled.

"It's Vince Ahlberg, Matthew. You still in bed?"

"It is six o'clock on a Saturday morning, Vince. Where did you think I'd be, hitting the bars?"

"Never can tell. I'm down on Sixth Avenue South, the twelve-hundred block, below the Kingdome. We've got a stiff."

"That's nice. Dead people are job security for you. I think I'm going back to sleep now."

"His name was Minh. Tran Loc Minh."

I sat up in bed and grabbed the phone from the headboard and put it in my lap. "That's interesting," I said carefully. "Why are you calling me?"

"Because the guy was an arsonist," he said, his voice becoming raspy with irritation.

"It still doesn't mean anything, Vince."

"Maybe not. Nonetheless, I'd like to see you down here. I'm sure you wouldn't mind, being a public-spirited officer of the court and all that."

"Duty calls," I agreed. "I'll be down there in twenty minutes."

"Good. And Matthew, I'm being nice about this. You know that."

"I know that. It doesn't mean I'm going to be nice back. I'll see you." I hung up the phone.

The twelve-hundred block of Sixth Avenue South was in the industrial section of the city near Boeing Field. It was built on what was once the Duwamish River mud flats. The avenues there run flat and straight, unlike the rest of the hilly city. They are lined with two- and three-story warehouses and light manufacturing plants. The buildings are nearly uniform in size, and as I drove down Sixth they appeared so evenly lined up that they seemed to disappear into the distant perspective.

The morning was softly wet, and I drove carefully past the rumbling semitrailer trucks that splashed through the streets around warehouses that held food and wine and furniture.

Three police cars were clustered around the south end of a grocery warehouse on Sixth, their blue lights flashing silently in the dim gray morning light. I parked well away from them and pulled a blue rain jacket over my heavy wool sweater before walking over. They were grouped around a dark-green garbage dumpster that leaned against the wall of the warehouse. Yellow crime-scene ribbons had been strung from the cars to keep anyone from approaching the dumpster. A camera crew was mounting photographic lights on a tall tripod so that they would light the inside of the dumpster. Two other detectives roamed around, taking sweepings of wet gravel from the broken-up asphalt surface of the parking lot.

I asked a tall uniformed officer to find Vince Ahlberg. He took me to an unmarked sedan parked away from the other cars and rapped on the window. The door popped open and Ahlberg leaned out.

"Be with you in a minute," he said. I stood and waited by the car, shivering in the light rain, wishing desperately for a cup of hot coffee. As I waited I saw a coroner's van pull up. Two coroner's assistants got out and strolled casually over to the dumpster. Everyone seemed calm, relaxed. Nobody was going to hurry for Tran Loc Minh.

Vince Ahlberg stepped out from his squad car while I was watching the coroner's men set up. Despite the early hour on a Saturday, he was carefully dressed in a light-gray suit with a fine pinstripe, blue shirt with contrasting white collar, red foulard tie.

I looked him over as he shrugged into a black trench coat.

"I still don't know why you dress like that," I said sarcastically. "Life is not a Hitchcock movie."

"My, aren't we bitchy this morning? You out late last night?"

"Not really. It's quarter after seven and I haven't even had my coffee yet. You can't expect a sterling grade of wit."

"No, but I can hope. You want to scope out the recently deceased?"

"Do I have a choice? You brought me down here. This is your game."

"Yeah, it is. Come on."

Ahlberg led me through the corral of squad cars parked around the crime scene. "Walk behind me, we're still taking samples from the parking lot. Not that we'll find anything. The rain has washed anything useful away."

We walked up to the dumpster. I looked inside. Tran Loc Minh lay sprawled on his back on top of the piled-up garbage, his limbs extending stiffly from the trunk of his body. His skin was a sallow yellowish gray. There was a single round hole, like a third eye, in the center of his broad forehead. His eyes were open but fogged over, and all sense that an intelligence lay within them gone. Whoever had dumped the body had left the top of the dumpster open. The rain had slicked down Minh's rather stiff hair and washed all the blood away.

I turned away from the body and looked at Ahlberg. "So?" I said coldly.

"You knew him, didn't you, Matthew?"

"Not really," I said evasively. "What makes you think I did?"

"He was an arsonist, like I said. Probably the best torch in the area, maybe for the whole West Coast. Knew his chemicals, knew how to hide the ignition points. Never been able to prove a thing against him."

"Now you won't have to. I'm cold and this conversation is beginning to bore me."

He ignored me and kept talking. "One of the Chinatown beat cops heard the call when the janitor at this warehouse found the corpse this morning. The janitor found the body about five o'clock and the officer was just about to go off duty. He came down here and recognized Minh. The officer told me what he knew about Minh, including a story about a couple of round-eyes that went into the Dragon Gate a few nights ago looking for him. One guy was tall and kind of lean, the other guy was tall, bearded and built like a freight train. Sound like anyone you know?"

"If this is supposed to be impressing me, it's not working. Why don't you finish? I'll buy you breakfast, and we can talk about the Sonics. I bet they'll make the play-offs."

"Bear with me, I'm almost done. Seems these two guys took Minh out in the alley and bounced him around a little. Like they were trying to get information."

"Get to the point."

"Guys like Minh get whacked because they know things people don't want them to know. What did Minh know, Matthew? What was so important that it got him shot? Or was it just to keep him from testifying against Prokop?"

"So that's it," I said in a cold tight voice. "If so, you can stick it. I did not have Minh killed and I don't know who did. Hugh Prokop, his girlfriend, and I were out to dinner last night. We can get alibis from a taxi driver, two waiters, a bartender, and a four-man Irish string band. Anything I might or might not know about Minh I learned while representing my client and is attorney work product. I don't need to tell you a damned thing. My best suggestion is that you might find out who killed him if you'd stop trying to tailor the evidence to fit my client."

"You could tell me that without acting like I was trying to put you on the rack," he replied angrily. "What's the matter with you?"

"You are. You haul me down here expecting to trade on friendship when you know perfectly damned well you'll use anything I say about Minh to try to hang Prokop. Jesus, you really must think I'm stupid, Captain."

His face reddened and anger flashed hot in his eyes, but his voice was cold, controlled. "I don't think you're stupid, counselor," he said softly, "but I'm starting to think you're a suspect. You and that thug from Montana you hang out with."

"He's not a thug. He's a nice Jewish boy with his master's in foreign policy from Columbia."

"And he used to kill people for a living. Come to think of it, you killed one guy two years ago. And almost killed another."

"That was self-defense."

"One of them wasn't. You slid out from under."

I shook my head. "You've taken leave of your senses."

"Maybe. We've always been able to get along because you're one of the few guys around who remembers that the point of the legal system is to put the bad guys away."

"That's not quite right, Captain. The point is to make sure that the innocent are not wrongly convicted. It works because it is an adversarial system. Which puts us on the opposite sides of this one, Vince. There's no statute on the books that says I have to answer your questions. And I'm not going to. So long."

CHAPTER 12

I awoke shortly after five on the first morning of the trial with my fists clenched so hard that there were red lines on my palms at the places where the fingernails had been driven into them. I reached onto the night table for cigarettes and matches before remembering that I hadn't smoked in years. I pulled on some sweatpants, then sat for a moment on the side of the bed, my toes digging into the carpet, until I was awake enough to go downstairs to the kitchen and make coffee.

I had been dreaming, and it was a bad one. In the dream I had been in court with Hugh Prokop, ready to try his case. When the time had come for my opening statement, I had started to speak and saw the jury looking at me as though I were mad. I was speaking, but no sound was coming out. I went to the easel and pad in the corner of the courtroom to draw my words. I wrote very hard, but no ink came out of the pen. The judge leaned down from the bench to admonish me. At first I could hear her, but as she continued speaking her words grew fainter, until I could see her lips moving but heard no sound at all. I stood in the courtroom as the judge and prosecutor and jury all talked and gestured with the extravagant manners of an old silent movie. I watched, horrified, until the light itself began to fade and the colors had drained away to a grainy sepia brown.

That was when I woke up.

After the coffee was made I sat down in the living room watching the black night sky fade to gray, and then to the orange and red streaks of dawn. The sky to the east was clear and I could see the Cascade peaks across the quiet waters of Lake Washington, still bearing a heavy white mantle of late-winter snow. I stayed in the dim, cool morning room until my watch said quarter after six, when it was time to dress and to pick up Hugh Prokop and start the first day of trial.

The criminal trial calendar is called at 9:00 A.M. each morning in the Presiding Courtroom on the ninth floor of the King County Courthouse. Presiding looks like a run-down Episcopal church, with its heavy oak bench, trimmed in a vaguely Gothic style, and rows of wooden pews marching up to the bench. Presiding's clientele is slightly tougher than the usual church crowd but in equal need of salvation.

The call of the trial calendar is ritual, drained of pomp. Cases are called and courtrooms assigned while prosecutors and public defenders banter about basketball and politics. In the back of the courtroom civil lawyers gossip about fees while their clients sit in the pews, sometimes chattering anxiously, sometimes silent, ashen and drawn. The lawyer reacts to it differently than the client. Properly understood, lawyering is a blood sport and calendar call is the opening bell.

Our case was fourth. "*State v. Prokop*, Case No. 86-1-44322-9," the presiding judge, David MacGregor, called out.

Elizabeth Kleinfeldt stood up, slender but imposing in a blue pin-striped dress tailored from a man's suiting fabric. "The State is ready, Your Honor," she said quietly.

I stood up in turn. "The defense is also ready, Your Honor."

MacGregor nodded from the bench. His white beard and narrow English features created the classic image of a judge basically fair, but as hard as the bench he sat on.

"The case is assigned to Department 12, Judge Detweiler," he said. "Courtroom East 724. Next case."

I sat down slowly, and a little carefully, as though I had the wind knocked out of me.

"How did we do?" Hugh whispered. "Is this the judge you wanted?"

"Not really," I said cautiously. "I guess we could have done worse."

"You don't sound convinced," Hugh said doubtfully.

I shrugged and picked up my briefcase to slide out of the pew. "Come on," I said, "let's go down to the courtroom."

Judge Margaret Detweiler was known to the criminal bar of King County as the Ayatollah, partly for her propensity for delivering decisions as if they were pronouncements of Holy Scripture, and partly out of the widely held belief that she cheerfully would chop the hands off petty thieves, if the law so allowed. She had been a policewoman before attending night law school, then had worked her way up the political ladder to a judgeship, starting as a deputy prosecutor, then becoming counsel to the Police Benevolent Association. The governor who had appointed her to the bench readily conceded that no one was going to rank Margaret Detweiler with Harlan Fiske Stone or Benjamin Cardozo. That wasn't the point. Nobody ever doubted which side Margaret Detweiler was on.

At the time of the trial she was a stocky woman of forty-five or so with large hooded eyes, a long straight nose, and thick, flowing black hair streaked with gray. As we walked into her courtroom she was pronouncing sentence on a small-time drug dealer who had run out of time and out of luck.

"I have heard your statement, Mr. Diaz," she said to the small trembling man in blue jail fatigues, "as well as the statements of your wife and mother. However, the Court's discretion is limited by the sentencing guidelines and the fact that dealing drugs is a truly heinous crime. I therefore sentence you to eleven years in state prison. We will be at recess." The bailiff gavelled the hearing closed, and the judge swept off the bench and into chambers. The unlucky Diaz and his family wept until a court detail officer led him away.

"That's my cue," I told Prokop. "I've got to meet with her and the prosecutor in chambers. Sit tight." He nodded and remained seated in the back of the courtroom, suddenly numbed by the sentencing he had just witnessed.

I walked toward the front of the courtroom, pausing to put my briefcase at the counsel table nearest to the jury box. The theory is that the closer you are to the jury during the trial, the more they will understand and identify with your client, making it harder to convict.

I heard the back door of the courtroom open and Liz Kleinfeldt walked in, accompanied by a young male junior prosecutor with long, light-brown hair and rimless glasses. The junior was carrying a brown banker's box of exhibits. When they reached the counsel tables he slid the box under the table so that the jury would not notice it.

"Good morning, Mr. Riordan," Liz Kleinfeldt said.

"Good morning," I replied cautiously. "The judge just finished her sentencing. I suppose we should go in."

"Yes, let's get started." There was a note of tension in her voice. I wasn't the only one who got nervous before trials.

I followed her to the door to the judge's chambers. Before either of us could knock, the door opened and the judge's bailiff, a plain-faced young woman of twenty-four or so, motioned us in. "Come on, counsel," she said impatiently, "The judge is waiting."

Kleinfeldt stepped through the door and I followed. Judge Detweiler was standing behind her desk, still wearing her robe.

"Good morning, counsel," she said, shaking hands. "Any matters before we begin jury selection?"

"I have some requests for jury instructions, Your Honor," I began. "Most are from the pattern instructions, but there are a couple of special ones."

"Give them to my bailiff and I'll consider them in due course," she said politely. "Why don't we all sit down for a moment."

When we were seated the judge cocked her head in my

direction and said, "Mr. Riordan, I don't think you've appeared in my court before. Have you?"

"Just on motions, Your Honor," I replied.

"Yes. Well, I want both of you to know I run a very tight courtroom. I expect you both to be on time, and when arguing a matter to be succinct and have your law at hand. I've barred television cameras from the courtroom for the trial, but both of you take care in what you say to the press, as I don't intend to sequester the jury until they retire. There's been some pretrial publicity, but not enough to be prejudicial." She paused, then asked, "What is your estimate of the length of trial?"

I looked at Liz Kleinfeldt. "I think I'll need four trial days. Possibly five," she said.

"I think I'll need three," I replied.

"That adds up to twelve," the Judge said, sighing. "At least by lawyer's arithmetic. Anything else? No? Good. I'll have the bailiff bring down twenty-four jurors. We should be ready to go in twenty minutes."

Jury selection in King County is done by the lawyers, who are free to question potential jurors about almost any subject to determine how their background, race, economic status, job, or sexual preferences might affect their decision on a case. Most of the questions must be indirect, to avoid offending a potential juror. At times the questions and answers can take on a Kafkaesque sameness, particularly when the potential jurors are all white and suburban and making airplanes at Boeing.

I knew the sort of jurors I wanted, people who had run their own businesses, made money on their own, or otherwise took risks in their lives by dancing, writing, acting, or painting. What I got, of course, was a panel made up of the type of people I didn't want: retired postal clerks, personnel officers, middle-management city workers, the sort of people who were born with the souls of hall monitors and lived their lives taking chances only when they had a safe sixty-forty bet. Such people, I thought, might have a hard time understanding that Hugh need not have panicked over his financial losses.

You don't always get what you want. Often the best you can do is to unselect a jury, getting rid of the jurors most likely to be biased against your client. After a day and a half of juror *voir dire* and excusals for cause, I used one of my peremptory challenges to get rid of a fat-faced federal bureaucrat who wore those big round tortoiseshell glasses and a look of insufferable self-satisfaction. Just looking at him pissed me off, and it was sure to become mutual before the trial was over. I hesitated painfully before deciding to retain a successful grocer and clothing-store owner living in the Central District. He was tough and honest, but he wore his blackness on his sleeve, and I was afraid he might resent Hugh's easy inheritance of a family business. Liz Kleinfeldt used a peremptory to knock out my favorite juror, a third-year law student from the University who had served as an army ranger and would understand and apply the presumption of innocence. He stepped from the jury box reluctantly, angry at being denied the chance to see what life in his chosen field would be like.

I had five challenges left. If I used too many challenges, the remaining jurors might think that we had a lot to hide. I looked down at my jury notes. Engineer, housewife, student, businessman, secretary, baker, computer programmer. Three retirees and the inevitable pair from Boeing. I turned to Hugh.

"Any deep feelings?" I whispered.

He shrugged in reply. I looked up at the jury and rolled the dice.

"The defense accepts the jury, Your Honor," I said.

Margaret Detweiler nodded. "Ms. Kleinfeldt?"

"The State accepts, Your Honor."

"Very well. Morning recess, with opening statements when we return."

In the end it is luck and art and artifice, combined. Throughout the jury selection I had created a warm family tableau in the first row of spectator benches, directly behind Hugh. Susan Haight sat closest, dressed conservatively but not too expensively, her arm often draped around Megan, Hugh's seven-year-old daughter from his first marriage. Megan was somber, wearing little dark dresses with white knee socks, not really understanding what was going on but possessed of a child's profound knowledge that something in her daddy's life had gone very, very wrong. Mary Alice Thierrault, Hugh's sister, sat next to Megan, dressed in a grown-up version of the same dresses, her hair pulled straight back, her face severe with strain. In a way I worried more about Mary Alice's demeanor than Hugh's; she was far more openly emotional than he was. I would have to remember to take a moment three or four times a day to see how she was doing and offer a calming word.

When morning recess was over the judge had the jury sworn, and I fidgeted expectantly, knowing that Margaret Detweiler hated to waste court time and would try to fit both opening statements in before lunch.

I took out a lined yellow pad and placed it on the bare counsel table as Liz Kleinfeldt stood to begin her opening. The single pad on the bare table was, I hoped, a visual reminder to the jury at just how alone Hugh Prokop really was as the State began to use its power to put him away.

Elizabeth Kleinfeldt began her statement in the same clear, warm voice that I had heard her use in conversation. I could see the jurors relax, legs uncrossing, arms unfolding as they got used to her presence in the courtroom. She explained the nature of the crimes of arson and felony murder, then outlined the evidence, freely admitting the chief weakness in her case, the lack of a witness who could place Hugh at the scene of the fire. She used her honesty as a springboard to her conclusion.

"Arson is not a crime that happens in broad daylight," she said. "It is inherently a secret crime, committed late at night when the criminal hopes that no one is watching. Because it is that kind of crime, we will prove our case by circumstantial evidence. Circumstantial evidence is indirect, rather than direct, proof. The judge will instruct you that circumstantial evidence is as valid as any other. That is the law, but it is also common sense. When you are standing at a window and see people on a busy street suddenly stop to raise their umbrellas, you do not need to feel the water on your face to know that it has started to rain.

"The facts we will be presenting to you are like threads. Each of them, standing alone, might not be conclusive. But just as threads are woven into cloth, these facts, when woven together, will prove our case. A single fact is nothing. But when you weave dozens of facts together, they will prove arson, and murder."

She left that harsh word hovering in the air as she sat down. It was a good opening, and I had to respond.

"Ladies and gentlemen," I began, still favoring the old-fashioned style of addressing jurors, "this is a case about a nightmare. A nightmare that could happen to you or anyone else. Hugh Prokop had a small business, selling marine products. He has run it successfully despite the depression in our economy over the last five years. Like most of you, he has taken his lumps, making money some years, losing money in other years. Hugh's business was in his family for over forty years. His business is gone now. The evidence will show, and we agree, that someone set fire to his warehouse. In the course of the fire, Walter Kessler died.

"The question before you is whether or not Hugh Prokop set this fire. He did not. Despite the personal financial losses he has suffered—and the evidence will show some— Hugh had his business, his health, his skills, and the ability to battle back. He had no motive to set fire to his building. That is the core of our case.

"There is simply no evidence that Hugh Prokop was anywhere near the warehouse building at or before the time it burned. There is no evidence that anyone was hired to set the fire, or that any kind of a timing device was used. In short, there is nothing that connects Hugh Prokop to this fire except his ownership of the warehouse.

"Hugh will take the stand and tell you where he was on the night of fire. He was having an evening much like you or I might have—a dinner out with his friend, Susan Haight, then home for a few hours of television before going to sleep. Hugh left his house in Broadview at ten o'clock to buy some beer. He returned home and stayed there asleep until the fire department called him to let him know that his quiet night had turned into a nightmare.

"We won't be able, like Perry Mason, to show you exactly what happened at the Prokop Marine warehouse on the night of the trial. We will show you that the man who died in the fire, Walter Keller, was Hugh's accountant. Walter Kessler had a key to the warehouse. He was to deliver to Hugh a lot of money, a quarter of a million dollars, money that Hugh was to use to invest in real estate. Walter Kessler needed money very badly. We believe that you will conclude that Walter Kessler decided to steal this money and set the fire to cover his tracks, knowing that Hugh, as the owner of the warehouse, would fall under suspicion. Walter Kessler then died in the fire he himself had set.

"The evidence will show you that Hugh Prokop, far from committing this crime, was its victim."

I walked to the front of the jury box and rested my hands on the rail. I looked into each of the juror's faces, pausing briefly to make eye contact. Finally, I lowered by voice and said, softly, "and that, people, is Hugh Prokop's nightmare. Whoever set fire to his building—whether it was Walter Kessler or someone else—took away Hugh's business. The State now proposes to take away his life. It is up to you decide if this nightmare ends."

I turned and walked back to the defense table and sat down. Hugh leaned his head over to me to whisper. "I think that was good," he said. "They really watched you."

I made sure my back was to the jury before I answered. "It's too soon," I whispered, shaking my head slightly. "Way too soon to tell."

CHAPTER 13

The State's first witness was Dr. Walter Johnson, the King County medical examiner. He was a tall, lean black man, with a seamed, taciturn face and graying, close-cropped hair. Liz Kleinfeldt's first questions meandered lovingly through Johnson's excellent medical credentials, an undergraduate degree from Cornell University and an M.D. from Harvard. She went quickly through the identification of the body as that of Walter Kessler, then slowed down as she marked the autopsy report and offered it into evidence.

"Dr. Johnson, did you determine the cause of Mr. Kessler's death in your autopsy?" she asked.

"Yes, I did."

"What was the cause of death?"

"Smoke inhalation."

"Does that mean that Mr. Kessler was alive at the time of the fire?"

"Yes, it does. We can determine that by examination of the lungs. As you can see from the report, carbonized particles and carbon monoxide were found in the lungs."

"Doctor, did you have occasion to photograph Mr. Kessler's body at the time of the autopsy?"

"Yes, I did. That is our standard practice."

Kleinfeldt walked up to the judge's clerk, sitting at a low desk below the bench. "Please mark these photographs as State's exhibits two, three, and four, for identification.'' She took the three photographs and handed them to the clerk. When the clerk had marked them, Liz turned and brought them to me.

I had seen them before. They were gruesome; the body had been charred. I dropped them casually on the defense table. "Are they being offered, counsel?" I asked.

"They will be.''

I nodded. "Your Honor," I said, rising, "may we approach for a side-bar conference?"

"Yes.'' The judge got up from her chair and stepped down, turning away from the jury, as we reached the bench. "We object, Your Honor," I began, whispering. "The defense is willing to stipulate that the fire caused Mr. Kessler's death. The photographs are cumulative and irrelevant.''

Judge Detweiler nodded. "I'm inclined to agree. For what purpose are you offering them, Ms. Kleinfeldt?"

"So that the jury can see the effects of the fire, Your Honor.''

"They are still irrelevant." I replied. "This jury is not a group of voyeurs," I added harshly.

Judge Detweiler narrowed her eyes at me. "That comment is not necessary, Mr. Riordan. But the objection is sustained. The photographs will not be admitted. Proceed, Ms. Kleinfeldt.''

Kleinfeldt merely nodded and walked back toward the jury box. She picked the photographs up from my table as she passed, rolling them into a tube as she continued her questioning. "Doctor, did you find anything else in your examination regarding Mr. Kessler's condition?"

"Yes.''

"And, what was that?"

"I found some signs of a subdural hematoma at the base of the skull.''

"What is a subdural hematoma?"

"It is a swelling of the lining between the brain and the skull.''

"What typically causes such an event?" The question

was objectionable on a number of grounds, but I let it pass. I had some plans for this testimony.

"Typically, a blow to the head."

"Thank you, doctor. Your witness."

I stood up and strolled over to the jury box, maintaining a careful yard between myself and the jury. "Doctor," I began turning to face the witness chair, "As King County medical examiner you are called to testify in court a lot, aren't you?"

"Yes. It's part of my job."

"How many times have you testified in court?"

"I couldn't say. Dozens of times, I'm sure."

"I see." First let the jury know he is a professional witness, then go after him. "Doctor, please take a look at your autopsy report. You wrote the report during and immediately after the autopsy was conducted, correct?"

"Yes."

"Please look at the third page. Does the statement appear, quote, 'signs of possible hematoma,' unquote?"

"Yes."

"And you wrote that?"

"Yes."

"Now, doctor, doesn't 'possible hematoma' mean that you weren't sure at the time of the autopsy that there was a hematoma?"

"As I said, there were signs."

"But you weren't sure what those signs meant, were you, doctor?"

"No. I was not."

"So you cannot testify today whether or not there was such a hematoma, can you, doctor?"

"No. That is, I cannot so testify."

"And even if you could say for certain there was a hematoma, you couldn't say what caused it, could you?"

"No, I couldn't."

"Thank you. No more questions."

"No redirect," Liz Kleinfeldt said. Dr. Johnson nodded and left the stand. I sat down, satisfied. We had at least revived the possibility in the jury's mind that Walter Kessler had been on his feet when the fire had started. The fact that the money was still inside the locked safe, after the fire began, made it less likely that Kessler had started the fire to cover his own theft, but I needed to keep that possibility alive.

The next witness was Lieutenant Walter Buehler, the fire department officer in command of the first unit to reach the Prokop Marine fire. Buehler was a short, swarthy man with a thick guardsman mustache and a wide, harsh-featured face. He testified with competent ease about the fire.

"We arrived at 10:04 P.M., about three minutes after the first alarm was called in," he began.

"What did you observe?" Liz Kleinfeldt asked.

"The building was not yet fully engaged, but there were two separate flame areas visible from the outside." He took a pointer and gestured to a drawing of the Prokop Marine building that had been mounted on cardboard and placed on the courtroom easel. "One was here at the northwest corner," he said, pointing to the corner of the building where Walter Kessler's body had been found. "The other was at the southwest corner of the building, here."

"Did you observe anything unusual about the flames?"

"Only that the rate of propagation was very rapid."

"As a trained fire officer, did that have any meaning for you?"

"Yes."

"What did it mean?"

"That some sort of accelerant was involved in the fire."

"No further questions," Kleinfeldt said. "Your witness."

I stood up to cross-examine. We weren't contesting the fact that the fire was arson, but I wanted to place the time that the fire started as close to ten o'clock as I could, in order to shore up Hugh's fragile alibi that he had been out buying beer at the time the fire started.

"Lieutenant," I began "who called in the first alarm?"

"A parking-lot attendant at the Harborside Restaurant."

"The Harborside is in the Warren Maritime building, isn't it?"

"Yes."

"Where is the Warren Maritime building?"

"Farther up Westlake Avenue."

"About a hundred yards north of Prokop Marine, correct?"

"That's right."

I moved up to the easel. "And the parking lot is between the restaurant and Prokop Marine, correct?"

"Yes."

"So the parking lot area of the restaurant would command a good, clear view of the northwest corner of the burning building?"

"Yes, it would."

"In your view, the fire started in that northwest corner of the Prokop Marine building, did it not?"

"I didn't perform the fire investigation, personally."

"But based on what you saw, is that not your opinion?"

"Yes, that's my belief."

"Did anyone ever tell you that your belief was incorrect?"

"No."

"Now, Lieutenant, at the time you arrived, you testified that the Prokop Marine warehouse was not fully engaged, correct?"

"Yes."

"And isn't it also true that the Prokop Marine building contained hundred of gallons of marine paints, varnishes and solvents?"

"Yes. We had a hell of a . . . sorry. Yes."

"So, isn't it true that you arrived on the scene only a few minutes after the fire had been set?"

He was unprepared for the question and he hesitated before answering, looking over at David Swenson, the fire inspector. I followed his look with my eyes and body language so that the jury could see where he was looking. "I'm asking for your testimony, Lieutenant," I said sharply. "Not anyone else's."

"Objection," Liz Kleinfeldt shot out, rising to her feet. "Argumentative."

"Sustained. Strike counsel's remark. But answer, Lieutenant."

He did. "Yes, I would say that is true. My estimate

would be that we arrived ten or fifteen minutes after the fire had been set.''

"Thank you, Lieutenant. No further questions.''

"No redirect,'' Liz Kleinfeldt said.

The judge looked at the clock on the courtroom wall. "Who is your next witness, Ms. Kleinfeldt?''

"Inspector Swenson, Your Honor.''

The judge shook her head. "It is ten of four. I have a special matter set for hearing in ten minutes. Let's call it a day. Members of the jury, I want to remind you that you are not to discuss the case among yourselves, or with others. You also should not watch the television news, or read about the case in the newspapers. We are in recess.''

The courtroom filled with the sounds of scraping chairs and clearing throats as the Judge returned to chambers and the jury filed out of the room. When they were gone Hugh Prokop sat down and leaned back, stretching out his arms and spine against the hard-edged courtroom chair.

He took a deep breath. "Oh, shit,'' he said, putting about three extra syllables into shit. "I never realized how tired you could get just sitting here. I'm beat.''

"You've got the hottest seat in the house,'' I replied. I drummed my fists against the courtroom table, still pumped with adrenaline from the cross-examination of Buehler. "We're going to get that alibi of yours put together yet,'' I said. "Kleinfeldt didn't want him to nail down the precise time the fire started, but we got him to place it at the exact time you were in that convenience store. I just wish to hell we could find somebody who remembered you there.''

"Is there any chance of that?''

"Not much, I'm afraid. The clerk on duty just doesn't remember you. But Bernstein said he might go back one last time. We'll see.''

Susan Haight and Mary Alice Thierrault came up to the table from the public benches to join us at the counsel table. "I thought things went well,'' Susan said quietly. "The jury seems to follow everything you do.''

I shrugged noncommittally. "At this point I don't know,'' I replied.

"Is there anything you want us to do tonight?" Mary Alice asked.

"Two things," I replied. "Make sure Hugh goes to the health club and works out. He gets a couple of beers afterward with dinner, and a lot of sleep. I'm not joking about that. This is like a very long race and he's got to be in good shape.

"The other thing I want you to do is think about today and ask yourself whether any particular juror is either turned on or turned off by what I'm doing. That will help me tailor my questions. And thanks for being here. You all looked great. Good night."

Hugh hoisted his daughter up into his arms and led the others out of the courtroom, humming a little tune to the child as he walked. I gathered up my notes and trial notebook to dump them back into my briefcase. As I turned to go I saw Sandra Kessler standing in the benches on the other side of the courtroom. She stared at me for a moment. Her large dark eyes seemed full of mourning. She took a half step up the aisle toward me, then lowered her head and turned away. I didn't move. I wanted to talk to her, but stayed away, fearing that my words would be taken as foolish, or empty.

On my way out of the courthouse I stopped at the law library to dig out a few cases on evidence points that I thought might come up before the trial was over. When I finished it was six o'clock and the daylight had faded to a soft gray-blue dusk as clouds moved in from Puget Sound and dropped a light rain on the city. I drove down through Pioneer Square to pick up the waterfront viaduct. Below me, to the left, the decaying piers on Alaskan Way were lit with colored lights that had the soft glow of old pearls against the black water. In my rational head I knew that the piers were filled with cheap tourist shops and fish shacks, but I never could quite lose the sense of wonder at how the tawdry could change to beauty in the night.

I picked up a sandwich and a soda at an all-night grocery on Northlake Way near my office. The office was peacefully empty. I switched on a desk lamp and a classical-music station, then settled in to read my notes and try to think through the next day's testimony. Liz Kleinfeldt's strategy for the case had become clear through the way she had ordered her witnesses; she would emphasize the fact of murder to the jury in order to minimize her weak proof that it was Prokop who had actually started the fire. The best way to fight her would be to push the fact of Walter Kessler's death as far into the background as I could while driving home the point that Hugh had no real motive to start the fire.

I was still working at eight-thirty. There was a knock on the door in the foyer that led to the outside stairs. The knock was so soft that at first I wasn't sure that I had heard it. When it came again I got up from behind the desk to answer the door. I paused in the doorway between my office and the waiting room to switch on a light. The unlocked door opened and a woman came it. It was Sandra Kessler.

She was wearing a tan trench coat over the same black jersey dress she had worn that day in court. She took off her coat and shook the rain from it. Her hair and face were damp and her mascara had run, leaving long black streaks on her face.

"You shouldn't be here, Mrs. Kessler," I said softly. "I'm sorry, but under court rules I'm not even supposed to talk to you. You'd better go."

"Please," she replied. "Just for a minute. I need . . . someone. No one knows I'm here."

"All right," I said dubiously. "Just drop your coat on that chair. There are some tissues on my secretary's desk."

"I must look awful," she said. "It's . . . I've been crying and I can't stop."

"Want some coffee?"

"I'd rather have a drink."

"I think coffee would be better," I said. I could smell liquor on her breath, and I did not want to have her get comfortable over a drink, if only for the way it might sound later, in court.

I poured some coffee into a cup and handed it to her as she sat down on my office sofa. She sipped at it. "Thank you. This is very good."

"Sandra," I said, "what do you want? I cannot discuss this case with you. I'm sorry, but I can't."

She placed the cup on the arm of the sofa and began to pace around the room. "I need your help, Matthew," she said. "Walter really left me in awful shape. We were behind on our house payments when he died, and most of his insurance had lapsed because we were behind on the premiums. After all the expenses and keeping the house from being foreclosed, I don't have anything left."

I hesitated. "I don't know what I can do to help you," I replied.

"Hugh is responsible for my husband's death. He should compensate me. My God, people collect hundreds of thousands of dollars for car accidents and things. Hugh should at least pay me that."

I shook my head, no. "Sandra, Hugh did not start this fire. That is what this trial is about. That is what the jury is going to say."

"I didn't mean that he started the fire. But it was his company. He should be responsible."

"I can't talk about any of this with you. If you want money from Hugh, you'll have to sue him when this trial is over."

"I want to know that I'm going to be taken care of," she said insistently.

I froze. "Sandra," I said carefully, "have you demanded money from Hugh?"

"No," she replied, "Hugh won't even *talk* to me. I thought Hugh was my friend, and now he refuses to help me. And he'd better."

"What are you talking about?"

"Ask Hugh," she replied nastily. "He knows." She reached for her coffee cup and knocked it over with clumsy, fluttering hands. And I knew she was drunk.

I stood up and took her by the arm. "I'm going to have to ask you to leave now. Please don't make it worse."

"No!" she screamed, twisting away from me, then turning back and slapping me as hard as she could. "You lousy bastard! You and Prokop. He killed my husband and now he won't even take care of me! What am I supposed to do? What?'' She collapsed onto the sofa, sobbing hysterically.

The phone rang. I kept an eye on Sandra and crossed the room to answer it.

It was Greg Van Zandt. "Hey, Matthew, it's Greg," he said. "Listen, have you seen Sandy Kessler? I had her out to dinner at Ray's with some people, trying to cheer her up. She drank too much and started to say all kinds of rotten things about Hugh. When I went into the bar to say hello to some other people, she split. There's no answer at her house. I called Hugh and Susan, but they haven't seen her."

"She's here," I said, sighing with relief. "She's hysterical, and much too drunk to drive."

"Oh shit. I'm sorry. Look, I'm right downtown, be there in five minutes." He hung up.

I waited. Sandra had fallen asleep on the couch, curled into the fetal position, worn out from alcohol and her frenzied accusations. Van Zandt, as good as his word, arrived within minutes.

"Matthew," he said, smiling sheepishly, "I'm terribly sorry about all this. I should never have let her out of my sight."

"It's okay," I replied. "But why has she started accusing Hugh? She didn't say anything like that before. Not in her deposition, anyway."

"I don't know. I don't think she means it. Maybe it's just the strain. Her finances aren't very good. Walter didn't have anywhere near enough insurance, I guess."

"Hugh can't possibly help her until after the trial, even if he had reason to. It'd look like hell."

"I know. I offered her a job, but it isn't going to come close to giving her the same kind of living." He shook his head sadly. "I'll take her home. Don't worry about her car, I'll send somebody for it in the morning."

"Thanks."

"No need, it was my fault." He slapped me lightly on the back, then moved to the couch and picked Sandra up in his arms. "Come on, Sandy," he said gently, setting her on her feet. "Time to go." She wobbled unsteadily as he wrapped her in her raincoat and guided her out the door. After a moment I heard a car grind to life and pull away.

I stood for a long moment in the silent, darkened room, listening hard but hearing only the ticks and sighs of the empty building, hoping to God that Sandra Kessler had nothing to sell.

CHAPTER 14

At half past eight the next morning I leaned back in my chair at the defense table and watched the courtroom begin to fill up with press and spectators. We had drawn reporters from both the Seattle dailies as well as the wire services. A couple of local television reporters sat on one of the back benches, looking lost without their camera crews. The judge had banished the cameras to the courthouse hallway. A group of police and fire types were clustered at the back of the room, drinking coffee and laughing uproariously over something involving the ex-wife of somebody's watch commander, her New Age spiritual advisor, and a cocker spaniel. Cop humor is one part irony to five parts acid, and I never really acquired a taste for it.

Hugh sat quietly beside me. On the surface he was holding up well, but there were little cracks beginning to form, as though the tension he was holding inside him was working its way to the surface. He stared straight ahead, tapping a pencil on the table.

"Hugh," I began quietly, "Sandra Kessler came to see me last night, at my office. She's broke. She wants money from you."

He turned to look at me, his eyes somehow not surprised. "What for? Does she think I'm guilty?"

"I'm not sure what she thinks, but she wants money pretty bad. Does she know anything about you, Hugh?

Something that would make her think it could be worth something?"

"Not that I know of. Like I said before, she's a good friend of Susan's, and I was out socially with her and Walter a half-dozen times, but we're not really close or anything. Maybe she's just desperate."

"Maybe. The prosecutor hasn't got her on the witness list. She didn't seem to know anything important in her deposition."

"What could she testify about? She wasn't involved in any of the work Walter did for me."

"I don't know. She said something like, 'Hugh knows.' I can't figure it out."

"Well, it beats me," he said. The pencil kept tapping.

The judge's arrival on the bench cut off our conversation as we got to our feet. "Bailiff, please bring in the jury," the judge as she settled behind the bench. "Ms. Kleinfeldt, call your next witness as soon as the jury is seated."

Liz Kleinfeldt remained standing. The jury filed in. Some of the jurors' faces were somber, others alight with anticipation. Kleinfeldt spoke as the jurors sat down. "The State calls Fire Inspector David Swenson," she said.

David Swenson took the stand confidently, with the practiced ease of a cop who had testified a dozen times and knew most of the tricks that defense lawyers might throw at him. He was carefully dressed in a two-piece gray suit, blue shirt, red tie, and polished black shoes. He looked more like a lawyer than a fire investigator and I knew the resemblance was not an accident. Liz Kleinfeldt would have prepared him well.

Swenson testified about his experience and training in fire investigation, then turned to the Prokop Marine fire. The evidence of arson was overwhelming: the nature of the flame spread through the building, the hot spots in the ceilings on the main floor above the points where paint thinner had been dumped and ignited, the blackened tins found near the ignition points, the samples taken from the floor and walls and analyzed for traces of thinner. I did not object to any of it in order to avoid highlighting the testimony for the jury. After a couple of dozen questions without an objection Swenson began to look disappointed. He had wanted to stick something in me and break if off.

The fire testimony was finished by lunchtime. After the noon break Swenson testified briefly about the statements Hugh had made at the night of the fire, including his alibi concerning the trip to the convenience store on Greenwood Avenue for a six-pack of beer at ten that night. Swenson, I knew, had gone to the store after the fire and interviewed the clerk working that night. He had not testified about the interviews to avoid the obvious hearsay objection; the clerk was shown on the prosecution's witness list and we would probably see him next. Bernstein, my investigator, had made two separate trips back to the store to talk to the clerk, but it had done no good. The clerk simply did not remember Hugh Prokop.

I was planning to cross-examine Swenson only about the threats he had made when I had shut down his attempts to question Hugh after the fire. As I was rising from my chair I saw Bernstein come into the courtroom. He gestured urgently.

"Your Honor," I said, turning back to face the judge, "I'd like a moment, please."

"What is it, Mr. Riordan?"

"One of my associates has come into court with a message for me. I ask the Court's indulgence."

"Very well," she said, "but keep it short."

Bernstein was standing at the bar, waiting. "What is it?" I whispered.

"I can't believe I was so goddamned stupid," he replied, exasperated. "There was something important about that convenience store that I just couldn't remember, so I went back this morning. And I finally figured it out. They've got a camera system in there, Matthew. It video-tapes everyone coming to the register."

"Why didn't you spot it before?"

"The camera is mounted inside a plasterboard box. The box is painted the same color as the wall. I figured it out only when I saw a little flash of light from the lens."

"Where are the tapes? Do you have them?"

"No. I asked the manager about them. He says he gave them to Swenson. Swenson looked at them and gave them back, saying he didn't need them."

"Did they keep them at the store?"

"No. They erase them at the end of every week."

"Did Swenson know that?"

"The manager says he told him. Swenson said that was fine, because he didn't need them."

"Where's the manager now?"

"He's working. I can get him in here tomorrow, if you need him. I had him write out a short statement." He handed me a single sheet of paper. "His name's Ralph Delvecchio."

"He can't come today?"

"Nope. Tomorrow's the best I could do. Am I too late with this?"

"I don't think so. I fact, I think Swenson just fucked up big time. Stick around, this is going to be fun."

I put Delvecchio's handwritten statement in my pocket and turned back to face the bench. "Thank you, Your Honor," I said. "I'm ready to begin now." I walked up to the witness box and put my hand on the wooden railing that surrounded it. "Inspector Swenson," I said softly, "did you do anything to check on whether Mr. Prokop's alibi was true or not?"

He was taken aback by the open question, and the target I was offering him. "Yes, I did," he rasped, a smile beginning to spread across his face.

"Did you go to the RapidMart convenience store on 125th and Greenwood?"

"Yes."

"And you interviewed the clerk who was working that night, Mr. Marston?"

The smile was wider now. "Yes, I did. He said he couldn't remember seeing Mr. Prokop."

I smiled back at him. "I move to strike everything after the word 'did', Your Honor, as nonresponsive and hearsay," I said casually.

"Motion granted. The jury will disregard Inspector Swenson's statement."

I knew the jury wouldn't forget that line. Hell, I was counting on it.

"Inspector," I said, continuing casually, "didn't you also talk to Mr. Delvecchio, the store manager?"

"I did." He said it casually, still not seeing the trap.

It was time to move in closer. "Inspector," I said, an edge creeping into my voice, "didn't you survey the store when you were conducting these interviews?"

"I looked around, if that's what you mean."

"That's what I mean. And isn't it true, Inspector, that the RapidMart Store has a hidden videotape camera trained on every customer at the checkout counter during the hours that the store is open?"

"I . . . I'm not sure. I don't remember." The color began draining out of his face.

"You don't remember. Isn't it true, Inspector, that Mr. Delvecchio told you that there was such a videotape camera and permitted you to view the videotape from the night of the fire?"

"Objection," Liz Kleinfeldt said. "Calls for hearsay."

"It's impeachment, Your Honor," I replied.

"Overruled. The witness will answer the question."

"I looked at the tapes. Prokop wasn't on there."

"Move to strike the comment," I said. "Unresponsive."

"Granted. The jury will disregard everything after the word 'tapes.' "

I walked back to the counsel table, feeling the jury's eyes watching me, not quite understanding what was going on but feeling the tension in Swenson's answers. I took the written statement Bernstein had given me from my pocket and read it for a moment, then walked back to the front of the courtroom, holding the sheet of paper casually in one hand.

"Inspector," I said, harshly, letting each word grate in my mouth, "isn't it true that after you looked at the videotapes you gave them back to Mr. Delvecchio and said you didn't want them?"

His mouth worked, as though it was very dry. "I told him something like that."

"So it's true, isn't it?"

"Yes."

"And isn't it also true, Inspector, that Mr. Delvecchio told you that the tapes would be erased and reused if you didn't take them?"

He hesitated and glanced around the courtroom. "I have his statement here, Inspector. In my hand. Don't look around. Do you want to read it?"

He shook his head. "He told me that."

I turned to the bench. "Your Honor," I said loudly, "The defense moves for dismissal."

The judge had seen the way the testimony was going and looked as angry as a Montana thunderstorm. She turned to the jury. "The jury will be excused," she said tightly. "We have some legal matters to attend to." The jury filed out. The bailiff shut the door behind them. "All right, counsel."

Liz Kleinfeldt and I walked to the bench. Swenson started to get up to leave the stand. The judge looked him back down. "Sit down, Inspector," she hissed. He sat quickly, like a puppet on slack strings.

She turned to me. "Make your motion."

"Your Honor, the motion is based upon police and prosecutorial misconduct. The videotapes were not listed in any of the discovery provided by the prosecutor. As she well knows she has a duty, under the criminal rules and under the code of ethics, to turn over to the defense any evidence which tends to negate guilt.

"The police misconduct is even more egregious. As Inspector Swenson is fond of telling people, he has been trained and sworn as a police officer. When the police or the prosecution destroys material evidence without notice to the defense and opportunity to inspect, a dismissal is warranted. If I might, Your Honor." I walked over to the rows of *Washington Reports* shelved along the north wall of the courtroom. "*State v. Wright*, Your Honor, is one of the leading cases. It's at 87 Washington Second, page 783." I opened the volume and passed it up to the bench.

The judge read a couple of pages. "Ms. Kleinfeldt," she said severely, "were you aware of what Inspector Swenson had done?"

"No, Your Honor," she said coolly, as if unconcerned by what had happened. "Assuming that Inspector Swenson did return the videotapes with knowledge that they would be erased, there are at least two reasons for not granting a dismissal. First, Mr. Riordan made no request for this evidence. He has a duty to do so, if he becomes aware of it. He cannot, as he has apparently done, simply wait to lay a trap at trial. Second, Inspector Swenson did not destroy the evidence, Mr. Delvecchio did. Since Inspector Swenson's testimony is the only evidence we have of the contents of the videotape, and he says Mr. Prokop did not appear, then the omitted evidence does not tend to create a reasonable doubt as to Mr. Prokop's guilt."

"A nice sophistry, Your Honor, but it won't wash. I made no request because I did not know the evidence existed until my investigator came into court and told me. He learned of the taping system today. As to what Inspector Swenson says, it defies any sort of logic. It is perjury. Had the tapes failed to show my client in the store, as Inspector Swenson says, Ms. Kleinfeldt and I would be battling over their admissibility into evidence. He gave them back to Mr. Delvecchio and let them be destroyed because they did show Mr. Prokop and thus tend to prove Mr. Prokop's innocence."

Margaret Detweiler frowned in thought. "Step back. I'm going to want to think about this for a minute. We're in recess." She walked off the bench and into chambers, black robes flowing behind her.

As I turned to go Liz Kleinfeldt caught my arm. "I didn't know about this," she said, her voice low. "I want you to know that."

"Bullshit," I said angrily. "Wait for the goddamned ruling. I've nothing to say to you." I stalked back to Hugh.

He sat bolt upright at the table, anxiously drumming his fingers on the bleached oak surface. "Am I going to get out of this?" he whispered.

"I don't know," I replied. "This judge is very anti-defendant. But the law is so clear I think she's going to have to dismiss."

I sat down beside him and waited silently, hands clasped together, staring at the courtroom clock high up on the mustard-yellow walls. The minutes walked by slowly. Judge Detweiler's courtroom had no windows and the harsh blue fluorescent lights burned my eyes. Hugh turned around to talk to his sister. I stayed where I was and waited.

The judge returned fifteen minutes later, toting a couple of brown legal volumes under her arm, her half glasses still perched on her nose. The courtroom was very quiet as she settled in at the bench.

"The motion to dismiss is denied," she said simply.

"Your Honor," I shouted, jumping to my feet. "With all respect, I believe your ruling is in error. The law is clear. When relevant evidence has been destroyed by direct or indirect police misconduct, the case must be dismissed."

"I do not find that the evidence, if it existed, would create a reasonable doubt," she said.

"The test, Your Honor, is a possibility that the evidence will create a reasonable doubt. That means a chance. Not six chances in ten."

"Sit down, Mr. Riordan," she said sharply. "The court gives the law here, not you. The point is close. I will let you argue the issue to the jury. If the jury convicts, I will permit you to move for a new trial or a dismissal, and will accept briefs on the issue then."

"Your Honor, may I . . ."

"No. I have ruled. Bailiff, bring in the jury. Mr. Riordan, do you have any further cross-examination?"

"Yes, Your Honor," I said, rising to my feet, fighting the letdown from losing on what should have been clear-cut grounds for dismissal. I waited until the jury was in place, then went after Swenson with everything I had left, getting him to concede that he had threatened Prokop after the initial interview on the night of the fire. It should have been good grist for the jury but it fell curiously flat, as though the jury had been distracted by their time in the jury room. When I gave it up at four o'clock on that Friday afternoon, a hint of a smile had begun to emerge from Swenson's correctly somber mask, the cold smile of a man who has lied and gotten away with it.

CHAPTER 15

There are times when I think weekends are the worst part of a trial. If you have prepared your case correctly, there is not that much real work to be done. But in the belief that you must do something, you fill the days by endlessly rehashing each day of trial, second- and third-guessing yourself amid boxes of evidence, sandwich wrappers and milk cartons scattered around the room.

Hugh took the judge's decision not to dismiss the case badly. He dragged himself into my office on Saturday morning, looking as though he had gone diving into an ocean of whiskey the night before. I found him ginger ale and aspirin. He swallowed the aspirin and belched painfully.

"I thought you were going to go easy on yourself," I said, by way of a greeting.

"Yeah, well, yesterday wasn't my best day," he muttered. "You got any coffee?"

"Out by my secretary's desk," I replied. When he came back with a cup, he looked angry.

"Are you having that private detective buddy of yours watch me?" he demanded.

"Of course not. Why do you ask?"

"Take a look out your secretary's window. There's a brown Honda sedan parked across the street, in the sail-maker's lot. I saw it behind me this morning as I was driving down here."

139

I got up and went to the window. The Honda sat in the parking lot, its windows covered with dark plastic sun-film. I couldn't tell if there was someone in the car or not.

"Wait here," I said. I pulled on an oiled-wool sweater and walked down the outside steps into a light rain.

I crossed Northlake Way at a trot and hurried up to the car. When I got within twenty feet, the car's engine ground into life and the Honda pulled away, tossing gravel in its wake.

I started after it. The rear plate had been artfully covered over with a smear of mud. Eventually I walked back to the office, thinking hard.

"Who was it?" Hugh asked pensively.

"I don't know," I said, shaking the beads of rainwater off my sweater and hanging it up in the entranceway. "If it was the cops they wouldn't have taken off like that."

"Then who was it?"

"Why ask me? You're the one they're tailing."

He stared at me for a moment, his bloodshot eyes darkened by some emotion I could not read. "Let's go to work," he said.

On Monday, the prosecution's case started quickly. Liz Kleinfeldt put Swenson back on the stand to testify, over my repeated objections, that Hugh Prokop had not appeared in any of the convenience store videotapes on the night of the fire. She was doing it less for its effect on the jury than to shore up the shaky factual basis for the judge's decision in the appeal we were sure to make.

By mid-morning Kleinfeldt had put on her main witness for the day, a pale, graying man named Atherton who testified as an expert accountant on how much money Hugh had lost through bad real estate, oil, and stock market investments. The testimony wasn't a surprise, but the numbers came raining down like mortar fire in the distance, each loss taking its toll: "CreekCo Oil I Limited Partnership, $17,000 lost; Alameda Apartments Partners III, $67,000 lost; Global Marine Common Stock, $25,000 lost." The list grew until the total reached nearly half a million dollars. I hoped the jury had eaten a big, heavy breakfast, the better to make them drowsy as Atherton droned on in the late-morning warmth of the courtroom.

After the lunch break, I cross-examined Atherton on Hugh's substantial remaining assets, especially his investments with Van Zandt & Company and the value of his real estate, showing the jury that for all the losses, Hugh was still reasonably well off. With a draw on the motive issue, I hoped, the jury would believe Hugh.

I finished with Atherton at three o'clock, a solid if not flashy job of cross-examination. I walked back to the defense table and gave Hugh a confident squeeze on the shoulder and a smile as I sat down.

"We're holding our own, Hugh," I whispered. "Hang in there, and by the end of the next week you're going to be clear, even if we don't get our dismissal." He nodded and smiled back, but his smile was false and shallow, his eyes quick and nervous. And I wondered for the hundredth time what was wrong.

When we returned from the afternoon recess, Elizabeth Kleinfeldt was standing in the well in front of the bench, waiting to address the court.

"Your Honor," she began, "the State would like to add a new witness to our list at this time. The State will call Mrs. Sandra Kessler, the widow of the victim."

"Mr. Riordan?"

"I think it's prejudicial, Your Honor." I said, rising to my feet. "Ms. Kleinfeldt has known of Mrs. Kessler's testimony for a long time. Why wasn't she placed on the list before?"

"I was just informed of new evidence by Mrs. Kessler at the recess, Your Honor. Mr. Riordan took Mrs. Kessler's deposition and had a full opportunity to question her in advance of trial."

I shook my head. "But not on any claimed 'new evidence,' Your Honor. I would ask the court to—"

"No," the judge said, cutting me off. "I'm going to allow the testimony. Bailiff, bring in the jury."

Sandra Kessler took the stand nervously, dressed in a khaki-colored skirted suit, white blouse, and paisley scarf.

The contrast from the black clothes she had worn throughout the trial looked to be deliberate. Had Kleinfeldt been lying when she said that she had just learned of the new testimony? I sat up on the edge of my chair, waiting pensively.

"Mrs. Kessler," Liz Kleinfeldt began, "do you know the defendant, Hugh Prokop?"

"Yes, I do," she said, her voice low.

"How did you meet him?"

"I don't remember, exactly. It would have been some social occasion. Walter, my husband, was his accountant, and he also worked with Susan Haight, who is a friend of Mr. Prokop's."

"When did you meet Mr. Prokop?"

"About a year ago, I think."

"After you met him, did your social relationship with him change?"

Suddenly warning lights came on in my head and I got to my feet. "Objection," I said, keeping my voice soft. "Any social relationship between Mrs. Kessler and Mr. Prokop is completely irrelevant. May we approach the bench?"

The judge cocked her head at Liz Kleinfeldt. "I think you'd better tell us where you're going with this, Ms. Kleinfeldt."

"Let me withdraw the question, Your Honor, and try it another way." She turned to Sandra Kessler. "Mrs. Kessler, did it come to pass that you had a discussion with Mr. Prokop about his company, Prokop Marine Supply?"

"Objection. Leading."

"Overruled."

"Yes. I talked to him about it."

"When was that?"

"Late in January, of this year. I can't recall the date, but it was a Wednesday night."

"What did Mr. Prokop say about his company?"

"Objection. Hearsay," I cut in.

"Overruled."

"He said that it had lost money in the past year. He said that he wasn't sure if he could continue to compete against the bigger companies. He said he'd like to sell the business but that it wasn't worth anything, except for the land. And he said he was very tired of working long days without much to show for it."

"Where did Mr. Prokop make these statements?"

"At his home."

"And where in the home were you?"

"We were in bed."

Her timing was perfect. The courtroom was silent. Hugh shook his head and slumped forward, staring at the table. I grabbed his arm and squeezed it as hard as I could. "Goddamn you, look up. Look at the jury," I commanded, whispering.

Liz Kleinfeldt paused to give the revelation its maximum dramatic effect, then went on.

"Mrs. Kessler, was that the first sexual encounter you had with Mr. Prokop?"

"No. We had been having an affair since the fall of last year."

"I see. Mrs. Kessler, what was the relationship like between your husband and Mr. Prokop?"

"Objection. Irrelevant."

"Overruled."

"They weren't friends. Mr. Prokop employed Walter as his accountant because Walter did good work. Hugh . . . Mr. Prokop, was always very contemptuous of Walter, whenever Walter wasn't around."

Liz Kleinfeldt nodded at the answer and moved closer to the jury box, resting a hand lightly on the rail as she posed her next question.

"Now, Mrs. Kessler, do you recall that Mr. Riordan took your deposition?"

"Yes, I do."

"And you didn't tell him about you and Mr. Prokop, did you?"

"No, I didn't."

"Why was that?"

"Well, he didn't ask directly, so I thought Mr. Prokop had told him. And I did not want to hurt Mr. Prokop."

"Why didn't you want to hurt Mr. Prokop?"

"Because I was not sure if he had done this."

"And did your opinion change?"

"Objection!" I exploded, jumping out of my chair. "Calls for a conclusion. No foundation—"

"Sustained," the judge said.

Kleinfeldt let the question drop. She had made her point. Everyone on the jury would assume that Prokop had confessed to Sandra Kessler, or at the least given some clue to his guilt away.

"Your Honor," she said, "it's past four o'clock and I have more questions for this witness. Should I save them for tomorrow?"

Margaret Detweiler nodded. "Yes. Court is in recess."

I sagged down in my chair as the jury filed out. I watched their faces as they left. Some looked bemused, some shocked. One or two looked angry. They would be angry, I thought, if they had bought a piece of Hugh Prokop's story, only to find themselves sold out. Hugh would never have their votes now.

Beautiful. By breaking for the day when she had, Liz Kleinfeldt had all but assured that the jurors would think about Sandra Kessler's testimony all night. Tomorrow, if I came back with a tough cross-examination on her sex life, Liz Kleinfeldt would have Sandra do an hour of tearful self-recrimination about the lifelong guilt she would bear for having slept with her husband's killer. And the jury would decide, even if they didn't like her, that Sandra Kessler must be telling the truth.

Beautiful.

"I swear to God it wasn't like that," Hugh said, his voice a low dull monotone. "It was never . . . I just went to bed with her a couple of times."

We were sitting in the empty jury room of a nearby seventh-floor courtroom. I had called in a favor from a friendly bailiff to use the room. It was a little after four-thirty. When the jury had left the courtroom, Susan Haight had stood up and walked calmly out of the room, saying nothing, not looking back. Hugh remained slumped in his chair, stunned, until I grabbed him by the collar and dragged him away to talk.

I sighed. The jury room felt hot and tight. It had been used that day in a robbery trial and there were half-empty coffee cups and dirty ashtrays scattered across the square wooden jury table. The room had a sour smell, of sweat and stale smoke and indecision.

"Tell me again about the relationship," I said coldly. "When it began, where you went, how many times you did it."

"It started last October. Late in October. We were all supposed to go to a cocktail party—Susan, me, Walter, Sandra. Susan and Walter were an hour late, then they finally called and said to go ahead out to dinner because they weren't going to be out of the office before midnight. Sandra and I drove over to the Red Lion to get something to eat and ended up taking a room. God, I can't believe she would do this to me."

"Don't be an ass. She's doing it because she wants a lot of money from you. If you get convicted, your civil liability for Kessler's death will be just about automatic. She'll take everything you've got. Now pull yourself together. How many other times did you sleep with her?"

"Jesus," he whined, "do we really have to go into all this? I need to get out of here and call Susan, apologize to her."

I jumped up and grabbed him by the shirtfront and shoved him against the back of his chair. "You held out on me, you stupid son of a bitch!" I shouted, pushing my face down toward his. "You let me walk right into a nice little trap that Kleinfeldt had all laid out and ready. Now you're going to stay here and answer every goddamn question I have for you, or I'm going to pull out of this case and let you swim down the rat hole. You'll love Walla Walla, Hugh. You're going to make somebody one hell of a roommate."

I let him go and his head fell forward into his hands and he wept. I stood over him, not bothering to hide the scorn in my face or my voice, putting the same questions to him all over again.

"How many other times did you sleep with her?"

"Three or four. No, three. I broke it off right before Christmas. My relationship with Susan was starting to go better and I wanted to give it a chance."

"Never after Christmas? She said January."

"Well, once more. It was late January, about a week before the fire. The twenty-ninth? Something like that. Susan and Walter and half their company were down in Las Vegas for some securities industry meetings."

"Why then?"

He threw up his hands. "How do I know? I was bored and feeling left out. And she's good in bed."

"Were you drinking?"

"Yeah, some. I had maybe four or five shots before she called me."

"She called you. You're sure of that?"

"Yes. I was just sitting around the house having some drinks and watching TV."

"Did she come to your place?"

"Yes."

I stopped asking questions and thought. I was down to grasping at straws and that seemed to be one of them. On cross I could portray Sandra as the rejected party, revenging herself through false testimony. I didn't necessarily believe it but that didn't matter. The jury might buy it. The hypocritical Victorian gentleman isn't as dead as everyone thinks.

"Did you talk to her about the business that night? On the stand she said you were tired of it and wanted out."

"Shit, I might have. I was pretty down. But it was just talk."

"Just talk." I laughed harshly. "You stupid jerk. You really don't understand what she's done to you, do you? Your whole case was built on credibility. The jury has to see you as a nice guy, the classic small-business owner who lives for his company. Goddamn it, they have to see you as a victim. We were doing well with that. But because you didn't tell me about her, all that good guy stuff is going to come back and make you look ten times worse. To the jury you're going to be just another sleazy creep, willing to grab whatever easy money and free-floating tail that comes by.''

Hugh sat staring down at the floor. "I don't have to listen to this shit," he said slowly, his voice filled with rising anger. He got up and slammed the chair against the table. "Just where in fucking hell do you get off judging me, anyway?" he shouted. "You want to tell me there aren't any pissed-off husbands or blacked-out nights in your past, Riordan? Don't hand me that crap, because I know better." He walked over to the wall and leaned against it, his fists clenched. "I thought you were my friend. I thought you'd understand."

"Understanding doesn't mean shit. I'm your lawyer and I'm trying to get you off. I don't know or even much care anymore if you burned the building, Hugh. I want to do my job, win this case, and every time I get close I find another lie from you blocking the way. So answer my goddamned questions. What exactly did you tell her about the business?"

"I told her that I was tired and that we'd had some losses. That's all I said. I didn't say anything about wanting to sell out."

"Did you tell her you'd gone to see Tran Loc Minh?"

"No."

"And Susan?" I asked sharply. "Did you tell her?"

He hesitated. "Only you," he said. I couldn't tell if he was lying or not.

"You'd better be right about this, Hugh. Or you're dead."

"I know that. I swear, that's all I told her."

I paused and walked aimlessly around half of the jury table, thinking hard about the next question. It was one I didn't want to ask. I turned back to face Hugh.

"The cops haven't tried to make you for the Minh killing because Susan and I both give you an alibi," I said slowly. "But I sent you and Susan home in a taxi around eleven. Minh was shot around one o'clock in the morning. Is Susan still going to say she spent the night at your place?"

"You're asking me if I killed Minh," he said bleakly.

"The answer is no. Susan won't change her story. It's the truth." All the emotion had gone out of him.

"You'd better hope she sticks to it."

"She will."

"Okay. Somehow you're going to have to persuade Susan to stay with you, at least through the trial. I'm going to talk to her but it's mostly going to come down to you. If she walks out on you, the jury is going to know that. And if she decides to testify against you, you have no marital privilege. Anything you've told her will come in."

"I'll talk to her. That's why I've got to get out of here. I'll call her tonight."

"All right. There's just one other thing. The same thing we've been dancing around for a month. If there's anything you haven't told me about the money in the safe, I need to know it now."

"Oh, for God's sake, Riordan, why are you bringing that up again?" He straightened up from the wall and walked back to the table. He sat down heavily, sprawling in the chair. "We told you where it came from. A hundred times. Greg and Susan put up the money for a real estate deal in Hawaii."

"You keep telling me that, Hugh. So what was the address of the house you were going to buy?"

"I don't know. I mean, I don't remember."

"You'd better know by tomorrow. Greg was supposed to provide me with the purchase papers and he hasn't given me all of them yet. Why not, Hugh?"

"Ask Greg."

"I will. But you might be on the stand by late tomorrow, and you'd better have them. And why cash? Why not a cashier's check, or a letter of credit?"

"The seller was going to leave the country. He wanted cash."

"Maybe. If he was leaving the country, a wire transfer to a bank in the Caymans or Switzerland makes a hell of a lot more sense. You'd better have answers to these questions because now I have to go into the money in very precise detail. I don't have any choice. You've got to be able to explain completely why it was there. And the explanation has to hold up under cross-examination. Kleinfeldt is going to come after you hard. She thinks you skimmed the money. There isn't enough left of your inventory records to prove you didn't skim. The jury has got to believe you, and Susan."

"Are you going to ask Susan about it?"

"In court? Hell, yes. I'm even going to have a subpoena served on her tonight, to make sure she shows up."

"Look, all I know is that the deal specified cash. Nobody asked why the seller, this Filipino guy, wanted cash. It was a good deal and we thought asking too many questions might screw it up."

I shook my head, trying to clear it. At that moment I had heard all of the bullshit lies I ever wanted to hear from Hugh Prokop.

"Forget it, Hugh," I said softly. "You skimmed the money, didn't you? And maybe you killed him and maybe you didn't. No, don't answer. It doesn't matter." I walked back to the jury table and slumped down in a chair.

An awful, aching exhaustion had come over me, and I yearned to do nothing more than stretch out in a long, soft bed and sleep for a couple of weeks. "Go call Susan," I said finally. "I'll try to keep you off the stand tomorrow. Tomorrow night we'll go over all the stuff about the money one more time." I yawned and shook myself trying to clear out the fog. "But listen, Hugh. You'd better have your story together by tomorrow. If you don't, you're going to do hard prison time. A lot of it. I won't be able to save you. Nobody will. Hell, you're almost there already."

I picked up my briefcase and headed out the door, not looking back.

CHAPTER 16

The next morning began as badly as the previous day had ended. I had spent most of the night going over and over the sparse information I had gathered about Sandra Kessler, trying to figure out a line of cross-examination that would undercut her testimony without triggering the jury's natural sympathy for her as the victim's widow. I considered questioning her about her other affairs, but I had no names, no places, only rumors and the nastiest sort of innuendo from the people she once worked with. In the end I decided that smear tactics would not work. Kessler's sexuality was not at issue. By questioning her about her affairs I might lose whatever credibility I still had with the jury.

That left the money. The way Sandra had pleaded with me for money, coupled with facts that Bernstein had dug up about the Kessler's finances in the weeks before trial—Walter's moonlighting for extra money, the mountain of credit card and mortgage debt they both had run up, the lack of life insurance—would probably do. By pinning the blame on Hugh, Sandra Kessler could hope to recover a large wrongful-death settlement. That would give her a motive to lie.

The ironic thing, of course, was that Sandra Kessler probably had not lied at all. I had no doubt that Hugh, tired and depressed and semi-drunk, probably made the statements she repeated on the stand. I would be using one truth to attack another truth in the hope that the jury would decide that Hugh was innocent—a conclusion I was no longer sure to be the truth at all.

I was so absorbed in rehearsing the cross-examination that I didn't notice that the courtroom had filled up and the time had advanced to five minutes before nine. And that Hugh wasn't in the courtroom.

The dry rasp in my throat got a little rougher, the ache behind my eyes a little worse. I turned around in my chair at the counsel table, scanning the rest of the courtroom. Susan Haight had arrived and was just sitting down at her usual place, in the first row in back of the counsel table, directly behind Hugh's chair. Her face seemed calm, even serene. It had none of the red-eyed sorrow or anger I would have expected, given what she had learned the day before.

"Susan," I said softly, gesturing to her to lean over the bar. I stood up and leaned over so that I could whisper in her ear. "Where's Hugh? Have you seen him?"

"No," she said, whispering her reply. "But I talked to him on the phone last night."

"Did you . . ."

"Yes. We talked about it. We agreed not to make any decisions until after the trial is over. Beyond that we didn't have much to say." Her voice, even in a whisper, was too calm, too controlled.

"Don't judge him too harshly, Susan. Please." I suffered a moment's self-revulsion as I began to plead Hugh's case. "I talked to him, and it wasn't the way Sandra painted it. Hugh said he regarded it as nothing more than a couple of one-night stands. He's well aware of the pain that he's caused you."

"I understand that. Look, Matthew, it really doesn't matter. Not until this trial is over. You didn't have to have the subpoena served on me last night. I'm going to testify if you want me to. I'm not going to create a scene that's going to prejudice the jury. I'll be warm and supportive and the jury will think I'm Donna Reed. So don't worry. You concentrate on winning."

I stared into her dark brown eyes for a moment, wanting to thank her for being there, yet jarred by her offhand tone and the way she had denied her own emotions. For just a moment I thought I saw a coldness, a calm, dispassionate self incapable of love or warmth. Then her eyes shifted away and there was nothing to see, and I told myself to stop being such an idiot.

"Hugh's late," I said. "Please get to a phone and call him and find out what the trouble is. If the judge comes in before he gets here, she's not going to like it."

"Okay," Susan said. She got up and slipped down the aisle and out of the courtroom. She was back a moment later. "There's no answer at Hugh's house," she said. "I let it ring ten times."

"He must be on his way," I replied. I heard a door open behind the bench. The bailiff came in. "Oh, shit," I cursed under my breath as the bailiff droned out "All rise."

The judge came in and sat down. She shuffled a few papers, then looked up from the bench and said, "Morning, counsel. Any matters before the jury is brought in?" The judge's eyes flicked casually around the courtroom. When she looked at the defense table and saw Hugh's chair empty, her eyes widened slightly and turned hard.

"Mr. Riordan," she snapped, "Where is Mr. Prokop?"

"Apparently on his way, Your Honor," I replied. "We've called and there is no answer. I don't know why he is late, but I'm sure there is some reasonable explanation."

"There had better be," Judge Detweiler said, "Or I will revoke bond and Mr. Prokop can spend the rest of the trial as a guest of the County. I'm sending an officer out to his home, Mr. Riordan, just to be sure. Bailiff, tell the jury there will be a delay. We're in recess." She left the bench and returned to chambers.

The courtroom buzzed after the judge had left. I turned again to Susan and she shrugged, a blank look on her face. "I'll go call again," she said, and left the room. Mary Alice, Hugh's sister, came over from her seat at the end of the first row. "What's happening, Matthew?" she asked, her plain square face, careworn and puzzled. "I spoke to

Hugh last night, and he didn't say anything about being late, or not feeling well."

"He's probably just on his way, caught in traffic or something," I said with an assurance I did not feel. "We'll be starting in a few minutes. Why don't you get some coffee or something? There's nothing to do but wait." She nodded and left.

I sat back down and fiddled with my cross-examination outline for a minute or two, then gave up and leaned back in my chair, lacing my fingers behind my head and staring at nothing in particular, wishing I could get the gut-twisting tension out of my belly just once before a day of trial. Out of the corner of my eye I saw Liz Kleinfeldt get up and walk over to my table.

"Okay, Riordan," she began, "What's . . ."

I put up a palm and cut her off. "Don't start with me, counsel, not today. Not after throwing the grieving, horny widow in our faces yesterday. Did you let her in on what I can do to her on the stand if I want to? I've had a detective on her. For all you know I have every lonesome salesman she's ever nailed out in the hallway. All the gory details should be out in time for the afternoon papers. Not that the emotional well-being of the victim's wife is anywhere near as important to you as winning."

Her face darkened with anger. "Damn you. Who do you think you are? The judge will never let you pull that kind of crap. Your client is guilty, Riordan, and now I know why and the jury knows why. And he's going down for it."

She spun on one foot and stomped back to her table. I was still mentally drafting up a nasty comeback when the judge's bailiff, Susan Strachan, came over to the table. Her young plain face was grim as she motioned Liz Kleinfeldt back to the defense table. "The judge wants to see both counsel in chambers," she said.

"What is it?" Liz Kleinfeldt asked, her voice suddenly hesitant.

The bailiff shook her head. "The judge wants you. Now."

We followed her into chambers, apprehension eating at

me like acid. Good God, could Hugh have been so stupid as to run? We were winning the case until yesterday, and with the right cross-examination on Sandra Kessler, we might still pull it out. Whatever private doubts I had about Prokop's innocence would not stop me from putting everything I could into his defense. What the hell had he done?

Judge Detweiler was seated at her desk. She had taken off her courtroom robes and was wearing a simple, but obviously expensive, gray jersey dress. Her strong handsome face was grim. She was smoking a cigarette, something I hadn't seen her do before. Standing behind her, his face half turned to stare out the window behind her desk, was Vince Ahlberg.

"What is it, Your Honor?" I asked.

"Please sit down. Both of you."

I shook my head, no. "Thank you, but please tell me what is wrong, Your Honor."

"I'm sorry, Mr. Riordan, but Mr. Prokop is dead. Apparently by his own hand."

I heard a sharp intake of breath and turned to look at Liz Kleinfeldt, shaking her head slowly from side to side, in disbelief or in sympathy I did not know. As I watched her I felt my guts turning slowly to stone, even as my head remained oddly clear.

"How did it happen?" I asked slowly.

Vince Ahlberg turned away from his window. He had been staring out at the rooftops of Pioneer Square as the hard gray morning rain had slowed and finally stopped. "All we have is the word of the patrolman Judge Detweiler sent," he replied. "It seems Prokop hanged himself from a beam in his living room. I'm sorry, Matthew. I have a medical examiner and his team going up to the scene. We are not excluding the possibility that you have been right, that Prokop was innocent and this may be a fake set up by somebody else. But we haven't got anything yet that goes against a finding of suicide."

"I'd like to go to Hugh's house," I said, speaking to Ahlberg.

"I figured that. I'll take you up with me when the judge is finished with us."

"Thank you." I turned to Judge Detweiler. "Mr. Prokop's friend, Susan Haight, and his sister, Mary Alice Thierrault, are in the courtroom today. I have to tell them what happened. I don't want them to find out from a courthouse whisper. I'd like to do it away from the press. May I use the jury room?"

The Judge shook her head. Her face was very somber. A sudden death is unsettling even to those who decide cases involving death every day. "I'll tell them," she said. "Go with Captain Ahlberg. Shall I tell them to meet with you later today?"

"Please tell them to be at my office at two o'clock, if they can. Thank you, Your Honor."

"I'm going to dismiss the jury now, Ms. Kleinfeldt," the judge said. "Both counsel can leave."

I stayed put, leaning against the back wall of the chambers, and waited until Liz Kleinfeldt had left, with Ahlberg following her. I turned to go after them, but the judge stopped me.

"Mr. Riordan," she said. "It was an able defense. More than able. You're not responsible for this happening. Remember that."

I looked back at Margaret Detweiler. Her severe judicial persona was gone. The look in her eyes had softened into something that might have been pity. I hoped it was not. I felt no anger, only the deep wrenching sadness that sometimes flows from guilt. Finally, I shook my head, no. "We all have to live with what we do," I said. Then I turned and went after Ahlberg, following him through the courtroom, where the sudden explosion of light and noise was simply too harsh to bear.

Hugh Prokop had lived in Broadview, a north-side neighborhood of 1960s vintage ranch-style homes set on a long ridge overlooking Puget Sound. Hugh's house was on the downhill side of his street, a long, comfortable-looking tan house with big windows in dark-stained frames and a weathered, almost silver-gray, shingled cedar roof.

The house was on a short, curving block of similar homes, each with fine lawns and gardens. Somehow it seemed still to be early morning. The lush green lawns were wet from the recent rain. Many of the people who lived in the neighborhood were retired, still at home on a weekday. Some of them stood around outside the police barricades in heavy wool bathrobes, gray hair still tousled from the pillow, clutching steaming mugs of coffee, staring quizzically at the silent flashing red lights of the ambulance and the M.E.'s van parked in the street.

Vince Ahlberg and I had been silent on the fifteen-minute ride from the courthouse to Hugh's home. We stepped out of the unmarked police car into a swarming mass of reporters and gawkers. Ahlberg shook off a couple of them and bulled his way past a camera crew onto the front sidewalk and up to the front door. I followed close behind him, knowing that even if I shoved him out of the way I could go no faster.

We went in through the paneled oak front door and into the small entry hall. I noticed every detail, as if going into the house for the first time. Carpeted stairs led through an archway into the living room. The living room itself was quite wide and extended to the back wall of the house. It was carpeted in the same beige wool rug as the entry had been. The walls were white and almost empty of pictures. The twelve-foot-high cathedral ceiling was made of cedar planks and beams stained a dark brown.

A two-foot length of rope dangling from the ceiling drew my eyes up to a large heavy-gauge steel hook that had been screwed into the highest beam, the one at the ridge of the ceiling. Beneath the dangling rope a kitchen chair had been kicked over on its side.

"Where's the body?" I said to Ahlberg, almost choking on the words.

Ahlberg turned to one of the medical examiner's men standing around the edges of the room and motioned him over. They whispered. I couldn't see why they needed to. Ahlberg turned back to me.

"It's in the dining room, on a gurney," he said. "Do you want to see it?"

"I don't know. Are they through in here?"

This time the M.E.'s man spoke for himself. "We've

taken photographs and measured the distances between the body and the rest of the stuff in the room, Captain. We've vacuumed and taken fiber samples from the rug. I can't think of anything else to try.''

"Prints on the chair?" Vince asked.

"Yes, but I think they're going to match the victim's. We found only one person's prints on the chair. I'd like to take another look at the rope and the hook, just to be complete." He shook his head. "It's suicide, Captain. We haven't found a note, but that hook wasn't there before last night; we found fresh cedar dust around the hook and in the carpet. I don't think anybody could come in here, set this up, and wrestle the victim into the noose without either a struggle or a lot of help. The only thing that could change my mind is if we find drugs or one hell of a lot of alcohol in the victim.''

Ahlberg shrugged. "Be complete and don't overlook anything.'' He turned to me and added, "You done here?"

"Not yet. I'd like a minute.''

"Okay. I'll be back in a little while." He left. I wandered slowly around the room, looking at the place where Hugh had killed himself, searching for a meaning I did not think I would ever find. As I see it, there are all kinds of suicides. Some of them are awful and some, as bad as they are, show mercy to the victim or to the survivors. A few suicides make eminent sense, as when a dying man chooses a cleaner, better death than what his fates have chosen.

Hugh's death fell into the awful category. It would be seen as an admission of guilt that would cause his family and his lover considerable pain. Hugh had surely known that. Sometime in the small hours between darkness and dawn, his will must have shattered and his fear or guilt driven him into a well of despair and left him too weak to climb back out.

As I circled the living room, I stopped and picked up the kicked-over kitchen chair and placed it below the hook in the beam, appraising the height of the beam and the chair as well as the length of the rope.

I bowed my head as the awful calculation I was making came clear. Hugh had saved himself no pain. He lacked the hangman's working knowledge of physics and anatomy. The drop from the chair had not been enough to break Hugh's neck and kill him quickly. Unable to get his feet back onto the kicked-away chair, he would have strangled, slowly.

Nausea came over me in waves. I left the house quickly and stood outside, breathing the cold, wet, clotted air until the nausea was under control. I never did look at Hugh's body. I did not need to see the blackened face to know that the dangle had not been a dance.

CHAPTER 17

The rest of the day crawled by like a wounded man, dragging its bloodied leg behind it. I left Hugh Prokop's house and stormed through the gaggle of reporters still clustered on the front lawn to a waiting taxi that took me back to my office on the north shore of Lake Union. When I got there I set to work with a raging will born of grief and guilt and a desperate desire to get away from anything to do with this case. By the time Susan Haight and Mary Alice Thierrault arrived at two o'clock, I had pulled Hugh's will out of my office safe and gathered his financial statements and insurance policies together. I had made phone calls to line up a wills-and-estates attorney to handle the probate, as well as three potential trial attorneys to take over the claims the Prokop Marine Corporation would press against the fire insurance companies for the loss of the Lake Union warehouse. Within twenty-four hours, if Mary Alice agreed and released me from my engagement, I would no longer have any involvement with any matter involving Hugh Prokop.

Mary Alice arrived first, accompanied by Peter Tobin, the wills-and-estates attorney whom I'd called. She came up the outside stairs like an old woman, each step a tortured bout between will and fatigue. The thin facade she had constructed for the trial was gone. Her face was a map of shock and grief. I helped her into a deep leather armchair and brought her coffee, saying nothing, hopelessly incapable of finding any comforting words to say.

She spoke first. "Matthew, I want you to know nobody blames you for anything," she said with surprising firmness. "I just wish I knew why he . . . did this."

I dropped to one knee and touched her arm. "Nobody knows why something like this happens, Mary," I lied, hoping to comfort her. "But the pressures that can build on people accused of a serious crime are enormous. Particularly when they are innocent."

She nodded. I got up and shook hands with Peter Tobin. Tobin was a sallow, dapper man in his mid-forties, an office lawyer clearly uncomfortable with the raw emotions left in the wake of Hugh's suicide. He took a copy of the will and was reviewing it when Susan Haight came in ten minutes later.

At first she seemed as calm and untroubled as she had appeared in court that morning, but there were little signs of tension in the way she walked and the oddly high, strained voice with which she spoke. When she entered the room she shook my hand briefly, then walked over to Mary Alice and leaned over to give her a brief hug and a sisterly kiss. Mary Alice stiffened at Susan's touch.

Susan had not come alone. A large pale man in a gray windowpane-plaid suit, with a wide bland face and an earnest, near-friendly smile arrived a moment later, huffing from the long flight of stairs. He extended a hand so big it looked like a white catcher's mitt. "Dudley Baird," he said, grinning while he looked around the office. "Nice office. Interesting. Terrific view, too," he added, pointing through the large south windows at the Lake Union collage of boats and water, with the downtown towers rising in the distance across the lake, their office lights shining against the dark clouded sky.

I left his hand in the air. "I don't understand why you're here, Mr. Baird. You have no invitation."

The amiable grin disappeared. "I'm an attorney for Van Zandt & Company, temporarily representing Ms. Haight's interests in this matter."

I put acid in my voice. "We're not talking about a

'matter,' Mr. Baird. We're doing the necessary cleaning up after the tragic death of a man who some of the people in this room loved. Very few of these matters even concern Ms. Haight. She's here because of her relationship with Hugh Prokop. Now get out.''

Baird's wide face set in a grim mask of suspicion.

"I'm not going anywhere until I know what's going on here," he said heavily. "There's a quarter of a million bucks in cash involved here. It's ours. I'm here to see that we get it."

"Then you're making this a short meeting. Fine. Hugh Prokop left a will. Ms. Thierrault and Hugh's daughter Megan are the primary beneficiaries; Ms. Thierrault is executrix. She has retained Mr. Tobin for probate work." I gestured at Tobin who sat silent and a little wide-eyed at the intensity of my outburst. "Ms. Haight is a legatee. She receives mostly cash and stocks, about twenty grand worth. Mr. Tobin will give her a copy of the will tomorrow. As for the quarter-million you're so interested in, Mr. Tobin will take the appropriate actions to have the court determine ownership when and if the money is released from police impound. Now get your fat ass out of my office before I throw you down the stairs. I've been wanting to hit someone all day and you'd do just fine."

Baird flushed to the roots of his hair. "Come on, Susan, let's go," he said. "This can all be worked out later." He edged his fat bottom toward the door.

She stayed where she was. "Go ahead, Dudley. Wait in the car. I'll be along." He left, sulking at being dismissed.

When Baird was gone Susan walked up to me and placed a gentle hand on my arm. "I'm sorry, Matthew. I knew it was a mistake for Dudley to come along. But Greg insisted since part of the money is his, too. Dudley has to please Greg. Don't be angry, please."

"Okay," I said, taking a deep breath. "I'm sorry. Truly. I know what you're going through, Susan, and I know how hard you're working to keep it all together." I gestured for her to sit down on the couch. She did, and I dragged my straight-backed wood desk chair away from my desk and turned it around so I could face Susan and Mary Alice.

"There isn't much more to add about Hugh's will," I began. "Peter here will take that over, and Mary has the names of some other attorneys to handle things related to the fire. If she will allow me to, I'm going to withdraw from any remaining duties I may have as Hugh's attorney and as the lawyer for Prokop Marine. Before I do, I'd like to know something. Both of you talked to Hugh on the phone last night. Did he say anything about the case, or that he'd learned something new, or bad, something that made him feel hopeless?"

"What are you asking, Matthew?" Mary Alice said. "Are you asking whether he confessed to setting the fire?"

"Maybe. I don't know. I just need . . . to know if there's something he didn't tell me."

"There was nothing like that," Mary Alice said. "He was down, and angry, mostly at himself for becoming involved with that Kessler woman."

"He felt very anguished about that," Susan said, her voice faint, as though she were speaking from a long way in the distance. "He kept apologizing. I told him not to, I told him it was all right, that I would still be there for him, testify for him. But he was very depressed. Perhaps he'd been drinking. He sounded like it." She shuddered. "He kept telling me I was all he had left, that I couldn't leave him. That I was all he had left."

Hugh's words burned like acid, eating away at the stone in my chest that kept the grief and impotence bottled up, under control. I got rid of them all as soon as I could, telling Mary Alice that I would forward my notes and files to her new attorney as soon as she had chosen one. When they were gone I walked around my office in a daze, neurotically straightening the piled-up copies of the *State Bar Journal* and the other junk people are always sending to lawyers. I tried to work but the words blurred on pages that I read over and over again. I left a message for Bernstein at the office of the law firm he was doing some work for, telling him to look me up for dinner if he had the time. I stared at the walls and the lake and the clock.

When I could stand it no longer, I closed up the office and drove downtown and walked through the swinging doors of a crummy courthouse bar called The Scales of Justice with the same cheerful expression that a condemned man uses when walking to his own execution.

The Scales was a riot of sweat and smoke, off-duty cops and firemen mingling with nervous lawyers waiting out verdicts by pouring booze down the gullets of fearful, twitching clients. I found myself a spot at the center of the bar and ordered double bourbons. The bartender tried once to be cheerful at me but put up his hands and withdrew when I fixed him with my eyes. I must have been sending off signals because the stools on either side of me cleared, fast. Nobody talked to me. The bourbon wasn't doing a thing. I was patient. Bourbon had worked before.

Perhaps forty-five minutes and four drinks after I got there, Elizabeth Kleinfeldt came in with one of the junior prosecutors, a kid named Howard Marks, who had helped her work up the case against Prokop. Swenson, the fire department inspector who had worked on the warehouse fire, trailed behind. Swenson was charged up. He'd obviously had a few drinks someplace else. From the way she looked at him, Liz didn't want him here any more that I did, but he'd tagged along like a spoiled child on an older sister's date.

Liz caught my eye in the barroom mirror and looked me a question. I shook my head, no. No company, thanks, no lawyer-to-lawyer chat about how we all lose one sometimes. She nodded and started to move away through the crowd, taking the junior prosecutor in tow behind her. But Swenson took the bait.

"Hey, Riordan," he cackled in a high, drunken voice, "heard we got some fucking justice today. Too bad your fucking client didn't have the stones to take you with him. That'd really have made it right."

He stood behind me, leering into the mirror like a mad wraith. I got off my stool slowly. I turned around, my hands loose and easy at my sides.

"Swenson," I said slowly. "Come a little closer."

"Take it outside," the bartender warned in a loud voice.

I half turned. "Okay," I said to the bartender. I looked back. "Swenson, you are an ignorant and cowardly pig and a perjurer. Let's go chat."

He strutted up to the front door. He thought I was going to fight fair. He was making a hell of a mistake.

I caught him by the collar as he went through the door, swung him around, and threw him face first into the rough brick wall outside the bar. When he turned around his hands came up feebly and I knocked them away. Then I slapped him, hands open, again and again, batting his head against the brick wall, moving in slow motion through a fine red haze that seemed to drift up like smoke from the ground, putting my weight behind each blow as the cuts opened up on his face and his blood began to flow.

The young prosecutor, Marks, came flying through the door and tried to grab my arms from behind. I bucked him off and turned back. Swenson put a shot straight into my face, but I slipped it a little and took it on the cheekbone. I shook it off and clubbed Swenson with a forearm to the side of his head as he tried to get away. He went down and stayed there. I took a step back and turned toward Marks.

"Get him out of here," I said, gasping for air. "Now. Or I'll kill him." Marks didn't move. "You hear me? Now."

Marks and I stayed frozen for a moment, each of us measuring the other. Finally he nodded. I turned back toward the door to the bar, shivering with sudden cold under the harsh blue-white light of the street lamps. Liz Kleinfeldt stood in the doorway. She looked a little sickened by the violence, but she did not turn away.

"Howard," she said firmly, "put Swenson in a cab and send him up to the emergency room at Harborview. They can patch him up. I'm sick of him." She turned back to me. "Riordan, this is not doing anybody any good."

I shrugged and walked past her, back into the bar. The bartender was just taking away my glass. I took a twenty-dollar bill out of my pocket and reached over and tucked it in the vest pocket of his shirt.

"Pour," I said.

"I don't know," he said dubiously. "What happened to that guy . . ."

"Pour," I repeated. "He'll live. You shouldn't let the riffraff in here anyway. You got any cigarettes behind the bar?"

"I got Kools," he said as he brought me my drink. I made a face. "Or Marlboros," he added.

"Gimme," I said. I dropped half the drink down my throat. I tore open the cellophane cigarette wrapper and lit one. I coughed. I hadn't smoked but a couple of times in the last few years. Vice requires more frequent practice.

Liz Kleinfeldt came back into the bar and sat down on the next stool. The bartender drifted over and asked her if she wanted anything to drink. She shook her head.

"Listen to me, Riordan," she said. "What happened to Prokop was his own decision. I know what you're going through. We always want to think they're innocent when we take their case. I know that. But nine times out of ten it turns out they're guilty. And you know that. That doesn't mean you don't take their case and fight like hell for them and feel like death when you lose. You have to. The system is more important than any individual case. When the case is over you have to go on."

"I think I've heard this before," I said nastily, waving my hand to order another drink. "Way back in law school. I thought it was shit then. Still do."

"You know I'm right. Stop acting like a child."

I turned on her in a sudden cold anger. "Lady, you don't know what the hell you're talking about. You don't know what I did." I gulped at my drink. It didn't help. "He never told me that he was sleeping with Sandra Kessler. Her testimony just flattened me. It wrecked our whole case, which was based on the lack of motive. And I sat there watching the whole thing go down, because Hugh hadn't told me about it."

"I didn't know either. She came to me at lunch and told me about it. I put her on because you blew Swenson up on the stand."

I shook my head. "Doesn't matter." I tasted something sour in the back of my throat and swallowed hard. "When the day was over I took him into an empty hearing room and read him out for not telling me everything. And when I was done with that, I went into my high-and-mighty lawyer act and told him that I was so mortally insulted by him I might just have to let him twist around slowly while you packaged him up and addressed him neatly and shipped him to Walla Walla, since he was ninety percent of the way there already. And you know what? He believed me. He thought he was gone and done for and abandoned. *And he killed himself.*"

The bourbon was getting to me now. It rose in my brain like dirty water in a flood and slurred my thoughts and feelings and speech. I turned blearily back to the bartender and gestured with my glass. I lit another cigarette. They tasted better now.

Liz Kleinfeldt was saying something. "You can't know that," she said. "Everybody makes their own choices. He made the choice to burn that building and ended up by committing suicide."

I looked back at her bleakly. "I know. I knew Hugh. Maybe he did light the fire and kill Kessler. But I still do not believe it." I dropped my head, feeling sick to my stomach. Then I raised my head and took a hit off the cigarette that still smoldered in an ashtray. "Please, just go home," I said drunkenly.

She got angry. "Damn you!" she hissed. "You like this, your self-pity. You want to wallow in it, drown in it. Because you cared for poor dead Hugh so much? I doubt it. Because it is easier for you to blame yourself for his suicide than it is for you to admit that you might have been wrong about the guy. To admit that he was guilty."

I drained the last of the bourbon from the shot glass in my hand. I turned the glass upside down, holding it in the air. I stared at it for a moment. Then I slammed it onto the top of the bar and it shattered into tiny sharp bits. I turned back to Liz Kleinfeldt.

"Why don't you fuck off," I said.

She stared back at me for a moment, then stood up and left. I watched her go.

I stayed and bribed the bartender to clean up the broken glass and drank bourbon until sometime after one o'clock in the morning, when Bernstein found me and took me home.

CHAPTER 18

On Sunday morning we ran through fog that had settled like thick braids in the meadows of Discovery Park, following the loop trail that wound through the wooded hills and down to the north beaches of this old fort on the western edge of the Magnolia district of Seattle. The wet winter air soothed our lungs as we churned into a sprint past the lighthouse and down the beach. It was morning low tide and a hundred yards of beach lay bare or scarcely covered by shallow tidal pools. The gulls wheeled away from us in search of quieter places for Sunday breakfast.

Bernstein slowed to a walk and finally stopped, bending forward from the waist, gasping for air. He choked and spit onto the sand, then slowly straightened up and walked in aimless circles, his hands pressed against the small of his back.

"Remind me," he demanded, "why I quit smoking and started doing this shit."

"You love it," I replied, breathing heavily. "It gives you a sense of achievement, control over body and destiny. It cleans your mind of meaningless debris so that self-actualization can begin."

"Fuck you," He raised an arm like a club.

"Truth, then. Because we're getting old. And we can't get by on good looks and charm any longer."

He turned his back on me and began to walk back up the

beach to the trail that climbed the bluff. "Maybe," he said to no one in particular, "but I'm damned if I'll admit it."

We walked slowly back up the trail, luxuriating in the rest after the long run and in the deserted winter silence of the park. Bernstein and I had been friends so long—ever since that VC mortar barrage in the early spring of 1970—that neither of us worried about filling the silence with words.

It had been a long four days since Bernstein had brought me home from the Scales at one o'clock in the morning. Drunk as I was, I could not sleep and passed into the next day in a fog, guzzling tomato juice and beer and then more whiskey, eating vitamins and aspirin like candy. The hangover was bad but held fewer pains than going to sleep, for I was afraid I would dream about Hugh as he lost his final battle with gravity.

After the second day I managed to stop drinking, but that was not much of an improvement. In bad times a person prone to depression, as I am, comes out of a drinking bout with a great silent crash into a despair so black that physical pain becomes a welcome relief. Too often the despair is replaced by a kind of fragile truce, a calm that is not more than a vivid dream or a harsh truth away from hysteria.

When we reached my car Bernstein took my keys and popped open the hatchback. He took out a couple of towels, tossed one to me, and began to wipe the sweat off his face with the other. As he was tucking the towel around his neck he said, "So where are you going from here?"

"Home to shower," I replied, "and then maybe we can stop at the Santa Fe Cafe for huevos rancheros."

"That's not what I meant, man," he said gently.

"I know. You meant the global question. Am I going to pick up the pieces? Am I an alcoholic because I got drunk for two days rather than confront my own failure? Maybe. I can't answer those questions. Not now. All I can do now is focus on each thing I do and try to handle it, one thing at a time."

"At some point you're going to have to look in the mirror, Matthew. Or go to sleep sober."

"True. But I don't have to do that now. And now is all that matters."

Bernstein shrugged and gave me an expression I always think of as Talmudic, not that Bernstein knows the Talmud any better than I do. When he uses that expression he is trying to get what he wants to say exactly right.

"I've got to get back home to Montana," he said finally. "I would solve this for you if I could. I think you're going to have to go back over every thing you've done about this case and satisfy yourself that there wasn't anything you could change. If you do that and you still can't make yourself believe that Prokop lit that fire, then you have to go out and find out who did. Not because you owe Prokop anything. Because you'll go crazy if you don't."

I stared into his black eyes for just a moment. Then I shook my head. "No. Not even to save my own life," I said.

Two weeks after Hugh Prokop had hanged himself from the ceiling beam I was back at work, struggling to catch up on the backlog of cases I had neglected during the trial and the period of collapse I had gone through in its wake. The case against Prokop Marine's fire insurers had been taken over by Hal Thiery, the senior partner in a new, hungry trial firm that needed the work. I had to meet with them a couple of times to answer questions as they learned about the case, but that was all. The chance of recovering on the policies was thin, but they would do a good job. As far as I was concerned, the case was as dead as Hugh Prokop.

The first few days back at work were bad ones. I forced myself through the work, my heart pounding anxiously as I dealt with the simplest problems, my mind filled with the thousand small things that could go wrong and lose a case, breaking the hearts of clients who had bet their last buck on a lawsuit they had hoped would make them whole again. For a while I wondered if I could handle the stress. In the end it was the routine that saved me, the repetitive, almost instinctive knowledge of the rules of court and the customs of practice that guided me as I sweated as never before over motions and depositions and the day-to-day horseshit that make up the small-time practice of law. I cut no corners and made no deals, following the rules and the statutes with the devotion of a priest to ancient dogma. Finally, I relaxed enough to feel almost normal again. Hugh's ghost had gone. The self-hatred had subsided. Even the courthouse clerks couldn't make me angry.

On Saturday morning after that first week back at work a cold Canadian wind blew out of the Okanogan and down through the city, pushing the dirty gray weather out to sea. The air that followed was bright and brittle and dry, suffused with the pale sunlight of late winter. I knocked off work at noon that day and drove down from the north side of Lake Union and over the Fremont Bridge to the downtown YMCA.

The gym was old and nearly empty. Sunshine filtered through the rafters and spilled onto the gym floor, the light dusty and aged by the dirty windows like light in an ancient church. I changed clothes and stretched and walked up the narrow spiral stairs to the tiny, steeply banked running track that was suspended from the rafters.

I ran three miles slowly, muttering cadence under my breath, twenty-five laps to the mile. When I was done I went to the basement and put in an hour on the irons, sweating and cursing, filled with secret envy for the muscular gym rats who handled heavy weights with such ostentatious ease.

For the last part of the workout I went back up to the main gym, and into the boxing area. I wrapped my hands with cut-up strips of an old Ace bandage and slipped on leather speed gloves. Then I worked the heavy bag, dancing at first, bobbing and weaving, finally settling down to the serious work, trying to drive each blow straight through the bag. The pounding of fists on the bag echoed off the wooden basketball floor. I worked the bag until my arms quivered from fatigue and the cuts on the knuckles of each hand had opened and bled. The cuts didn't bother me. Eventually, with enough work, the knuckles would scab over and calluses would form. They had before. It was as close to religious belief as I came in those days.

When I was done it was nearly three o'clock. I walked down the steep hill of Madison Street from Fourth to First, feeling the workout in my knees and thighs as I took each step. The neighborhood below the terraced plaza of the federal building on First Avenue had recently been rebuilt, the old buildings sandblasted clean, and new compatible buildings raised in the vacant lots that once had divided the longshoremen's bars and sailors' hells along First Avenue. Even Post Alley, where the whores had plied their trade, had been steamed clean and paved with brick, recast as a European lane in the heart of the city. I found it hard not to like the old buildings in their gaudy new guise, the quiet, clean streets and the smart stores that lined them. The sidewalks were filled with well-dressed people shopping and talking and eating ice cream while they enjoyed the mild winter sun. But I knew that the resurrection had been accomplished at a price, pushed through by a thousand tons of political pressure and a wave of corporate money that had swept the old, poor, tired people who once lived here clean away.

I stopped for a beer at the Mark Tobey, an upscale tavern with pastel walls and bleached oak woodwork that stood on the corner of Madison and Post Alley, down below the Alexis Hotel. The Tobey is a quiet, spacious place, named for the painter whose paintings captured the oyster light and muted colors of the Pacific Northwest far better than anyone else ever had, or would. The tavern had deep old mohair couches and scarred wooden tables imported from England, a half-dozen local beers on tap and more in the bottle, and the best collection of newspapers from around the country to be found in the city. I love saloons and the Tobey had been like a second home to me when my office had been down in Pioneer Square, but as I walked in the door I felt a wave of apprehension. If I could stop today after one beer, fine. If not, I could never set foot in a saloon again.

I ordered a pint of Ballard Bitter at the bar and scooped up a handful of peanuts from a jar beside the cash register.

The bartender, a thin kid in his twenties dressed up in bright cotton clothes, pulled down the draft beer from a spigot mounted on the back bar. As he turned around, beer in hand, I saw his eyes widen and he set the glass down hastily, slopping beer on his hands and the top of the bar.

I turned around slowly. Henry Cruz stood four feet behind me, tall and painfully thin, his hatchet face dark and somber.

Two men with the bulky chests and shoulders of serious gym rats hovered silently behind him. Each was dressed in casual Saturday clothes, khakis and sport shirts and light-weight jackets, the kind of clothes nobody remembers when they're asked. They moved silently, and well. They had probably played linebacker on the same team as War, Famine, Pestilence, and Disease, the Four Horsemen of the Apocalypse.

"Mr. Riordan," Cruz said softly, a thin smile beginning to play across his sun-weathered face.

"I had hoped that you'd forgotten about me," I replied quietly. I turned to the bartender and held out a five-dollar bill to pay for the beer. The bartender was making himself very small and very busy down at the far end of the bar. He didn't make a move toward me. I sighed and put the bill on the bar and picked up my glass and tasted. The beer was very good. I put the glass down on the bar and turned back to Cruz.

"Your call," I said. "Where do you want to go?"

Cruz glanced around the tavern. It was still empty. "This will be all right, I think. Perhaps in back." He gestured to a table in an alcove at the back of the room. The two soldiers went behind the bar and helped themselves to bottles of seltzer, leaving a bill on the bar in payment. One man set himself by the front door, placing his drink on a small shelf at his elbow. Anyone trying to get in would be told politely that the tavern was temporarily closed. The other man waited calmly at the bar, his eyes moving constantly, watchfully.

As Cruz led me to the table in the rear alcove I chewed over in my mind what I knew and remembered about him. A long time ago he had been an enforcer with the San Jose mob, but in the late 1970s he had moved to Tacoma, the aging, gritty industrial city south of Seattle. Picking up the pieces after a local crime war had broken the old Pierce County gangs, he had reorganized the trades of loan sharking, prostitution, and wholesale and retail drug distribution. He was smart enough to insulate himself from the actual running of the businesses and tough enough that nobody crossed him. Not twice. Three United States Attorneys had taken their best shot against him. None had even gotten close.

I knew Cruz because we both had gotten involved in the serial murders of a group of former radical students a couple of years before. Cruz had unwittingly supplied a deranged businessman with the services of a professional killer. When most of the story had been brought out, Cruz and I had cut a deal that kept his involvement secret. I had done it to save a couple of lives, including my own. But the nasty feeling that I'd bargained with the devil had never quite gone away.

We sat down facing each other across a plain wooden pub table that was scarred with years of use. Cruz folded his long, elegant hands on the table and stared at me impassively, as if waiting for me to begin, so I did.

"I'm puzzled by this visit," I said, taking another swallow of bitter and wiping the foam off my upper lip. "I understand you've retired from running the Pierce County rackets. Not even the cops talk about you anymore. Yet here we are, sitting in a tavern with two guys who looked like pals of George Raft watching the door. Why?"

Cruz's small smile returned. His facial expressions were affectations, not caused by emotion. As near as I could tell Cruz never had any emotions. I tried to look bored and waited.

"Retired," he said at last, repeating my word with quotation marks around it. His speech, as always, was careful, precise, and cold. "Yes, I am retired in the sense that I no longer actively manage certain businesses in the South Sound area. They have been turned over to others. But I retain certain interests and assets, some my own, others that are . . . joint ventures. A problem has arisen in one of my personal holdings. I need your assistance with it. You will be very well paid, with all funds in the form of legitimate legal fees from legitimate businesses.''

"No," I said briefly. I got up to go.

"Please sit down, Mr. Riordan. Hear me out."

"Why?"

"Because my problem may bear on the reasons why your client, Hugh Prokop, killed himself.''

I thought about that for a long minute, then I shook my head. "Not good enough, Cruz. Hugh is dead. He left enough money so that his daughter won't ever want. I don't see any point in poking amid the bones.''

"Even if he was innocent?" he inquired softly.

I stopped and stared at him. "I'd like to go with you on that one," I said sadly, "but even I can't see it that way anymore. Hugh torched his business. When he'd lost hope of getting away with it, he killed himself. A nasty story but not one I can change. I'm leaving. If the monster at the door touches me its going to get messy. Good-bye.''

As I turned to go, Cruz said in a soft deadly voice: "Take him." There was a blurred, half-seen movement to my right, and something hard crashed into my shoulder and dropped me to my knees. My arm went dead to the fingertips. I used my good arm to brace myself on the wall as I got up. The other arm hung useless. The nerves in it burned. I looked up. One of Cruz's two bodyguards stood nearby, holding a woven leather sap. He had no particular expression on his face but seemed pleased with his work.

Behind me I heard Cruz say: "Now sit down."

The bodyguard shoved me roughly against the table. I stumbled and sat down in my chair, hard. My head was filled with a helpless, impotent rage.

"You son of a bitch," I said in a hot angry whisper. "I ought to break you in half.''

Heartfelt but futile. Cruz's nameless bodyguard stepped back into the alcove, one hand already reaching into his jacket. Cruz waved him away.

"I don't have time to sit here and bargain with you," he said. "You need your memory refreshed as to what I can do. If you listen to what I have to say, no harm will come to you, no matter what you decide to do about what I tell you. But I insist that you listen.''

I nodded. "I'm listening," I said shortly.

"When you were defending Mr. Prokop at his trial," Cruz began. "One of the most damaging facts must have been the discovery of the $250,000 cash in his office safe.''

"It didn't help," I told him. "The cash made Hugh look like just another crooked businessman, and since his defense hinged on lack of motive and on shoring up a weak alibi, any damage to his credibility was a tough blow.''

"Mr. Prokop provided you, I would imagine, with a number of fanciful explanations as to where he obtained the money. You did not really believe them. Correct?''

I looked for the percentage in lying to him and didn't see any. "Correct," I replied grudgingly. "The story was that the money was to be used to buy a house in Honolulu in some kind of desperation sale. The details were kind of sketchy.''

He continued with his cross-examination, trying to nail down the point. "Mr. Prokop gave you no explanation, other than the tale about investing in a Honolulu building?''

"No.''

"Interesting. I think I know whose money that was in his safe, Mr. Riordan. I think it was mine.''

The world started to pitch and yaw like an airplane going out of control. "I don't understand," I said finally, a massive understatement. "Did you have a hook in Prokop's business?''

"No. I don't understand it either, Mr. Riordan, and I admit I am speculating. I want you to find out if the money in Prokop's safe was mine.''

I shook my head, trying to clear away the same aching feeling of helplessness that I had the last day of trial, when Sandra Kessler's testimony had blown Hugh's defense to shreds.

"Why do you think it's your money?" I asked.

"Several months ago I began placing some funds with a brokerage firm called Van Zandt & Company, usually in their foreign currency funds. One point four million, in total. The last installment was $250,000, in cash. It was to be placed in the names of several nominees and broken into a number of small separate accounts.''

"All of which would just happen to be less than the $10,000 reporting requirements set out in the money-laundering and tax statutes, I suppose?''

Cruz made a small, irritated gesture with both hands. "We're not children here, Mr. Riordan," he said testily. "If I could continue? Fine. The last funds were reported to me as having been broken up and deposited shortly after Mr. Prokop's arrest. I have since compared the dates of the deposits with the arrest date. Of course, I made no connection at the time between Mr. Prokop and Van Zandt.

"I continued to receive fund statements on the deposits. But the more recent statements have made no sense. The rates of return are shown to be different on dollars supposedly deposited at the same time, in the same currency trading funds. I have looked at some of the other Van Zandt investment programs that I have placed money in. The investments being reported now are not consistent with the original objectives of the programs, as set forth in the offering prospectus. One other thing troubles me. On these currency trading funds, the monthly balance sheets used to be prepared by an independent accountant. Now they are being prepared by an internal bookkeeper working for Van Zandt & Company.

"When Prokop's trial began, much was made of the $250,000. And then I learned from press reports that Mr. Prokop's lady friend, who sat so faithfully with him at his trial, was an employee of Van Zandt.''

I sat still through his long monologue. When it was over I allowed myself a smile.

"So," I said, "you think somebody may be stealing your money?''

He grinned back, the only true expression I had ever seen on his face. "I was once a thief, Mr. Riordan. I was a good thief. I can smell this.''

I said, "Do they know who they're stealing from?''

"I think not. The original approach was made by an

accountant from a land company that I control. He actually delivered the funds to Van Zandt. I have never seen Van Zandt or any of his employees.''

I looked at Cruz. The fleeting grin had faded into a small thin smile, without mirth or mercy.

"God help them," I said.

CHAPTER 19

At ten-thirty on the following Monday morning I was sitting in the basement cafe under the Elliott Bay Bookstore in Pioneer Square, drinking my fifth cup of coffee and rereading *The New York Times*. Ordinarily I don't mind doing those things, but on this morning I was waiting for a lawyer from the local Securities and Exchange Commission office named Colleen Westfall to show up and give me the dirt, if any, on Van Zandt & Company. She was just over an hour late.

It was a slow news morning and not even the sports page was any fun. The New York press was holding its usual spring autopsy on the collapse of the Jets in the NFL play-offs. The Knicks had lost six straight and missed the play-offs. The Yankees' best pitcher, who was paid slightly over two million dollars a year, had sued to go on the disabled list, claiming that the psychological stress of playing baseball in New York had ruined his slider. I laughed. None of those people knew what true anguish was. None of them had spent an entire season watching the Seattle Mariners.

Colleen finally showed up at five minutes to eleven. She was wearing a stylish silk dress that draped over her in all the correct places. She is a strawberry blonde and still very English even though she hadn't lived in London since she was six. She looked so good I was glad to see her, even an hour and twenty minutes late.

"Sorry, love," she said as she swept into the cafe. "Our great leader scheduled a meeting for 9:45 without taking the pain of letting people know in advance. I couldn't even call."

"No sweat. Nice dress. What happened to squarish little blue suits and white shirts with frilly ties?"

She smiled, a little sharply. "When you've got my trial record, sweetheart, you can wear anything you want. I need coffee."

I went up to the counter and got her some and brought it back to the table. I shuddered slightly as she dumped milk and sugar in it until it looked like a milk shake.

"So," she said, taking her first sip, "is this a date, albeit a cheap one, or business?"

"Business. We went out a couple of times last year and you decided we were fundamentally incompatible. You said so. Twice."

"You're too easily discouraged. If it is business, it means you're looking for information about someone. Who?"

"Man by the name of Greg Van Zandt. Van Zandt & Company. Local investment house. They're supposed to be hot stuff."

"They are. They've got two facets, really. On the one hand, they're an ordinary boutique brokerage, the kind that serves a small but wealthy clientele looking for investment advice and not bothered by the higher commissions. But the real glamour for them is in their trading funds. Van Zandt is a brilliant currency trader. He averages a pretty steady twenty-to-thirty percent annual return, quarter after quarter. Very hot."

"How are they set up?"

"Closed-end limited partnerships. You get twenty people together with the kind of money I'd like to have, take a hundred thousand from each one, set up a fund. Van Zandt trades for the fund, takes a surprisingly small commission for his work, and the investors share the profit or loss. The sales and operating expenses aren't too steep, either. There's no registration with the commission, since the partnerships are sold on a private placement basis. All their offerees are qualified under Reg. D."

Regulation D is a Securities and Exchange Commission rule that assumes rich people are bright enough not to get conned when they invest their money. Consequently, SEC registration of a securities offering that is sold only to rich folk is not required. Reg. D is probably fair, since rich people can afford to lose money, but it has no basis in reality. Rich people are as gullible as anyone else and will buy all sorts of weird, stupid investments. Rich doctors will buy absolutely *anything*.

"That's the basics, " I said, "but what's the gossip? You got any bad stuff on these people?"

"Even if I did, I couldn't tell you. You know that. What are you fishing for, anyway?"

I ignored the question. "Come on, Colleen," I said, "I'm not asking to see the formal investigative order or something. All I'm looking for is a little dirt. I'll even take rumor."

She shook her head. "Tell me why."

"I can't."

She laughed. "You don't ask much, do you? Okay, I'll guess. Does this have something to do with the murder trial you had where the guy killed himself? His girlfriend is a vice president and broker at Van Zandt."

It must have shown in my face. I never have been able to play poker.

She looked sharply at me. "I'm right, aren't I? What's going on, Matthew?"

"I don't know yet. I honestly don't," I told her. "I'm just trying to settle one or two questions, things I couldn't get from that client before he died. Give me four or five days. If I turn up anything rotten, I'll give the lead to you." And hopefully not get my ass shot off by Henry Cruz, I added silently.

"Deal," she said. Colleen never dawdles. "I don't have much. Their paperwork is pretty clean, and most of what they do is Reg. D anyway, so we don't get involved that deeply. But we're getting complaints now, just a trickle. Mostly slow payment on settlements, and one dentist in Bellevue is going absolutely bonkers because Van Zandt won't let him liquidate his limited partnership share in one of the funds. He swears that Van Zandt personally told him it would not be a problem. But it doesn't necessarily add up to anything.''

''What about Van Zandt personally? Anything on him?''

''I haven't heard of anything.''

''Can you get me his 204 forms?'' 204 forms contain personal information about stockbrokers. The National Association of Securities Dealers requires that they be filed. The industry would rather not do it, but since the alternative is direct policing of brokers by the SEC, the securities dealers do it themselves.

''This could be getting a little sticky,'' Colleen said.

''You can get them from NASD in one phone call. And what are Xerox machines for?''

She broke into a sudden smile. ''Sure, guy,'' she said brightly, in the endearing way the English talk when they try to use American slang. ''How about this afternoon?''

''That would be perfect. I owe you for this.''

She gathered up her stuff and got up to go. ''Yes, you do, Matthew. Make me look good or I'll be truly rotten every time I see you.'' I nodded. She turned and walked out. I watched her go and sighed happily. The greatest improvement in the practice of law in the past four hundred years has been the addition of women lawyers. I don't know why in the hell somebody didn't figure that one out years ago.

I needed a lot more information about Greg Van Zandt and Susan Haight before I did anything else. Working up a good dossier is a job for a pro. If Colleen could guess at what I was up to so could anyone else. I thought about calling Bernstein but I knew he was following the snow down to the Alta and Snowbird ski resorts and generally lowering the moral tone of the Salt Lake City, Utah, metropolitan area. When Bernstein is in party mode he regards requests for anything short of cardiopulmonary resuscitation as an intrusion. I also wanted the information collected quietly, and Bernstein's methods usually involve a fist in somebody's face. Subtlety is not his strong suit. So I called Paul Schaeffer.

Schaeffer used to be the classic *Front Page*-style reporter: a hard-drinking, skirt-chasing, heavy-smoking bastard who would commit his own crimes and report on them before he'd let a deadline go by without a story. He had been a gypsy, hired and fired and hired again by most of the papers up and down the West Coast. When he was forty he had a reasonably serious heart attack that put him in the hospital for several weeks and caused him to rethink some of his pastimes. He had to quit drinking and smoking, of course, but he didn't stop there. He started on the Pritikin diet and lost forty pounds, then went to macrobiotics and holistic medicine, acupuncture and shiatsu massage. Now he had the chest and arms of a small bear, a thirty-two-inch waist, and the sort of nut-brown tan, even on his balding skull, that in the Pacific Northwest you can get only by sitting naked in the snow on top of Mount Rainier.

Paul now made his living as a free-lance researcher, drawing on years of contacts with city cops, state officials, federal bureaucrats, media types, and even the phone company. Much of his work was legitimate factual research for writers and attorneys needing to flesh out a book or a brief. The rest of it involved invading people's privacy and doing nasty little chores like the one I had in mind. That's why I planned to pay Paul in cash.

When he got to my office I was still eating lunch at my desk, reading the 204 forms that Colleen Westfall had sent over. "Nice to see you again, Riordan," he said breezily. "Still poisoning yourself, I see."

I looked down at my desk. I saw a half bagel with lox and cream cheese that I had bought but not eaten at Elliott Bay and a Styrofoam cup of black Starbucks' French Roast coffee. "That is not poison," I replied, pointing. "It is called, 'lunch.' Lots of people do it with no ill effects."

He suppressed a shudder. "You're young," he said ominously, taking a chair. "What do you need? You weren't too specific over the phone."

I passed over the 204 forms for Greg Van Zandt and Susan Haight. "I need a couple of people checked out," I said. "These 204s should give you a fair amount of background information, including employers and education.

Van Zandt is the owner, and president, of his own brokerage firm. The woman, Susan Haight, works for him as a
vice president and broker.''

He nodded. "You have any photos?"

"No. You'll have to get them from the newspaper
morgues. I'm sure they'll have them."

"Probably." He squinted at one form and said, "Isn't
this the woman that was dating the guy who torched his
building and killed himself?''

"Yeah," I said sourly. If everybody I talked to kept
making that connection I was going to be blown before I
could find out what the hell was going on.

"This have anything to do with the fire?"

"The one thing I like best about you, Paul," I said
sarcastically, "is that you're not a reporter anymore, and I
don't have to answer your questions.''

He grinned. "Too bad. I used to love shit like this. But
I gave it up along with red meat and whiskey." He sighed
at the memory. "You want the standard job? Or the
deluxe?''

"Deluxe. Spare no expense. And put me at the head of
the line. I want it as soon as you can get it.''

He looked at his watch. It was one of those black plastic
styles that can give you the date, weather, and your quarter-
mile splits in the marathon. In Greenwich mean time. "It's
three-thirty. Suppose we say five o'clock Friday for the
main stuff, with a follow-up the day after. I can't get it
any sooner because I'm looking over some surprise witnesses
in a case that's already in trial. Fair?''

"Sounds lousy. But I'll take it, if it's all I can get.
What'll you do with the money?''

"Honolulu Marathon's next month. I think I'll send my
entry in now.''

I rolled my eyes toward heaven and swallowed some
more coffee. "Enjoy," I said as he skipped out.

I spent the rest of that day and part of the next one
wading through the private placement memoranda that had
been prepared to meet legal disclosure requirements when
interests in Van Zandt & Company currency funds were
sold. The lawyers and investment bankers who write these

things work long and hard to prepare documents that meet the technical letter of the law while seeking to bore, bamboozle, and frustrate anyone who actually attempts to read them and understand what is going on. I found it slow going, but no worse than, say, the commentaries on Gray's Rule Against Perpetuities. In Latin.

The trading scheme outlined in the memorandum was actually quite simple. Van Zandt created, through sales of limited partnership interests, pools of funds that speculated like commercial or investment banks in the vagaries of the European currency markets. Van Zandt monitored the movements of currencies against one another, taking positions that could yield thousands of dollars of profit out of small movements in German marks or Swiss francs or the mighty Japanese yen. He might make dozens of trades a day; if each yielded even a small profit, the overall rate of return on the partners' investments could reach thirty or forty percent a year. According to the quarterly performance reports that Hugh had received and retained in his files, in a year and a half Van Zandt had never had a worse quarter than a profit equaling a twenty-five-percent annual yield. Not bad. Nearly as good as loan sharking.

I dug out a couple of other interesting facts. The first was that it was relatively hard to pull your money out of a trading pool; you either had to wait six weeks, or else pay a penalty of thirty percent for immediate withdrawal. The second was that most of the trades were being executed through banks on the Caribbean island of Montserrat, a British Crown Colony in the Leeward Islands with dozens of small, offshore banks and very strict bank-secrecy laws. Not even the IRS could pry records out of Montserrat banks. I began to understand why the deal had looked so good to Henry Cruz.

I spent the rest of my free time that week on the telephone or having drinks with lawyers and brokers I knew or could get an introduction to, asking questions about Van Zandt. With most of the calls I used the line that I was considering making a major investment in a Van Zandt limited partnership and wanted to check the company out before taking the plunge. With just about every broker that meant I had to suffer through a lengthy sales pitch on why they could run my nonexistent money better than Van Zandt.

It is amazing how much people will tell a total stranger who is plausible, polite, and who listens. I got the names of the last five women Van Zandt had dated, including a married Merrill Lynch analyst with whom he'd shacked up at a conference in San Francisco two weeks before. I also got a lot of improbable guesses as to the reasons for Van Zandt's considerable success in securities and currency trading. Like many successful traders, his was apparently a native or at least self-learned talent, with a gut instinct for the inner workings of markets that couldn't be taught in business school.

Out of the witless chaff of gossip I began to get a rough picture of Van Zandt, like seeing a face emerge from the shape of a cloud. Despite the warm public persona I had seen at the football game on New Year's Day, Van Zandt emerged as a tough, secretive man easily angered by challenges to his control. In less than four years he had scrambled up from a broker's desk at a middle-sized regional brokerage to owning his own company, a half-million-dollar house, a string of Jaguars and Ferraris, and a private plane. He made large contributions to several private schools and colleges, the symphony, and the Washington Repertory Theatre.

To me it made no sense that a man like that would try to steal from a customer, particularly one as dangerous and vindictive as Henry Cruz. Perhaps if he knew who Cruz was, it was the danger that appealed to him. Either way, I felt as though I was trapped in my usual dilemma. The more I learned, the less I felt I understood.

broker that meant I had to wade through a lengthy explanation why they could not leg, conscientiously recommend a stock...

CHAPTER 20

On Friday I told Paul Schaeffer that after a hard day of
listening to stockbrokers try to sell me the stuff that dreams
are made of, I needed a beer and was going to get one
down at F.X. McRory's, at the south end of Pioneer
Square, near the Kingdome. If he had anything to tell me,
he could come along and sneer if he wanted.

When I got down to McRory's he was already there,
drinking a blackberry seltzer and looking scornfully down
the retread *Belle Epoque* bar at the other customers sipping
whiskey and smoking and talking. It was a little after six
and the roar of the after-work crowd bounced off the bare
tile floors and high ceilings. I ordered a pint of Bass Ale
and took a long, sweet swallow, ignoring the look on
Paul's face. Hell hath no fury like the reformed.

"So what have you got?" I finally asked. "Enough to
put them both in federal slam?"

"Not hardly. But it is interesting. Interesting."

Paul was being cryptic. It was his way. I sighed. "Start
at the beginning," I said.

He put down his seltzer bottle and looked at the top
page of his notes. "I'll start with the usual stuff. Neither
Van Zandt nor Susan Haight has any outstanding warrants
or convictions. They aren't parties to any lawsuits, except
that Van Zandt is a nominal defendant in a suit against the
brokerage in federal court. It's just a customer suit, com-

plaining that a broker, who's since been fired, churned the account. No big deal.''

I nodded for him to go on and drank more ale.

''As far as their personal lives go, that's also pretty quiet. If there's a relationship between the two of them, nobody knows about it. Haight was dating Hugh Prokop, your late client, steadily for five or six months, with the wedding march playing in the background, at least to her friends. Van Zandt is a little more lively. He gets around some, but nothing steady.''

''I heard that,'' I said, cutting in. ''I've already got a list of names you can check out if we need to. Keep going.''

He nodded. ''Neither of them uses drugs or alcohol to any excessive degree, but as you know, all of that stuff is poison. Van Zandt is rumored to keep a little Peruvian marching powder around the house for social occasions, but he's not one of those high-strung suburban business types who's constantly checking into the john to dilate his nostrils.''

As he paused for breath, I said, ''Tell me about their finances.''

He glanced down at another page. ''Haight's got a fair amount of money put away, some in cash, some with Van Zandt's own accounts, some with another brokerage house. She's pretty conservative. If she had to get liquid fast, she could lay hands on two to three hundred thousand, I'd say.''

I raised my eyebrows, surprised. Two hundred grand wasn't much by Wall Street standards but it was enough to impress me. ''Where did she get it?''

''She made it. Legally, as far as I can tell. She's been working for the last six years as a registered reptile and made good money, too. Before she joined Van Zandt she was making nearly a hundred grand a year at Alystine, Woods.''

I smothered a laugh. The correct corporate title of most stockbrokers is ''registered representative.''

''What about Van Zandt?''

''He used to work at the same firm. They started about

the same time, but it seems like Van Zandt could sell oil to the Arabs. He was making a hundred grand a year even before the bull market started back in '82. I don't think he missed any meals when he set up his own shop in 1985." Paul checked his notes and referred to a couple of Xerox copies. "I couldn't get his tax returns, but just looking at some of his expenses, the guy spends it at least as fast as he makes it. Over two hundred grand in charitable donations last year, plus he had about a hundred grand worth of gadgets added to his house. He's paying thirty bucks a foot for the Bellevue office, which looks like shit but costs like it was decorated by the guy who did the Palace at Versailles. Add in the cars, the airplane, and the women, which to my certain knowledge are unlikely to come cheap. A rough guess would be he needed over a million in income last year just to stay even. He must have made it because he doesn't owe anybody any money."

I shook my head. "I'm glad he's rich and all that, Paul, but that doesn't tell me what I want to know. I thought sure you could find me something at least moderately rotten. Next you're going to tell me that he was a high-school football star and she was the queen of the senior prom."

He grinned a high, wide, nasty grin. "Ah, but that's where it gets interesting, Riordan. I couldn't tell you that. Or even where they went to high school. You see, those Form 204s you showed me check out perfectly. For six years. And beyond that, nothing. *Nothing.* I even paid a handsome bribe to see their social security records. As far as the government's concerned, Greg Van Zandt was born on July 1, 1980. And Susan Haight came into this world in February of 1981."

The next morning was a Saturday but I was up early anyway, going for a long, slow, reflective run down the Burke-Gilman Trail, an old railroad right-of-way on the hillside above my house that the city had converted into a biking and hiking trial. It was gray and cool, but there was no rain and the Cascades looked blue-white under a heavy mantle of late snow. I thought longingly of the skis in my basement, edges filed and bottoms waxed, gathering dust because I had been too busy or too messed up for the last two months to take even a day in the mountains. A big part of me wanted to load the car that morning and disappear for a few days to Stevens Pass or Mission Ridge, but Bernstein had been right. The essence of sanity in a less than sane world is to finish what you've started.

When I got back to the house I kindled a fire to take the morning chill out of the air and put on the coffeepot and showered while waiting for the coffee to brew. When it was done I carved up a melon and made toast and ate sitting down on the living-room rug in front of the fire, scarcely glancing at the morning papers. My mind was still caught up with the question of who the hell Greg Van Zandt really was, and just what he had done that led to the quarter-million in hot cash being stuffed in Hugh Prokop's safe.

The fact that he had changed his name and adopted a new identity didn't bother me that much. Name changes are fairly common, a safe way for unhappy people to try and solve their problems quickly. Using a name that doesn't belong to you isn't illegal if there's no intent to defraud, and whatever Van Zandt had done before his rebirth in 1980 hadn't seemed to influence his conduct afterward. He was a legitimate success by the measure that everybody in American society uses. He'd made a ton of money.

After breakfast I brought the coffeepot into the living room and dug out the sketch pad that I used whenever I was preparing for a trial. Most lawyers use those eighteen-inch yellow legal pads, but the scale is too small for me. When I was in college, before I dropped out and went to Vietnam, I had an economics professor named Abramowitz who used to lecture from the blackboard. The ideas poured out as fast as he could scrawl them, little puffs of chalk dust flying off the green slate as a new insight into money velocity or some damn thing came roaring into his head. I never was any good at economics, but I loved the whole motion of ideas racing across a big empty canvas.

I started slowly, putting everything I knew about Van Zandt's business into numbered points, writing each one in block letters, the felt-tip marker squeaking on the page as I began to write faster. When I got done the points looked like this:

1. Currency trading hard, complicated. People don't know how it works.

2. Van Zandt uses fancy sales pitch, brochures, offices.

3. Very high rates of return. Twenty points above one-year treasury bills. Easy money.

4. Hard to get money out.

5. Different returns for same investment.

6. Accounting firm changed from national Big Eight to local. Monthly statements now prepared inside company by staff bookkeeper.

7. Van Zandt secretive. A control junkie.

8. Some funds starting to change type of investments. One fund bought stock in Van Zandt brokerage.

9. Willing to launder money for Cruz.

10. Nobody knows who Van Zandt really is.

I drew a line under these points when I had written them down and waited for the conclusion to pop into my head. Nothing came. None of the things I had learned seemed to have any connection with Henry Cruz or his suspicions that his money was being stolen. None of them even suggested that any sort of illegal acts were taking place, with the exception of the fact that Henry Cruz's anonymous cash apparently was being washed and dried and ironed with extra starch. But why even that? Van Zandt had every luxury and toy that any sane man could desire. Was he simply greedy, willing to take in dirty money to have that much more to bet in the international currency markets, the computer-driven casino of flashing electronic screens that made all the gambling halls in Las Vegas and

Monte Carlo look like the two-dollar window at the local racetrack?

It beat the hell out of me.

I was still blundering around the house in near-total confusion at three o'clock that afternoon when the phone rang. It was Liz Kleinfeldt. Her voice was unexpectedly shy.

"I just wanted to see how you were doing," she said. "I was worried. When I saw you in the bar that night I realized how much Prokop's suicide had shaken you. I would have called sooner, but I couldn't think of much to say."

"I'm okay," I said, embarrassed by her simple kindness after the way I had treated her. "It's awfully nice of you to call. Especially after the way I acted. I'm sorry, Liz. Words won't quite do it, but I'm truly sorry. I know you meant well. By the way, is Swenson all right?"

"He's fine. He had a couple of pretty good cuts around the face and he looked like a raccoon for a couple of days. He's not too cheerful when your name is mentioned, but he admits he had it coming."

"I'm glad he's not too angry. I kept waiting for the cops to come around and bust me for assault. I respect the guy because he wants to fight fires so much, and I'm glad he puts his soul into his work. But I still think he was pushing too hard to get a conviction. And I didn't like his attitude after Hugh was dead."

"I know. I think he does, too."

I didn't know what else to say. "Thanks for calling me," I said. "It means a lot."

"Hey wait a minute," she replied. "What about dinner? Now that we're not at each other's throats anymore."

"Fine with me. I'm buying. Not because I'm male. Because I was a jerk. When?"

"How about tonight? I'm supposed to go skiing tomorrow morning but we could make it an early night."

We chatted about where and what kind of food. She said to pick her up at six o'clock at her Capitol Hill apartment. I agreed and rang off.

I took her to Adriatica, a small restaurant on the hill

above Dexter Avenue, overlooking the dock lights of Lake
Union. Adriatica is located in an old house full of warm
woods and crisp white tablecloths, gleaming silver and
shining crystal. The food is more French than Mediterra-
nean and is very good. It costs a lot but is cheap to me
because I'm always happy to pay their bill. I couldn't quite
decide if I was hoping to impress her or not.

She impressed the hell out of me. She wore a simple
black cocktail dress that did her no harm, showing off her
strong, slender shoulders and neck. Her dark eyes and
short dark hair shone in the light. We settled in at the bar
to wait for a table. As we were waiting she saw a couple
of people she knew and wandered away for a moment,
then returned. I watched her dancer's walk, as supple and
proud as a cat's. She caught me watching. She smiled.

"It is just purely a pleasure watching you walk, ma'am,"
I said. "I wanted to tell you that in court, but I was afraid
you'd move for a mistrial."

"I was beginning to wonder if you'd noticed," she said
with mock severity.

"I noticed," I said. "Believe me, I noticed."

The restaurant was full despite the early hour. We stayed
at the bar for a while. I nibbled at a dry vodka martini and
learned a little about where Liz had come from and who
she might be. She was raised in Shaker Heights but left at
sixteen to dance with the junior company of the American
Ballet, then danced with companies in Los Angeles and
San Francisco. She had finished college at UCLA in two
years while recovering from a bad knee injury, then at-
tended law school at Berkeley and Columbia. She had
joined a Wall Street firm just about the time I was getting
ready to chuck corporate law and move to Seattle.

"Why did you leave Wall Street?" I asked. "Boredom?"

"Pretty much. When I came out here three years ago
from New York, I picked the prosecutor's office because I
wanted to practice in court every day, with something
more than money at stake. I've done that, and so now I've
been looking over offers to join the litigation departments
of a couple of Seattle firms. First I may take some time off
from the law and dance. I'm thirty-three, and it would be

nice to dance one more time before the knees won't take the strain." She smiled and said, "You've got me talking about myself, you rat. What about you? What are you going to do now?"

"The same thing I was doing before. Taking whatever comes in the door and looks interesting."

She mulled that one over while a waiter came and took us to our table. When the menus had been scanned and the wine ordered she said, "Don't you wonder if you're not reaching the level of work you could be doing if you were a partner in a major firm?"

"Of course I do. But Lincoln worked in a two-man law shop above a street corner store in Springfield, Illinois." I shook my head. "I'm sorry. That sounds pompous. Explaining myself is not something I do well, even when I want to. I tried a big firm, Winthrop, Seward, for three years. Some of it was fun but I'm not cut out to handle the internal politics and the other crap that goes with being in a big law firm. I take on clients I think I can help. Or if the case interests me. Or, sometimes, when I need the money. I don't need or want to be rich or famous."

The wine came and she tasted it and pronounced it drinkable. "I shouldn't pry," she said. "I just thought you were very good in court, yet when I checked you out, not too many people had heard of you. The dissonance intrigued me."

I smiled, a little ruefully. "I appreciate the compliment. But it's not true. If I had been better, Hugh Prokop might still be alive. He might be in jail, but he'd be alive."

There was a moment of awkward silence before she gracefully changed the subject. Dinner came and she ate with an appetite that belied her size. Perhaps she practiced starvation during her off-hours. We talked about politics and business and ethics and books. We talked about Melville and Conrad and Cather until I admitted to a low taste for high-finance thrillers with lots of sex, and she confided that one of her secret ambitions was to write one of those thick hardcover romances about women of questionable moral character with an unlimited supply of backless dresses.

We laughed and shared a growing sense that what we had was a chance for a friendship and perhaps more.

Somewhere over coffee the conversation took a fatal turn back to the Prokop Marine fire and the trial. "I don't understand," she said slowly, after I'd explained a little about why I was checking into Haight and Van Zandt. "What possible connection could they have had to the fire? They weren't there, and they had nothing to gain."

"You don't know that. You never did establish where the quarter-million bucks in the safe came from, or what it was really for. Hell, I never really knew. Hugh told me that story we were going to use in court, that the money was for a hush-hush real estate buy over in Hawaii. I accepted the story because I had to. Any other guess at where the money came from made it worse for Hugh. Running a full-scale investigation on him would just turn up evidence for you to use. There are damn few legitimate reasons for keeping that kind of cash around. But it never really figured. I was there when Prokop opened the safe and found the money. I *saw* the surprise in his eyes.

"The money is the trout in the milk, Liz. Last Saturday I got a tip that the money may have been from Van Zandt & Company, in the process of being dry-cleaned. A couple people had access to Hugh's office, even the combination to the safe. Kessler did. So did Susan Haight. The only thing I can't figure out is how the money relates to the fire. But it does. It has to."

She shook her head with the infinite patience of an old woman saddled with a mad husband. "No, Matthew. It doesn't have to be related. Suppose, as you think, Kessler and Van Zandt are laundering money. Kessler could have been using Prokop's safe to hide cash even as Prokop was planning to solve his own financial troubles and maybe get Kessler out of the way, so he could dump Susan Haight and take up with Sandra. Don't look at me that way. These things happen. Passions that seem almost laughable from the outside can drive people fiercely."

"I disagree, at least on this one. That was the case you had to sell to the jury, Liz, and maybe you even believe it.

I don't. For a long time I had doubts, but I knew these people. A little, anyway. That wasn't the way it happened."

"Well, we're not all blessed with your omniscience. The rest of us just deal with the facts as best we can. What did you want us to do? Not charge Prokop? Walk away from a murder case when we've got means, opportunity, motive? Because you say so?"

I took a couple of deep breaths and bit back a sharp reply. "Liz," I said. "Let's drop this. I wish it had never come up. I'm not trying to challenge the decision you made to prosecute Prokop, and I'm sure as hell not trying to pick a fight." I smiled ruefully. "God, what you must think of me. You always see me at my worst."

She looked at me somberly, her dark eyes shining. "And your best. I've changed what I thought of you. At first I thought you were oddly charming. And cold. I don't think that now. You liked Prokop and cared about him. You fought very hard for him, even when you began to have doubts. But this obsession about the case, trying to change the outcome when it is over, has to be wrong. You're not cold. But I think you are, in some very central part of yourself, alone."

She fell silent. The silence had weight and substance and a life of its own. For lack of anything better to say I invited her back upstairs to the bar for a cognac. She shook her head, no. "Thank you," she said, "but, remember, I've got an early skiing date tomorrow. You'd better take me home." There was no anger in her voice, but it had changed. It was the cool, correct, distant voice that she had used when we first met to negotiate the terms of Hugh's bond. I know very little about women, but I knew enough to realize that I had driven her away.

The silence continued. Good waiters know what that kind of silence means when it is between a man and a woman dining alone. The check came in record time and I paid it, then took Liz to her apartment and went on home to an empty house and an empty night.

CHAPTER 21

Sunday dawned dreary and wet, too cold for beach hiking and too windy in the mountains for skiing to be the kind of pleasure it should. I woke up feeling oddly anxious, as if there were something very important to do that I had forgotten about. The sense persisted as I dressed in long underwear and a goretex rain suit for the jog down the Burke-Gilman Trail to a neighborhood store near Magnuson Park that carried the Sunday *New York Times*. As I trotted down and back I replayed the previous night's conversation with Liz Kleinfeldt, trying to figure out if there was any sort of apology I could make that would lead her to give me a second chance. I decided there probably wasn't and pushed the thought of her from my mind, leaving a small gnawing ache in the place of memory.

When I got home I kindled the fire and showered and made coffee, determined to take the day slow and easy, maybe work my way through the fat Sunday papers and then see if the pro basketball games were any good. For just this one day I was not going to think about the Prokop Marine fire or Hugh Prokop or Henry Cruz.

I am a Sunday paper freak. I usually get three of them. I know what's going to be in them but I read every damned page anyway. On that Sunday they were full of the usual nonsense. The president's staff was lying to the special Iran Committee. A new spending bill was stalled by an obscure Oklahoma congressman with a wallet full of special-interest money and the soul of a lizard. There were brushfire wars around Asia and Africa that, like most people, I thought about only when I gave thanks I wasn't fighting in them. The stock market was ignoring the creeping rise in unemployment and consumer debt as it roared past twenty-four hundred on the Dow–Jones average. The magazine section of the *Times* featured a historically significant Park Avenue apartment that had been spray-painted battleship-gray by an Italian contessa who was married to a twenty-three-year-old investment banker. He was famous for having made a million bucks in fees on a junk bond issue that had gone into bankruptcy within five days of being sold to the public.

I worked my way through the business pages, munching on a Danish, reading the essays of two professors arguing over whether the dollar had fallen far enough against other countries' currencies. It was not the kind of thing I usually read, but all of the work I had put into understanding Van Zandt's business had created a little curiosity. The argument was a little too abstract for me to really follow—something about trade flows and Latin American currency fluctuations—and then I sat bolt upright in my chair. The back of my neck burned with excitement, as though I'd been struck by electricity.

"The commonplace view," the fellow arguing for greater declines in the value of the dollar was saying, "is that the dollar has fallen far enough, particularly after the sudden, crashing devaluation agreed on at the third meeting of the western economic ministers in Brussels last December. While that sudden turn in economic policy wreaked massive havoc in the foreign currency markets, the trade balance has not yet been restored. The dollar is still far too strong against Latin currencies, in particular."

I dropped the paper on the floor beside me and thought hard. The dollar had been pushed down by all the western countries last December 4, according to the chronology that accompanied the essays. Cruz had made his first investments with Van Zandt's currency funds around Christmas. I went over to the dining room table and dug out the earnings reports from two of Van Zandt's currency funds. The reports for December, as well as for the last quarter and all of last year, showed a smooth progression of earnings from trading. If the reports were to be believed, Van Zandt had been one of the only traders in the country not to take a serious loss on the plunging value of the dollar.

The key question was whether the reports were believable. If Van Zandt had taken Cruz's dirty money to stave off losses in the currency funds, his company books would have to be cooked prior to the end of the year, or at least before the auditors began their customary examination in early January. Suddenly my mind skipped backward for what seemed like years, not months, back to the New Year's Day party at Van Zandt's house. I remembered the ashen look on Walter Kessler's face when he came down to the bathhouse, the exhausted slump of his shoulders, his oddly bitter insistence that Van Zandt personally help him in preparing the year-end financials.

I flipped open my big sketch pad to the list of points I had written down the day before. I ran through each one in my mind. Currency trading was *hard*, a mysterious black box. People didn't know how it worked. The funds had very high rates of return, so high that people left their money in and watched it grow on paper. The funds were sold by fancy sales pitches. Van Zandt was secretive. Nobody knew his real name. Van Zandt had dropped his well-known national accounting firm for a new local firm. It was in December that Van Zandt had needed money bad enough to take in Henry Cruz's dirty laundry. I took down the felt-tip pen and wrote in a new item, the eleventh, in boldface letters: BIG LOSSES?

As I was running through the list I remembered something else, something very old. I thought of a dapper little Italian immigrant given to fine suits and jaunty straw boater hats. He had sold investments in a scheme that was supposed to make money through the difference between currency rates and the value of international postage stamps. The plan had never worked. He kept it going by paying high interest to some investors out of the capital of others.

But the illusion of success had swept the public. For a few months in the early 1920s that little man had most of the State of Massachusetts toasting his name and calling him a genius, until the scheme finally collapsed and landed him in Walpole State Prison. In the old pictures I had seen in books the little man was laughing, even in prison. Always laughing. The little immigrant's name was Carlo Ponzi.

For the first time in weeks I began to laugh, sweet laughter for joy and irony and simple relief. The thing that had misled me for so long was the notion that if Van Zandt had been stealing, he was stealing only from Cruz. That was wrong. Van Zandt had followed in Carlo Ponzi's timeworn footsteps. He wasn't stealing from just Cruz. He was stealing from *everybody*.

A Ponzi scheme works on the principle of taking in money from a group of investors and using part of that money to pay high returns. When the word gets out about the hot new prospect, greed follows a course as natural as gravity, and other investors line up to put their money into play. The scheme can be based on almost any plausible-sounding investment program. Ponzi did it with postage stamps and currency exchange. The Homestake Oil swindle was based on exaggerated reports of oil well production. Homestake actually drilled very few wells and most of those came up dry. When anxious investors asked to be shown the oil fields, the Homestake people painted up irrigation equipment out in Kansas to look like working wells. The Equity Funding scandal in the 1970s was made possible by computers that generated thousands of nonexistent insurance policies. The premiums reported as "earned" by the fictitious policies were used to prop up the price of Equity Funding stock in the market until the company executives could dump their stock back on an unsuspecting public. Even more recently, a San Diego stockbroker named J. David Dominelli had lightened the wallets of the Southern California gentry by nearly a hundred-million bucks in a currency trading scheme that sounded suspiciously similar to what Van Zandt was doing.

Some Ponzi schemes are frauds from the beginning, like

the pyramid games that swept up every car salesman and bartender on the West Coast during the summer of 1980. Others, like Equity Funding, begin as desperate attempts to shore up an otherwise legitimate business and protect the money that the insiders have in the company. From the little I knew I guessed that Van Zandt might have started like that, using the dirty money of new investors like Cruz to cover the trading losses and make payouts to earlier investors who insisted on taking their dividends in cash, rather than reinvesting them.

Every Ponzi scheme collapses of its own weight. How long the scheme works depends on how much money is being diverted by the swindler for his own use, how many of the initial investors demand to be cashed out, and how many new marks line up to take their place. In the long run the mathematics of robbing Peter to pay Paul inexorably chews up the funds taken in, especially when the swindler has expenses. I had tried criminal cases against several swindlers when I was with the Justice Department. They all had very, very high expenses.

The life span of a Ponzi racket can range from a couple of weeks for a simple pyramid scam, to months, or even a year, for a complex corporate or investment-based financial fraud. In more complex scams there are definite warning signs when the end is near. One clue is when the sales effort becomes more frenzied than ever, and depends on fancy trappings and mysterious hints about what the resident genius is doing. Another clue is the degree of difficulty the investors have in getting their money out. From what Colleen had told me in the Elliott Bay Cafe, Van Zandt's sales force had been glitzy from the beginning, and the restrictions on withdrawals were set out right in the prospectus. It was hard to read anything into those two facts. But there were other, more ominous signs. Van Zandt's switch from a well-known national accounting firm to a new, hungry, local firm, Draper & Brockett, could be a signal that he was after a less intensive, more understanding review of his books. The most definite sign was Cruz's statement that some of his investments in the same funds were receiving different returns. That told me

that Van Zandt was trying to conserve cash by paying out
only the amounts that he felt certain investors needed to
keep their capital tied up in his funds.

It was now over four months since the dollar had crashed
in the currency markets. If there was any connection between Van Zandt's scheme and the fire, it could be proved
only by exposing the scheme. If Van Zandt had ridden the
roller coaster down, he might be starting to run very short
of cash. To break the racket open before he cut and ran
would require a lot of pressure, applied quickly. I was
fairly certain I knew where to start.

I finally reached Colleen Westfall late that afternoon.
The phone at her apartment was answered by a male voice
I didn't recognize who grumbled a little when I insisted
that Colleen answer. She came to the phone sounding
slightly cross.

"Matthew," she said severely. "Your timing is lousy. I
was just about to make another toddy for a youngish
partner in a very good law firm that I might well want to
join this year."

"Tell him to put his hormones on hold, Colleen, and
listen. I may have something for you. Besides, you told
me to call you back within a week."

"That's true, but can't it wait until tomorrow?"

"I don't think so."

"Well, what is it? It had better be good."

"I don't have hard evidence," I explained, "but I've
got a lot of little threads that weave together."

"Damn it, Matthew—"

"Darling," I said, cutting her off, "Can you say 'Ponzi'?
As in Ponzi scheme, Ponzi racket, Ponzi fraud?"

"Oh my God. Talk."

I explained to Colleen the information I had and how I
thought it fit together. I was careful to leave out Henry
Cruz, only saying that I had been tipped by a major
investor who had large worries about his money. When I
was finished, she asked, "How much longer do you think
it has to run?"

"Not long," I replied. "It's been going for perhaps four months, and the structure might not hold too much longer."

"I'm inclined to think you're right. What should I do? You haven't given me enough to get any sort of formal investigation order."

"Just put on pressure. Nothing public, no press. Let a couple of people in the office know you're wondering about Van Zandt. And give his lawyers and accountants a call. They're exposed on something like this. If the investors were defrauded and Van Zandt splits, the lawyers and accountants are going to be the only deep pockets around, and they'll be holding the bag. You might remind his law firm of how much the guys who represented Dominelli's company paid to settle the class-action suits against them."

"I will. Anything else?"

"Let my name slip once or twice, or somehow let them know very subtly that I'm a source on part of this. I want Van Zandt to come back to me."

"Matthew," she said sharply, "what are you planning?"

"Nothing you need to know about. I'm not going to steal any of your thunder, if that's what concerns you."

"Not exactly. I was thinking of the consequences if you're wrong."

"I'm not."

"I hope not. Or I'll hurt you where it will hurt the most."

I laughed briefly. "Colleen, it is purely a pleasure dealing with you. I always know exactly where I stand."

"You'd better, love. I'll call you tomorrow and let you know how I do."

She hung up without saying good-bye. I put down the phone slowly and let another warm luxurious wave of laughter wash over me.

CHAPTER 22

Monday morning was quiet. I spent the morning going over the books and getting out the February bills, an ugly but necessary chore if I had hopes to continue eating. Since I had spent most of that month preparing for trial with Hugh, or drunk and then recovering, there weren't too many new bills to send out. There were quite a few reminder notices. I often laugh when I get brochures from consultants who want to teach me the fine art of getting clients. I have never had any trouble getting clients. It was getting clients who paid that was the problem.

The phone finally started ringing after lunch. The first call was from a lawyer named Clemens who was a partner in the law firm that had prepared the offering documents for the various Van Zandt currency funds. He was pompous and abrupt and wanted to know where in hell I got the crazy notion that there was something nasty going on at Van Zandt & Company. I listened to him for a few minutes and then cut him off, telling him that anything I had to say on the matter he would find out in good time. Perhaps it would be testimony. Perhaps not. I was vague. He was still sputtering angrily when I hung up.

The second call was from Colleen, wondering if anyone had taken the bait. I gave her a summary of Clemens's call. She said his timing was pretty good, since she had only hinted about who her source was, and his call to me had come within three hours of the time she first called him. I told her to let things hang for the rest of the day, until I knew whether Van Zandt had taken the bait. She agreed and rang off.

It took until nearly five o'clock to get the call I wanted. When it came it was Susan Haight, not Van Zandt.

"Riordan," she said angrily, before I could even say hello. "What the hell are you doing? We had calls from the local office of the SEC this morning, asking about the currency funds. Then our lawyers and accountants got called. They said you might be involved. Now what is going on?"

"Nothing much. I've been asking around about you and Van Zandt, that's all. Doing a little thinking about where that quarter-million dollars in Hugh's safe came from."

"We told you where it came from," she said, exasperation in her voice. "It was for a real estate deal in Hawaii. Greg and I put up the money. The deal never came off. We kept it in Hugh's safe because he was the one who would fly to Hawaii to make the deal."

"You told me all that, Susan. Before the trial. And I accepted it because any other explanation made Hugh look even worse. But it seems to me that you were all kind of reluctant to provide bank records or some other hard evidence that would prove it." I hardened my voice. "Why don't you cut the crap. The money came from the brokerage. What were you doing, laundering it?"

"That's not true. Hugh told you—"

"Stuff what Hugh told me. He would have told me bears had wings if you wanted him to."

"Why are you doing this to me? Is it just the money? Maybe you think it should all go to Hugh's daughter and his sister. Maybe I could talk Greg into that."

"Nice try. You forgot to mention what I'd be getting out of it."

"What do you want? I'm not going to—"

"Yes, you are," I said harshly. "You're going to do what I say. Meet me tonight for a drink, around nine. There'a nice anonymous pick-up bar in the Bellevue Black Lion Hotel. Meet me there."

"But—"

"At nine." I hung up the phone satisfied. Susan had been halfway panicked into a bribe without even really trying. She would be there.

I thought about calling Hugh's sister Mary Alice and letting her know what I was doing. There was still a chance that Hugh had been involved in the money laundering, and any other evidence against Hugh would hurt her lawsuit against the fire insurance company. But I couldn't prove a damned thing. I was working with small shards of evidence and trying to make something out of them, like an archaeologist trying to figure out an ancient civilization from a single broken pot. I could be too far wrong in too many ways. There would be time enough to tell her.

I went out around six for take-out teriyaki from a stand over on Fremont Avenue and brought it back to the office to eat. When I was finished I worked a little more and watched the office clock until it would be time to go, trying to decide whether I had to be ready for Van Zandt if he came along to the party. When it was eight o'clock I shrugged and opened the office safe and took out a flat, inconspicuous .32 automatic. I clipped it to my belt and put on a tweed sports coat to hide it. I don't much like guns, but there was very little point and even less humor in walking into a trap that I had set for myself.

The bar at the Bellevue Black Lion looked like a museum piece, a perfectly preserved example of a suburban West Coast meat rack, circa 1977. You entered through a limed-oak doorway into a long, L-shaped room. The lights were so low I had to stop in the doorway and let my eyes adjust. There was more light in the average coal mine. Such light as there was came from fluorescent tubes hidden behind panes of purple and gray stained glass. The purple-and-gray theme was picked up again in the wallpaper and set off nicely by the dark wine-red carpet and the burnt-umber vinyl on the bar stools and cocktail chairs. At the corner of the L there was a Plexiglas dance floor outlined with small, twinkling lights. A globe studded with hundreds of tiny mirrors was suspended from the ceiling. Instead of live music they had a house disc jockey spinning records that I thought had all been destroyed in the "I Hate Disco" riots at Comiskey Park in Chicago. The jock was dark-haired and slender but he still didn't look much like Travolta. He had on very tight knit slacks and a Quiana shirt that a textile museum would have paid plenty for.

The bar was organized along the same social rules that I had learned at Great Falls Cathedral High School in 1965. Boys on one side, in this case bellied up to the bar, girls on the other, gathered in little groups at the tables, clutching tall glasses of something with gin and pineapple juice and flashing frozen smiles at anyone who walked into the room lacking a major paunch or a wedding band or other obvious signs of social defects.

I took my place with the boys at the bar, ordered a club soda in the hope of doing this thing right, and looked around. Many of the boys were showing obvious signs of age or serious intoxication or both. Once in a while the brave ones would get up and ask one of the women to dance. The men had razor haircuts and health-club tans that looked pallid in the strange low lights. They took out packs of Vantage or Kool ultra-milds from suit coats or short leather jackets, but there was something furtive in the way they smoked. Bogart would have told them all to go to hell.

When I got done surveying the room I decided there wasn't anybody, male or female, who looked like they planned on whacking me out, so I relaxed and drank my soda and waited.

Susan Haight came in about nine-fifteen. She stood at the doorway peering into the gloom as she tried to find me. I got up and led her over to a quiet corner table where we could talk. A waitress in a very short skirt with very high heels tottered over and took our drink order and went away.

When she was gone I said, "I want to know about the money, Susan. Where it came from, where it went to get cleaned and pressed, how it ended up in Hugh's safe. For a start, anyway."

She looked straight at me, her face calm, impassive. "I've told you before that I don't know what you're talking about. I want you to stop this. You could ruin my reputation, and as a broker my reputation is my living. I assure you, I'll fight back.''

"With what? If you don't like those questions, I've got others. Just how badly did the Van Zandt currency funds get burned when the finance ministers got together last December to drive down the value of the dollar? Is that when Van Zandt started to dip into the customer accounts to cover the shortfalls?''

She looked at me, wide-eyed with horror. "My God, is that what you've been telling people? That's absurd. There is nothing wrong in our accounts. Even if he had lost money for a while, Greg could always make it back. He has losses on lots of days. But as he says, every day in the market is a new day, and you start even.''

"Unless you haven't got anything left to start with," I shot back. "Save me the sayings from Chairman Greg, Susan. Maybe you don't know what's going on. Okay, I'll assume that. Then take my questions as a warning, please. Try to find the answers for yourself, if no one else. And if things don't add up, call me. Quickly. When something like this breaks open, there is a very small window of time when someone who knows only a little can testify and get immunity and walk away. When the window closes the prosecutors from Justice or SEC or King County won't be cutting any deals." I softened my tone and added, "During the trial I had the strange sense that Hugh was trying to protect you from something, despite all that he did that hurt you. Let me help, now that he can't.''

The look on her face was cold, almost contemptuous. "I don't need any help, Riordan," she replied. "From you or anyone else. Tomorrow I'm calling my lawyers to see what we can do about you. Perhaps libel.''

I smiled briefly. "To me that's not much of a threat. I've heard it before. People who sue for libel often get the truth thrown in their faces." I looked at her straight on, filled with sudden anger at her cold self-possession. "You know," I added acidly, "in this whole conversation the only person who has mentioned Hugh Prokop was me. I think that says a hell of a lot, don't you?''

She stood up to go, her movements jerky with anger. When she turned back I thought she was going to say something, but she swung her hand around and slapped me in the face. She had gotten a lot of hip into it and the blow nearly took my head off. Susan stormed away.

I glanced quickly around the room to check how many people had seen or heard the slap. Everyone seemed thoroughly anesthetized by booze and Barry Manilow, which suited me fine. I reached for my wallet to pay for the drinks and then realized that they had never been delivered. Just as well. I walked out of the bar past a group of what looked like Sunbelt executives, mean, skinny men with western-cut suits, cowboy boots and blow-dried hair. Nobody even noticed that I was gone.

I got back to the parking lot just in time to see Susan's BMW do a rolling stop at the exit to the I-405 access road and flash away into the night. I ran to my car and followed. It was a hell of a long shot that she would be going any place interesting, but the rest of the evening had been a total loss, so I thought I might as well roll the dice.

They came up craps. I followed Susan down the access road and onto I-405. She got off at the Coal Creek exit and we wound for a mile or two down Coal Creek Parkway. The road was nearly empty and I hung well back, hoping she wouldn't spot me. She finally turned into a town-house development off the parkway. The row houses were built of wood, painted gray with blue trim. They clustered like a child's building blocks around a center common with a pool and tennis court and putting green. Big deal. She had gone home.

The driveway circled around the outside of the development past the garages attached to each unit. I drove down it and stopped at the far end. I wanted to see if Susan might have been upset enough to have anyone come and meet her. I parked, got out of the car, and walked to the corner of the end garage. I could see Susan's front door in the center of the complex.

Nothing doing. After an hour Susan's lights went out. Most of her neighbors were asleep. Not even the flickering blue glow of television invaded the night. I gave it up a half hour later. As I drove back to Seattle I thought about how easily Susan had been able to checkmate me simply by denying everything. In order to prove a connection between Van Zandt & Company and the fire, I needed a crack, a crevice, any kind of seam in the smooth blank rock wall of denial.

I had searched and found nothing. When I got back to town I stopped at an all-night restaurant on Denny Way and ate scrambled eggs and drank coffee laced with rum, feeling as mean and useless as a rattlesnake with a sprained tail.

CHAPTER 23

By ten o'clock the next morning I had dialed Susan Haight's house three times, and her office twice, feeling more foolish every time I punched the numbers on the telephone. My approach to her had been about as wrong as you could get. Pressed for time, I had gone straight at her with little more than guesses and smoke, and she had seen it for what it was. If I had still been with the Justice Department I would never have allowed an investigator to talk to her. The right way is methodical. First get the facts and check them until they are correct and cold and inescapable. Then do the questioning, leaving the witness the stone choice between indictment and cooperation.

Now I was stuck. Van Zandt ran his business on the managerial principle used by Jesus with the twelve disciples: there was one head guy and everybody else got The Word from him. Only Susan, having started the business with Van Zandt, had the kind of access to records and conversations that could provide usable evidence.

The dossier information that Paul Schaeffer had given me shed very little light on Susan's background or personality. I had learned next to nothing about her during the trial. The few times I had been with her she had seemed to me to be a very fine actress, in roles—devoted lover, spur-of-the-moment cook, dedicated, hard-driving businesswoman—that she had learned all the lines for but never quite understood. There had been something in each of those performances that was ever so slightly mechanical, as though the words she spoke were written for others but never for herself. Perhaps if I looked at her as her own person, rather than as Hugh's lover or Van Zandt's corporate officer, I might find something that I could use as a key.

Mary Alice Thierrault worked as a free-lance graphic artist, managing her own small studio out of a warehouse loft above the Alaskan Way Viaduct on the central waterfront. I found her there at mid-morning, hunched over her drawing board, casually dressed in jeans and an oversized shirt held in by a khaki web belt. When working she wore reading glasses that threatened to slide off her nose. Her hair was long and she wore it loosely tied back with a black ribbon.

I paused in the open doorway and rapped on the door frame.

"Mary?" I called. "It's Matthew Riordan. Can I come in?"

"Of course," she said, sliding off the tall stool and standing to greet me. She took off the glasses and folded them but let them dangle at her throat like a pendant, held in place by a string around her neck. The smile on her wide plain face was cautious. "What brings you down here?" she asked. "Something wrong?"

"Not really. I've learned some things that might interest you. I need to talk to you before I can go any further with them. Do you have time right now?"

"Sure. Would you like some coffee? We can stay here or go someplace down in Pioneer Square."

"Staying is fine with me. Can we talk here?"

"I guess so. Julie, my partner, is out making a presentation to a new client. She won't be back for at least an hour." Mary stepped over to a white cabinet standing against the far wall and poured coffee from a steaming open pot into an earthenware mug and brought it to me. "We're a little short on sitting space," she said. "Why don't you drag that chair in the corner over and I'll sit on the windowsill.'' I got the chair while she sat on the foot-wide sill, her arms wrapped around her raised knees, her back leaning on the wall. The big steel-framed windows beside her looked past the elevated concrete highway and out to Elliott Bay.

"Okay," she said when we were comfortable. "Tell me what's going on. I assume that you're here about Hugh." There was a trace of hesitation in her voice, as though she were bracing herself for more bad news.

"It's a little complicated," I began. "Let me just lay it out for you and then I'll answer any questions you might have."

I told her about the visitation I'd received from Henry Cruz, the suggestion that the money in the safe was either stolen or being laundered by Van Zandt and Susan Haight, my suspicion that Van Zandt was running a fraud on the investors in his currency funds, and Susan's unwillingness to answer any questions. She listened patiently. When I was through she looked more puzzled than concerned.

"I'm sorry," she said, "but I don't really understand why you're telling me this. Did you want me to pull what was left of Hugh's money out of Van Zandt & Company?"

"That's part of it. If the investors are being defrauded, any investor still in the funds is going to have a hard time getting his money back. I'm afraid there won't be much left."

"I see. Don't worry. I told Mr. Tobin that I wanted to do that—get out of those funds—at the second meeting we had. I don't know why I did. I didn't understand the investment, and I just didn't want to have any more contact with Susan, I guess. They weren't too happy about it, but we got the money back yesterday."

"Good. I didn't want to have you and Megan lose anything because I was poking around. But that's not really why I'm telling you this. The main reason I'm here is that if Van Zandt and Susan are involved in something criminal, it might appear to a lot of people that Hugh was also involved. I didn't want to take the chance of hurting you or his daughter any further."

"Was he?" Her question was cold, blunt.

"I don't think so. Not actively anyway. If I'm right, they were using his office safe as a place to park hot money. You see, they must have needed a place away from the brokerage, so they wouldn't get caught in a surprise audit. Both Susan and Walter Kessler had access to the building and to the safe. Hugh might have known what was going on, or found out what was going on after the fire, when he found the money in the briefcase. But he didn't tell me or anyone else. Looking back on it I believe he was trying to protect Susan."

"But what does this have to do with the fire? Are they connected?"

"I'm not sure. If the money was from Van Zandt—forgetting the story about the real estate deal—it helps explain why Kessler was there. He may have set the fire himself then been crossed up and killed. Or someone else may have killed him and set the fire to cover up the killing."

She started to speak but her breath seemed to catch in her throat. She took a sip of her coffee. "So there is a chance Hugh didn't set the fire after all," she mused.

"It's a chance," I agreed. "Whether we could ever prove Hugh innocent, after his suicide, is another matter. I don't know the answer but I'd like to try. I've already started to put pressure on Susan and Van Zandt. They're not taking it well. It might lead to something. If we can prove that someone else set the fire, you'll be able to collect the fire insurance. It's an awful lot of money for you and Megan."

"I don't much care about that. But if there is a chance to clear Hugh's name I'd want you to do what you can. The estate should retain you to investigate. I'll call Mr. Tobin."

I shook my head. "That's not necessary. All I need is your permission to keep going. I owe this to Hugh, I think."

"I don't agree, but we can discuss that later. Is there anything I can do?"

I nodded. "Susan is the key to this. Even if she doesn't know who killed Kessler she probably has facts that might

ell us something. I don't know how to reach her. When I
start thinking about her I realize that I know next to
nothing about her."

Mary Alice shrugged. "I don't know much either, to
ell you the truth. She never talked about her background,
at least not while I was around, which wasn't often. Hugh
never said anything about her family even though they
were reasonably serious about each other, giving some
thought to getting married. She didn't seem to have many
friends, outside of work. Most of the people she introduced to Hugh were either stockbrokers or her clients.
Hugh told me once that most of the parties they went to
were either for her business or were the kind of charity
functions where a lot of business gets done." She fell
silent. The muted rumble of the cars on the viaduct filled
the silence, a low sound that I felt as much as heard.

"I can't say I like Susan," Mary continued. "She was
always nice, but remote. I'm not used to that. For all its
troubles our family was open. We yelled and swore and
then always laughed about it later." She looked down, as
if falling into her memories. For a moment I thought she
might weep. Then she looked up. "I'm sorry. This isn't
helping, is it?"

It was my turn to shrug. "It does and it doesn't. It
confirms a few things I felt about Susan. It doesn't tell me
how she'd react to pressure, or where she would go. I tried
to call Susan a half-dozen times this morning. She isn't
home and her office doesn't know where she is. Somehow
I've got to persuade her that if she doesn't tell me the truth
she could go to prison for fraud or worse. If she's taken
off, I haven't a clue as to how to find her. The only thing I
can think of is to search her apartment. I hate like hell to
break in. If I got caught, I'd be in very bad shape."

She thought about that, then brightened. An unaccus-
tomed, devious smile played across her face. "Hugh had a
key to her apartment," she said. "I've still got it. Suppose
we both go over there. If we get caught we tell the truth.
You talked to her last night. She was distraught. We're
worried. You're the respectable attorney and I'm the upset, concerned almost-sister-in-law. Think it would play?"

I thought it over for a minute, and nodded. "It'd play," I said. "If I can't reach her by six o'clock today, let's do it."

At seven-thirty that night Mary Alice and I walked calmly through the center courtyard of Susan's condominium complex. I was dressed in a blue courtroom suit and a light-gray wool topcoat. Mary wore a black business suit and an expensive dress cape. As we walked we met a couple of other people coming or going, upwardly mobile latecomers from the office or the health club. They smiled politely in passing, nodding vaguely as though we were the neighbors they hadn't time to meet, or at worst a couple of visitors from someone's office. Nobody asked us what we were doing. Nobody called the cops. Appearances are everything.

Susan's apartment, number 12, was in the center of the complex. It was a three-story town-house, like the others, with its own stained-wood front door.

The door opened to a tile-floored entry at the middle level of the house. From the entry, carpeted steps led down a half flight to an open recreation room, up the same distance to a wood-floored living room.

"Susan?" Mary Alice called out. "Susan, are you here?"

The answering silence was marred only by the sounds that always leak through party walls—the mutter of a radio voice reading the news, the bass rumble of a Bob Seeger album being played two doors down, muffled, high-pitched shouts of canned laughter from a television next door.

"Thin walls," I said to Mary Alice. "I'd prefer not having to explain this to the neighbors, so don't call out to me. If you want me, come and get me."

She nodded. "What do we do now?"

"I'm going to search. If you want to help, put on some gloves so you don't leave fingerprints."

"What are we looking for?"

"Anything that might help us find Susan."

I began in the living room, which is the worst bet for finding anything useful but always has to be covered. Susan's living room was surprisingly traditional, given the modern architecture of the buildings. Wood floors had been installed and polished. There was a fireplace with a traditional mantel, a room-sized Chinese rug, a sofa, and chairs upholstered in white silk. The coffee and end tables were more modern, with vaguely classical lines but made of brass, black lacquer, and glass. The walls were hung with framed posters and lithographs in pastel colors but no particular style. There were no photographs, personal objects, or books. It looked like a room set up for a catalog photograph or the lobby of a good, small hotel. It wasn't a room anybody lived in.

I searched the living room quickly and moved on to one of the two upstairs bedrooms. The larger of the two was Susan's bedroom. It had a large brass bed covered with a puffy white down comforter and an elaborate, frilly white dust ruffle. I quickly checked the dresser and the closet, but they were used for nothing but clothes. I went back downstairs and found Mary Alice searching the basement recreation room, empty except for a striped cotton sofa and a TV/VCR combination standing in an open wood cabinet.

"I don't think you're going to find much down here," I said quietly. "Can you come upstairs for a minute? I'd like you to take a look at the bedroom and bath and see if you can figure out if Susan has been packing for a trip. I can't tell by looking at her clothes."

"Okay," she replied. "Did you find anything?"

"Not a thing. You?"

"Nothing. It's almost as if she really lived someplace else."

I moved on to the second bedroom. It had been fitted out as an office, with a reproduction rolltop desk and matching chair. I began to work the pigeonholes of the desk, checking each one carefully to make sure nothing had been pushed through and caught in the small gap between the dividers and the back panel of the desk. I needn't have bothered. Most of the items were bills or financial statements from one of Susan's several investment accounts. There were no personal letters or even cards from friends. In the last pigeonhole, on the far right side of the desk, I found an empty, note-sized envelope.

The cheap paper was pushed out at the bottom fold and there were faint creases, as if it had once held something bulky. I took a dollar bill out of my pocket and smoothed it flat against the desk top, then held it up against the envelope. Whatever had made the bulge in the envelope was the same size as the dollar. If Susan had been hoarding a little emergency money, it was gone.

Mary Alice came in from the bedroom. "I think she's gone," she announced. "There are two canvas suitcases missing, from what I think was a matched set of four. A lot of her makeup and toilet things are gone, too. There are also some gaps in the way she arranged her clothes, but I'm not sure that means things are missing. Did you find anything?"

"Maybe." I showed her the empty envelope and explained that it had probably held money. "What we need now is some idea of where she might go."

"There are a hundred and fifty-two countries in the Untied Nations," Mary Alice said. "Do we pick?" Her voice was heavy with frustration.

"No, we keep looking. Did you find anything downstairs? Letters, a diary, anything?"

"Unh-unh. There was a basket of what looked like old Christmas cards in Susan's closet. Want me to get it?"

"Yes."

We sifted through the basket of cards quickly. Most of the cards were simply signed or printed. Quite a few of them were from businesses. Near the bottom of the stack was a small card with a snowy Christmas scene that was badly printed on cheap stock. I opened it. Inside there was a clipping and a note.

The clipping was an obituary, dated early December, from the *Aberdeen Daily World*. Aberdeen is one of the dying lumber towns on the Washington coast. The death notice was for a woman named Pirovich. It was simple and dignified, listing only the fact of death and the names of the survivors, a husband and several children and step-children. The note was equally brief, addressed simply to "Susan." It read:

I'm sorry that we couldn't find you in time so you could come to the funeral. Your mother died quickly and as peaceably as you could expect from the cancer. I found this address for you in her things and hope this card reaches you. Please come see me. I don't know why you've stayed away, but you're always welcome here.

The card was signed by an "Aunt Rose." I looked quickly through the pile of cards, but there was no envelope matching this one, and no address on the card or the note.

I showed the note and the card to Mary Alice. She simply raised her eyebrows as she read, then returned the card to me. "It sounds like her family wouldn't know where she is either."

"Maybe not," I said. "But she might have gone back to them. It looks like Susan has gone to ground. There are worse things she could do than go back to Aberdeen, if that's where she's from. Home has lots of advantages."

"Such as?"

"Home," I replied, "is where they gotta take you in. Even if you're in trouble."

CHAPTER 24

I left for Aberdeen a little after dawn the next morning, fighting the morning commuter traffic streaming toward the aircraft plants in Renton and at Boeing Field. There was a second, smaller rush hour on Interstate 5 as it wound through Tacoma, Seattle's aging, weary industrial neighbor on the South Sound. The traffic thinned as I passed through Olympia, the state capital, and swung left on U.S. 12, the old coast road to the Pacific shore.

The morning was gray and rain-heavy clouds clung to the low ridges of the coast hills. At Satsop the twin cooling towers of an abandoned, unfinished nuclear project loomed like derelict giants over the highway. As I drove farther west the road seemed to narrow, hemmed in between the stands of fir and hemlock that had been force-grown in the woodlots of the big timber companies. The country here had a raw quality to it. The economy of southwest Washington was based on farming and timber and fishing, industries that extracted raw wealth and left wide slashes of destruction on the land. The cars on the highway now were older and rusty, many of them dating from 1979 and 1980, the last fat years before timber had gone into the tank during the Reagan recession.

Searching for Susan Haight in her home country was a fool's errand, long on guesses, even longer on odds. Even if I found her, there was very little chance that she would admit the money laundering or the Ponzi scheme, especially if she had been the one who had killed Kessler and set the fire.

And that was possible, I thought. Very possible. Susan had been alone on the night of the fire, from the time she and Hugh had left the restaurant. Susan was tall and strong. She could have slugged Kessler with a tool, a piece of wood, anything heavy that might have been consumed or charred in the fire. To Minh, driving past the warehouse parking lot on a rainy night, a tall woman bundled in a coat, running to a car, might well have looked like a man.

I didn't like the thought. I could understand why Susan might have killed Kessler. But she seemed to have cared for Hugh. Could she have sat by and coldly watched as Hugh's life collapsed in court?

It was possible.

I was sure of one thing. Susan had run because she knew that the money in Hugh's safe had been dirty money. If I found her, she would have to tell me that. With her testimony I could give Vince Ahlberg reason to reopen the case. If Susan would not give me that, then I was going to turn away and leave her to Henry Cruz.

There were sun breaks in the low clouds as I neared Montesano, a small town of about twenty-five hundred people that was the county seat of Grays Harbor County. I stopped there to play a fairly long hunch. If Susan really was from Aberdeen and named Pirovich, she might have changed her name legally. Name changes have to be approved by court order, and records of name changes are kept at the courthouse in each county. The Montesano courthouse should have the records from Aberdeen.

I pulled off the highway and wound my way on back streets through the town. It was still early. Small children in rain slickers and quilted jackets played in the muddy school yard beside the old red-brick school. Dirt-streaked pickup trucks were parked beside the cafes on Main Street. The windows of the cafes were steamed up, warm against the cold, wet morning.

The county courthouse was on a side street at the north edge of Montesano, built on a slight ridge so that it would stand above the town. The courthouse dated from the turn of the century. It was finely built of gray local limestone with a gold-leaf cupola dome that shone even in the weak winter light. I parked and walked up the stone steps that divided the rolling green courthouse lawn. The front double doors were thick heavy oak, dark with years and a dozen coats of varnish. Rich brass plaques with the names of dead men from four different wars were set into the limestone walls beside the doors. Courthouses like this were built as civic temples, and every inch of limestone and marble and oak testified to the sure belief that the community stood in harmony with the individual, and that justice would be discovered and done without passion or prejudice. I wondered if anyone thought that way anymore.

Inside the courthouse the air was warm and muggy. Big cast-iron steam radiators blew and hissed. I walked up the worn marble stairs to the central hallway that divided the building and searched for the County Clerk's office. I passed magnificent old courtrooms with benches and jury boxes of carved oak that made me think of Darrow and Bryan, Lincoln, and Oliver Wendell Holmes. The first three courtrooms were empty. In the fourth, a clerk's droning voice could be heard reading the matters on morning calendar call.

The Clerk of Court's office was behind a door of painted wood and pebbled glass. The legend CLERK was stenciled on the glass in wide, old-fashioned letters. The gilt paint was chipped. Behind the door was a small waiting room furnished with low benches and a Formica counter. I stepped to the counter and rang the bell. A matronly lady with steel-gray hair and a cast-iron disposition answered the bell.

"Yes, what is it?" she said impatiently.

"Good morning," I answered. "My name is Matthew Riordan. I'm an attorney from Seattle. I need to verify a few things in your county records."

"Real estate is done in the basement," she said briefly. "Any other court matter is kept up here. What are you looking for?"

"Name changes," I said. "I understand state law requires that a record of name changes be kept in the county where the petitions are heard.''

"If the law says so, we've got it," she said severely. "But we don't get too many of those here. They would be recorded in the civil books. I think we also keep them on a card file index, and then if you want to see the actual petitions, we can probably dig those out.''

"That would be fine. How does the index work?"

"Names should be listed by the name the person changed to, then cross-indexed by the original name. What's the last name you want?''

"Haight. Susan Haight." The clerk disappeared behind a wall of case files. She returned a moment later.

"Here's the H file," she said, placing a wooden, library-type card file drawer on the counter. "Let me know if you find the name and want to see the petition." She stepped to the far end of the counter and took a pile of pleadings from her in-box and began pounding them with a rubber stamp, pausing now and again to glance at me sideways as I worked.

I leafed through the card file quickly, my mind filled with the expectant buzz of a man playing a hunch. Some of the cards were more than fifty years old. The thick paper stock was yellow with age but still readable, written in India ink by the fine cursive hand of a long-dead deputy clerk. There were far more cards than I had guessed there would be. I should not have been surprised. Grays Harbor County stretched from the Olympic foothills to the Pacific coast. When the land runs out and people have traveled as far as they can go, the only thing left they can change is themselves.

I found it on the second try, misfiled ahead of Hague and Hagerty and Hagland. Susan Haight. Formerly Shirley Cowper. A married name. Her birth name was Shirley Pirovich, the same as the woman in the obituary. The name was Russian or Ukranian, I thought. I had been right about the Slavic touch in her high cheekbones and dark, slightly oval eyes.

I walked back along the counter to the clerk, carrying

the card drawer. "Excuse me. Can I see the petition on this name change, please?"

The elderly clerk took the card file and squinted at the name through her bifocal librarian's glasses. "This one's from 1980. It'll be in the basement for sure."

"I'd really appreciate it. It is important."

"With you lawyers, it always is," she sighed. "Wait here." She took down the name on a piece of scrap paper and disappeared behind the wall of files. I paced and studied the worn, cracked linoleum floor. I blew out my anxious shallow breath in a thin whistling sigh.

The clerk returned ten minutes later, carrying a yellow manila court file. I took it from her and opened it. The petition was there, handwritten in a looping feminine hand on the sort of quick-and-dirty legal form they sell in stationery stores. Shirley Cowper, née Pirovich, a divorced person. A form affidavit, denying any fraudulent motive for the name change. Last address given was 304 B Street, in Aberdeen. A court order changing her name was attached, filled out in the same looping hand but signed by a county judge. The name change was only a frail link to Susan Haight's past, but it was one more link than I had before. I copied the petition on a courthouse Xerox machine and continued on for Aberdeen.

In 1912 my maternal grandfather left his home in Stillwater, Minnesota, and went to work as a logger and cook in the timber camps of southwest Washington. He left the camps in the war boom year of 1917, a draftee private headed for France with Black Jack Pershing. As an old man at home in Montana, he remembered this wet country of rolling green hills and wide slow rivers, and with a dry chuckle he had said that the four hottest places on a Saturday night were Aberdeen, Chehalis, Hoquiam, and Hell. In that order.

No more.

The depression in the fishing and timber industries had hit Aberdeen like a neutron bomb; most of the buildings were still there, but all of the people had gone away, probably for good. The offices and warehouses of the timber brokers still stood along Water Street, looming above the shallow tidal slough of Grays Harbor like ruined forts. One block over, on Main, the few remaining department and furniture stores advertised permanent sales. The cardboard signs that shouted "Close Out!" had become faded and fly-specked with age and hard times. Only the taverns and poker parlors still showed signs of life.

B Street was a few blocks north and east of downtown Aberdeen. The houses along the streets here were mostly mill cottages, slapped up in the hurry to house the workers who once had labored in timber and pulp. Here and there a vacant lot showed a crumbling foundation where one of the shacks had burned down. No new houses had been built. Nobody wanted to live there anymore.

Number 304 was a mill shack like the rest, with a plain front door squarely in the middle, windows on either side. It was painted a particularly nasty shade of dull green. A landlord color. Take the color paint you've got, mix it with whatever paint they've got on sale at the hardware store, slap it on. It keeps the place from falling down.

I parked and walked up to the front door of 304. There was no doorbell. I pulled the sagging screen door open and pounded on the cheap wooden inner door. After about five minutes of pounding, the door finally flew open.

"What in hell do you want?" The growling question came from a woman about thirty. Mornings were not this woman's best time of day. Her hair was snarled and matted from the pillow, her eyes still filled with sleepy confusion. She was wearing a worn yellow bathrobe that she clutched with one hand, holding it closed. Her large heavy breasts sagged against the robe.

There was no point in trying to be charming. "I need some information about a woman who used to live here," I said. "I'm not going to hurt her and I'm not a crook. And I'm willing to pay for whatever information you can offer."

That got her attention. "Hunh," she said, bemused. "What are you, a cop?"

"No. I'm a guy who needs information. My name's Riordan."

She thought that over. "Okay. Come in. God, I probably look like hell. I'll be back." She turned and disappeared into the house.

I stepped into the living room and closed the door behind me. The room was small and stuffy. The furniture wasn't quite as old as the house but the couch looked like it had been around since Truman was President and the rest wasn't much newer. There were very bright, very bad paintings of beaches and oceans on the walls. I waited.

The woman came back with her hair brushed out, wearing jeans and a heavy sweater. She walked into the kitchen, which was just an alcove off the living room, and made instant coffee with hot tap water. She asked me if I wanted some. I said no.

She came back into the living room and sat on the sofa with her mug of lukewarm coffee. She motioned to a chair. I sat.

"So how much money are we talking about here, anyway?" she said, lighting a cigarette.

"Enough," I replied. I smelled the smoke and my stomach flip-flopped a little. Even during the ten years that I smoked heavily I could never light one in the morning. "How long have you lived here?"

"Forever," she said, a slightly bitter tone to her voice. "Seriously, I've lived in this house off and on since 1978. Why?"

I took Susan Haight's picture out of my wallet. "Do you know this woman?"

She laughed lightly. "Sure. I've known her forever. Shirley Pirovich. She was a senior in high school when I was a freshman. Except you weren't supposed to call her Shirley. She went by Susan. And she made sure everybody got it right, too."

"She used to live here, didn't she?"

"Unh-hunh. She got married a couple of years after high school to a guy named Cowper, Steve Cowper. He was a big jock, went down to Portland State to play football. Linebacker. I heard he tried it with the pros, St. Louis or something, but he never made the team. Anyway, they broke up, and Susan came to live with me. She only stayed a couple of months. Too bad. The place was never so clean as when she lived here."

"What happened to Susan then?"

"Beats me. When she lived here she worked real hard, as a secretary out at the Satsop power plant, and worked cocktail waitress at night, too. I guess when she had enough money saved up, she split."

"Have you seen her since?"

"No. Come to think about it, nobody's ever said she came back to Aberdeen, even for a visit."

"Is there anybody here who would know where she was?"

"I don't think so. Her mom's dead. I don't know where her ex-husband would be, but if he's anything like my ex he's long gone. She had a sister, though. Allison. Ally. Her last name's, unh, shit." She paused. "Wheatley, or something like that. She'd be older than Susan. I've heard she lives on the coast, up near Pacific Beach." She paused again, thinking. "I think that's all I know."

"It's a help," I said. "What's your name, in case I need to find you?"

"Mary. Mary Jacquard."

I went to my wallet and was going to give her twenty, but I relented and made it fifty. I gave it to her and said, "If I find her, you'll get fifty more."

"Thanks." She smiled again, a bawdy smile. "You come by with a hundred and we can party any way you want, Riordan. I work nights at the Harbor House Lounge, but I get off at twelve."

"Thanks yourself," I said gently, standing up to go, "but I . . ."

"Hey, don't sweat it," Mary Jacquard said. She gave me a big, wide go-to-hell grin. "What's Susan done, anyway, that she needs to be looked for by someone like you?"

I paused at the door and looked back at Mary Jacquard. I shrugged. "What everybody's done, I guess. Too much, or else maybe not enough."

Pacific Beach is the last in a string of small coastal towns that stretches north of Grays Harbor. The coast has beautiful, wide beaches and towering haystack rocks, but is too cold and remote to interest the developers of big vacation resorts. The town gets by on tourist cabins, roadside shops, and the trickle of money from retired folks who live in small houses and trailers set back from the beach. It has the same sleepy look that the northern California coast had in the late 1950s, when my father had packed my mother and me into the '54 Chevrolet wagon for happy all-night drives from my aunt's house in Seattle down to San Francisco and Carmel.

Ally Wheatley wasn't listed in the local phone book and none of the morning drinkers in the Seaview Tavern knew who she was, so I was reduced to cruising up and down the state highway, checking mailboxes and name markers on the private roads that led to houses built on the headland above the beach. I found her house on my third pass down the highway. The name Wheatley was stenciled in small letters on a metal mailbox painted sea-green, with a spray of painted wildflowers on the side. The mailbox stood beside a gravel path heading into a stand of pines on the bluff above the beach.

The house was nicer than I expected, a weathered-shingle bungalow with big glass windows on the side facing the sea. As I drove up the path and parked, a woman with long, kinked brown hair, wearing a loose cotton dress, walked around the side of the house. She stared at me quizzically. She had on cotton gardening gloves and carried a trowel.

"Ms. Wheatley?" I said, getting out of the car. The woman smiled a little, but still looked curious.

"I'm Ally Wheatley," she replied. "Who are you?"

"My name is Riordan," I said. "Matthew Riordan. I've come to see your sister, is she here?"

"No. Why would Susan be here? I haven't seen her in years." She spoke calmly, politely. She had a bland round face that showed little emotion. If she was lying I would never know the difference.

"I'm an attorney, Ms. Wheatley. It's very important that I speak to your sister. Would you mind if I asked you some questions?"

"I . . . no. I'm thirsty. Would you like some tea?"

"Sure."

"Well, come in, then."

I followed her into the house. It was small and well kept. The plank cedar floors were clean and polished. Bright cotton fabric with Indian print designs was spread over the sofa and chairs in the living room. Potted plants in macramé hangers hung from the ceiling in front of the windows. There was a beach-rock fireplace on one wall. Fresh flowers floated in bowls of water on the mantelpiece. Between the flowers there was a grammar-school photo portrait of a small boy with wild brown hair and a mischievous face. Framed posters were hung on the other walls. One was from an old Dylan album, the other from a concert at the Fillmore in San Francisco. The concert had been held in 1967.

Ally Wheatley came back into the room with tea in two hand-thrown earthenware mugs. I took a mug from her and sniffed it. It smelled like licorice and flowers. Maybe the sixties weren't dead after all.

"I don't know if I can be much help to you, Mr. Riordan," Ally said as she sat down on her sofa, curling her legs beneath her like a cat. "Susan and I have been on different paths since we were children. She is very concerned with the material world, with things, with money. I never have been. I care more about the spiritual and the philosophical. As a result I have no insight into Susan at all."

"But have you spoken to her recently?"

"She calls about once a month. She tells me very little about what she does, although I know it is financial. Mostly we talk about Ben." She gestured at the picture of the small boy on the mantel.

"Your son's a handsome boy," I said.

"But he's not my son. I wish he were. He's Susan's boy. You didn't know that?"

"No. She never mentioned it."

"Somehow I'm not surprised," she said dryly. "Why is it so important that you find Susan?"

"Because she's disappeared. She may be involved in a

fraud. One of the people ripped off in the fraud is a powerful criminal. The criminal wants his money back, or he wants the people who stole from him. If Susan is involved, she is in danger."

She took that calmly enough. "I haven't felt Susan to be in danger," she said. "As I told you, we are not close, but we are sisters. I would know if she were in trouble. I see a great deal, Mr. Riordan." She leaned forward and reached into a cigarette box on the table in front of her and took out a sizable joint. She lit it. I heard the dry sinsemilla buds crackle as they burned. She took a lengthy hit and offered me the joint. I shook my head.

"Ally," I pleaded. "I'm not kidding about the danger. Maybe it hasn't shown itself yet. Maybe Susan doesn't even know about it. But it's real."

"Perhaps. How do I know that you don't work for these people threatening Susan?"

"You don't, really. You'll have to trust your insight."

"I do. I asked that merely to see how you would answer. You are a kind man. I'm sure you wouldn't hurt Susan."

At least not until I find out what's going on, I thought grimly. "Look, you don't have to tell me anything now. If you know where Susan is, and can get in touch with her, set up a meeting between the two of us. You can bring the cops, the FBI, a couple of oversized hippies, anyone you want. Just help me talk to Susan."

She took a last contemplative hit off her joint. "I believe you, Mr. Riordan," she said. "But I just don't know where Susan is. Poor Susan. Poor Susan." Her voice trailed away, then erupted in a sudden surge of watery, stoned laughter. I moved over to the sofa and took Ally Wheatley by the shoulders, shaking her gently. "Ally, please. Isn't there anyone else I can talk to who might know where Susan is?"

"Steve might know."

"Steve. Her ex-husband? Where is he?"

"He tends bar, down on Ocean Shores, at the big motel there. Steve might know."

"Okay. I'll try Steve. I'm going now."

"You're sure you won't stay for more tea? I have cookies and cake, too."

"No, I'm going." I stood up and left. As I closed the front door behind me I heard her singing a little song, followed by more giggling laughter. She was, I thought, Susan's exact opposite, Mother Nature's child, a prisoner locked into time and an aging body, laughing to herself in a neat doll's house by the edge of the sea.

CHAPTER 25

The town of Ocean Shores lies on a sand spit perhaps seven miles long and two miles wide, a flat seaside prairie of sand and sea grass that separates Grays Harbor from the open sea. Ocean Shores is a town with no history, or not much, anyway. Born in a land fraud scheme in the early 1960s, it has grown up as a poor-man's resort, an unsightly jumble of condos, house trailers, tract homes, and restaurants in flat-roofed shacks with weathered signs promising surf-and-turf every night, a fish boil on Fridays.

The sky had turned dark and the wind had risen during the drive down from Pacific Beach. Rain splattered on the windshield of my car as I drove through the empty streets. I stopped at the Chamber of Commerce and picked up a tourist guide. According to the guide, The Tides' Inn was the largest and flossiest motel in town.

I found The Tides' next to the convention center, on the broad, treeless boulevard that ran through the length of the town. The motel consisted of a large A-frame building of brown stained cedar, with a long, low wing of rooms trailing off to one side.

I parked in the asphalt lot in front of the place and glanced up at the large white reader board at the front of the inn. The Morticians' Association was in town. They probably enjoyed the brooding clouds and bitter ocean winds.

The bar was upstairs and nautical, with hemp fishing nets with colored glass floats hung from the ceiling. Phony ships' wheels and winches were tacked to gray-stained plank walls or randomly mounted on posts around the room. The tables all had captain's chairs of stained wood and naugahyde. Even the bar stools were small captain's chairs on long spindled legs.

I crawled onto one of the bar stools and glanced around the room. A group of men sat in one corner. They wore dark suits and badges and hunched over their drinks, probably discussing the price of dying. In the center of the room two tables had been pulled together for a large family group, ranging from Grandma to babies. They squabbled sullenly over their lunch. I heard "goddamn rain" and "California" a couple of times.

The bartender looked about right to be Steve Cowper: mid-thirties, medium height, the strong shoulders of somebody who lifted weights and the burgeoning paunch of somebody who didn't lift them often enough. He stood off at the far corner of the bar, staring at the morticians and the wayward tourists and the rain beginning to hammer at the windows.

Eventually he drifted over, putting a little white napkin on the bar in front of me.

"Drink?" he asked.

"Beer. Whatever's on draft will be fine."

He pulled down a glass of Budweiser and set it in front of me. "What brings you to Ocean Shores?"

"If I said the weather, you wouldn't believe me."

He laughed hollowly. "I probably wouldn't," he said. "It sure isn't tourist season."

"I'm not much of a tourist. Your name is Steve Cowper, isn't it?" I kept my voice friendly and even.

It didn't do much good. He backed away from the bar, his eyes narrowing. A man with a working knowledge of bill collectors and angry husbands and cops. "Who wants to know?" he asked in a tight, tough voice.

"Take it easy," I said. "My name's Matthew Riordan. I'm a lawyer from Seattle. I'm a friend of your ex-wife's. She may be in some trouble, and she split from Seattle without telling anybody where she went. I want to help her, but in order to do that I need to talk to her.''

He swept my untouched beer away and dumped it in a sink below the bar. "Get out," he said.

"No. I don't know what it was like between the two of you, or why you broke up, but I think you owe it to her to help her if you can.''

"That's not your business. I don't know anything about you. And I want you out of here, now.''

"No. Listen to me. The trouble she has is real. She may be involved in the theft of a large amount of money. The man it was stolen from is powerful. He—''

Cowper came around the bar in a rush, grabbing at my arm, and yanking me off the bar stool. He threw a clumsy roundhouse punch at me. I set it aside with my left hand and hit him with two short hard jabs to his belly. The blows knocked the wind out of him and he sagged back against the bar. I grabbed his arms with both hands and straightened him up.

"I don't want to fight you," I said. "Nobody's going to get helped, and one of us might get hurt. Now let's just go someplace and talk." I held him for a minute or two longer, then let him go.

"Okay," he grunted, pressing a hand cautiously against his belly. "There's an office back behind the bar, but I share it with the motel manager. Let me get a busboy to take over the bar and we'll go outside."

He went behind the bar to telephone. I felt the presence of people behind me and turned. The four morticians from the corner table were standing there like a choir of fates. I smiled.

"Political disagreement," I said politely. "Sorry, fellas. No business today." They nodded and walked away.

A gangly kid in a busboy's uniform showed up from the office behind the bar. "Just cover the bar till I get back, Danny." Cowper said. "Lunch rush is over and there sure as hell isn't anybody in the motel today. Don't take any shit. I'll be back as soon as I can." Cowper turned to me. "Okay, Riordan, let's go."

We walked downstairs to the parking lot and stood

eneath a covered portico at the entrance to the motel, watching the rain hit the empty streets.

"Tell me again what kind of trouble Susan's in."

"It's a long story," I replied. "You sure you want to now?" He nodded. I told him about the fire and the money and a little about Henry Cruz. "I'm still not sure ow it fits together, but if she was involved, this guy will eed one of two things. He either gets his money back or he people who took it from him are history. He'd have her killed without any second thoughts at all."

Cowper shook his head. "Money. With Susan it was lways the money. When we got married everything looked ike it would go. I got picked in the third round by St. Louis; I was a little small to play linebacker in the pros but was fast and they tried me at strong safety. It was vorking out until the third exhibition game. I blew out my knee making a tackle. The team paid for my cut job and he signing bonus plus a year's salary. I tried to come back he next year but the knee was too screwed up. We came ack to Aberdeen together, but I wasn't much good at anything else. The football money lasted another year. When the money was gone, so was Susan." His voice was bitter with the memory of what he saw as his failure.

"What about your kid? He looks like a good one."

"He's great. Susan pays for Ally to take care of him. I vant him with me, but not until I know I won't drink nymore. I thought I was clean but I fell off last week."

"I'm sorry," I said. I couldn't think of anything better o say.

"Yeah," he said. "Me, too. I feel kind of dumb telling ou this stuff. It's kind of like meeting a stranger on a park ench and talking about God, you know?"

"I know. You know where she is, don't you, Steve?"

"Yeah," he said. "I do. She's at the Neah Cove Inn. 'll take you to her. But I hope to hell that what you're aying is true. I don't want to let her down again." He hrugged, a man learning to deal with life in his own slow, painful way. "Come on. Let's take your car."

We drove back up the coast road. The Neah Cove Inn vas on the beach between Copalis and Iron Springs, not more than ten miles from the home of Ally Wheatley in Pacific Beach. The inn had been built sometime before World War II of split and peeled cedar logs, weathered silver by time. There was a main lodge with a dining room and a string of cabins spread out along the beach. There were no lights and no cars. A small Closed for Season sign had been stuck in the front door to the lodge.

I turned to Steve Cowper. "If you've got notions about jumping me, do it now," I said tightly, "because this sort of wild-goose chase just purely pisses me off."

"Relax, Riordan, okay?" he said. "The place belongs to my cousin and I live here rent-free during the winter to keep an eye on the place. This is where Susan is, or ought to be. Look." He pointed to a thin wisp of smoke coming from the third cabin in the row, only dimly visible in the gathering afternoon dusk. "She's here."

"Okay. I think you should bring her outside to talk. I'm trusting you on this one, because she's got to listen."

"I'll do what I can. But I'm on her side, man, not yours. Keep that in mind."

"I will."

He got out of the car and walked over to cabin number three. I waited a minute, then followed him and stood outside the cabin. The western sky was darkening again, another rain squall poised to come ashore. I listened to the gulls and watched the rollers hit the beach, marveling for the hundredth time since childhood at how the peak of each wave seemed to pause for a brief moment before toppling over and surging against the beach.

I heard the sound of a door opening and turned to see Susan Haight standing beside me on the beach. Her blond hair was pulled straight back and banded into a ponytail. Her face was scrubbed free of makeup. She wore faded blue jeans and a windbreaker over a heavy oiled-wool sweater.

"Mr. Riordan," she said bitterly. "I see you've persuaded my ex-husband that he knows what's best for me. No matter. I think you would have found me eventually."

"If I hadn't, Susan, someone else would have."

"Why?"

"You know why. That's what you're going to tell me. ome on, let's take a walk up the beach."

We walked in silence for a moment. Steve Cowper llowed along, fifty yards behind, close enough for help, r enough back so he didn't have to hear anything he dn't want to hear.

"Let's start where we left off before, okay?" I said. Somehow this all goes back to the money. The two- ndred-fifty thousand in the safe that Hugh found after e fire. Whose money was it, Susan?"

"We told you. It was ours, Greg's and mine."

"Let's stop kidding ourselves with that story, okay? ere's a man named Henry Cruz who says the money is s. He thinks you and Greg and maybe Hugh were steal- g that money and maybe more. Cruz is the sort of ganized criminal who has a lot of money. But he has wer to match his money and he takes this kind of thing rsonally."

"We weren't stealing his money."

"No? Then why was a quarter million in cash—that uz can probably identify down to the serial numbers— t into Hugh's safe?"

"How do you know that? Are you working for Cruz?"

"No. As far as I'm concerned I'm still working for ugh Prokop's sister and daughter. But Cruz figures that clear Hugh's name and get the insurance proceeds for s daughter, I have to find out where that money came om. And he's right. He told me as much as he has cause he thinks I'll have to do the work eventually, and is way he can stay out of it."

"It sounds like you've got all the information you need. hy come after me?"

I grabbed Susan's arm as hard as I could and swung her ound. "Goddamn it," I shouted, "is that how you want play this? You want the SEC and the King County osecutor and Justice sitting at the table telling you just w much prison time you're going to pull on fraud and nspiracy charges? Fine, you've got it. But you walk on e street after you've been hauled in to talk to the feds d you are one dead woman. I am your only way out of

this, lady. The only way. Now you talk to me or I leav
you to the wolves.''

I let go of her arm abruptly and she stumbled backwar
catching the heel of her rubber shoe and sitting dow
heavily on the wet sand. She tucked her legs underneat
her knees and sat Indian-style, holding her ankles an
rocking back and forth.

"The money wasn't ours," she said in a low voice. "
belonged to an investor. I never found out who. Not unt
now, anyway.''

"What was it doing in Hugh Prokop's safe?''

"The investor—Cruz, you called him—didn't want t
to report the cash investment to the government. We ha
to set up small accounts, but we couldn't hold the cash i
our office because we might get audited. We needed t
find a neutral place to hold the money until we could s
up additional accounts that would show balances of und
ten thousand dollars.''

"I suppose this wasn't the first time you'd laundere
money. Did you always park it in Hugh's safe?''

She nodded. "We'd done it before. Walter Kessler or
always handled the movement of the money, since he ha
a key to Hugh's business office and the combination to th
safe. Kessler was still Hugh's accountant.''

"And Hugh never knew anything?''

"Not until the fire. Sometimes Kessler and Greg and
worked all night to break up the cash into separate ac
counts. We always wanted to be out by morning.'' Sh
paused. "When Hugh found the money, he guessed it ha
to be from Greg. He told me. I begged him not to sa
anything.''

"You got your wish, Susan," I said bitterly. "Hug
never told anybody. Not even me, not even to save himself.

I walked along the beach in silence. Somehow the know
edge that Hugh Prokop had been innocent of this stupi
money laundering scheme did not help. I should have bee
able to protect him.

"All right," I said angrily, turning back to confro
Susan as she got up from the sand. "You were runnin
dirty money. Kessler was the bag man, taking his cut an

eeping his mouth shut. That doesn't tell me who killed im. Or why. Who killed him, Susan?"

"I don't know," she said quietly. "Perhaps Hugh and Walter got into a fight over what we were doing. Or maybe Kessler found out about Hugh and his wife."

"That was *nothing*," I said. "Less than nothing. So ugh got drunk and fell into bed with her. So what. It urts you. I understand that. But it wasn't anything either f them really cared about. I don't believe Kessler would ave gotten into a fistfight with Hugh, or that Hugh would ave killed him. What about Van Zandt? Or you?"

"That's ridiculous," she said scornfully.

"What's ridiculous about it? That was money you couldn't dmit to having and couldn't afford to replace. You had ccess to the warehouse, motive, opportunity. And no ibi. Once the police understand why the money was in ugh's safe, it is going to start looking very plausible to em."

"*No!* We had nothing to do with it. I don't know why essler was killed."

"I think you're lying. No matter. Tell me about Van andt. How does he work the steal? Is it a straight-ahead onzi scheme?"

"There isn't any steal," she shouted, flaring up with ager. "Greg is a brilliant trader. In foreign currencies. I ld you that."

I shook my head in frustration. "Come on, Susan, face ality. You've already confirmed that Van Zandt is laun-ering money through the brokerage accounts. That's enough shut the business down, right there. When the auditors back through the accounts they're going to be checking determine the adequacy of the funds and securities in e accounts. The money just isn't going to be there, is it? an Zandt's operation has all the classic signs, Susan. The fferent interest payments to different customers, the scram-ling over the year-end audits, the shift from a big ac-ounting firm to a smaller one that needed the business to ep going. It's coming apart at the seams, Susan. All it is ing to take now is time."

"You don't know that," she said, desperation in he
voice. "It just isn't true."

"Then why did you run?"

"I don't know," she said miserably. "I don't know
You came around making accusations, and then when
asked Greg . . ." she hesitated.

"He didn't satisfy you, did he? That scared you whe
he couldn't explain. What's Van Zandt doing now? Is h
getting ready to pull out?"

"I don't think so," she said slowly. "I don't know.
didn't tell him why I was leaving. I just took off."

We had reached a headland perhaps half a mile dow
the beach that blocked our progress, the rising tide swirl
ing over the rocks at its base. We turned and began t
walk back to the old resort. Steve Cowper stood up th
beach, waiting. I felt old, tired, spent. I finally had som
solid proof against Van Zandt, could finally show that
was his dirty money, not Prokop's. But I was bothered b
what Susan had said about Hugh Prokop. He had betraye
her in one way, but he had protected her in another, fa
more important way. She seemed not to recognize that
Her words had been precise and cautious and ultimatel
cold. No remorse, no anguish for his suicide. Any sympa
thy she had she was keeping for herself.

"Why was Van Zandt so eager to take dirty money?"
finally asked. "He's tough and smart and gifted. He coul
have made it legitimately. What's he after?"

"The money is the same color, Riordan. It buys what h
needs, what I need. The money is there. We didn't as
where it came from. I never asked where it went. I don'
expect you to understand that."

"I do. Some, anyway."

"No, you don't," she said with sudden bitterness, turn
ing to face me. Her eyes flashed with anger that I coul
see in the fading light. "You don't know what it's like t
be divorced and broke with a kid to support, coming bac
to your home country and seeing it cut over and empty, th
mills shut down, the town you grew up in rotting away
The only work you can find is sitting in an office doing th
typing, watching the bosses take their long lunches whil

you keep the business running for a dollar an hour over the minimum wage. To get ahead you work the cocktail shift from six until two every night in a crummy uniform that's cut down to your navel and up to your ass, having the same old men feel you up while you put their drinks down on the table, feeling their hands slide up your legs, touching you. And keeping your mouth shut about it, because if you complain they'll fire you." Her voice began to break but she kept talking. "Keeping your mouth shut because you hope they'll leave a lousy extra buck on the table when they've gone." She stopped talking and breathed heavily. Her mouth worked but her eyes held mine defiantly.

"I'm not judging you, Susan," I said. "I don't know how. I can't say that what you've told me would have saved Hugh from the murder charge. Or from himself. I know something about how hard it is to remake yourself into the person that you need or want to be. But you're all out of choices now. The man whose money was in that safe is for real. You can come with me now, go into the U.S. Attorney's Office and make your statement. If you're telling the truth you will get immunity from prosecution and they will protect you. If you don't, it will be too late."

"All right," she said, finally, lowering her eyes to the sand. She seemed less persuaded than defeated. "I'll come with you. I'll do what you say. Come on. I've got to get my clothes."

I walked with her back to the cabin she had been staying in. Her ex-husband, Cowper, followed and watched, but even he seemed to relax. I waited, standing in the cabin door, watching while she packed. The cabin was a simple one-room tourist cabin; a bed, an old, sagging green sofa, a table with two mismatched chairs. A small driftwood fire burned lazily in a beach-rock fireplace. When Susan was done packing she poked at the fire until it was reduced to smoldering chunks of coal and ash.

When the fire was banked, Susan turned around and picked up her suitcase, then put it back on the bed. "Riordan," she said, "would you mind if I said good-bye to Steve? Alone? He's done a lot for me that he didn't have to."

"I understand. I'll go get him, then wait outside. Come out when you're ready."

"Thanks."

I left and got Steve and walked down to the beach, mesmerized as always by the sea, the light mist and the calm, steady pounding of the surf. I was still waiting and watching the sea when the blow on my head burst into my consciousness like a blinding white light that faded to red, and then to black.

CHAPTER 26

A rain as cold and bitter as a painful memory woke me up an hour later. I spat sand back on the beach and got to my knees, then was felled again by the relentless retching nausea that often follows a blow to the head. I was drenched to the skin and shaking with cold. When the retching subsided I managed to get up and stumble to my car, an endless tenth of a mile away from the cabin Susan Haight had used. I got there breathing hard, my stomach jumping around and threatening to make a run for it. I found my keys, fumbling with them in the darkness, and got the trunk open. Inside the trunk there was an overnight bag with clean, dry clothes, a half pint of brandy, and the hope of salvation.

I took the bag and walked back to Susan's cabin. She had locked it on the way out, but the lock was flimsy and I kicked the door open with no trouble at all. I rekindled the fire and stripped out of my clothes, toweling myself dry. The driftwood fire burned high with lots of flame, but the wood was so bleached out from its time in the ocean that it gave off little heat. I huddled as close to the fire as I could, my pale skin raised into goose bumps in the light of the flame.

When the shaking in my arms and legs had stopped and the room had warmed from the fire, I put on clean jeans and a great old wool sweater that was surplus from the

British Navy. I heated water on the two-burner hotplate in the kitchen nook of the cabin and made instant coffee, double-strength and cut with brandy. Then I sat down on the cabin bed to think.

I was nearly certain that at least some of what Susan Haight had told me was true. I believed her when she said that Hugh Prokop had known nothing about the money being stored in his safe. They would have gained nothing by telling him. He was an added risk they could not afford. But Susan knew more than she was telling about the money laundering and possibly the Ponzi scheme. The trick to professional money laundering is to move the stuff in volume, into the accounts, out through wire transfers to those funny little chartered banks in the Cayman Islands or Antigua. To work in volume you need lots of runners and accounts and activity. Van Zandt & Company just didn't show that kind of activity. Aside from Van Zandt and Haight, they had only about a half-dozen retail brokers and a support staff of about twenty. That suggested that money was coming in but not flowing out, that they were keeping any dirty money in their own investment accounts. There was only one thing that could justify that sort of risk: Van Zandt was running a Ponzi scheme, and needed that cash to pay the returns on his early investors and keep new investors coming in the door.

Finally, no matter what Susan said, I did not believe that Hugh Prokop killed Walter Kessler. Without the money, Hugh had no motive. There was the chance that the death was accidental, that Kessler had died setting the fire himself or had been caught when Hugh lit the blaze. I didn't believe that either. The medical examiner's suspicion that Kessler had been hit on the head and knocked unconscious might not hold up as courtroom proof, but I believed it. And Hugh, if he had wanted to burn the warehouse, wouldn't have done it himself. He would have had Minh do it. Ironically, the fact that Hugh had contacted Minh could now be used to prove his innocence.

Henry Cruz was a possible but unlikely candidate. There was almost no way he could have guessed that his money was being diverted at the time of the fire. He did not take

he risk to actually deliver the cash himself; he hired it
done. The people he had used would know their business.
At the slightest sign of a problem they would have picked
up the money and walked away—and that had not happened. The money had made it into the safe.

Liz Kleinfeldt must have been half-right. Kessler—
unhappy, broke, scared at being involved in a fraud that
could only end in a collapse, ready to leave his wife and
maybe head south to grow old peacefully in the sunshine—
decides to steal the biggest chunk of ready cash he knows
of. Hot cash that nobody can afford to call the cops on.
The money was not Hugh Prokop's; it was Van Zandt's.
Van Zandt could not report that theft, nor could he let it
happen. Somehow Van Zandt finds out about Kessler,
goes to the Prokop Marine Supply building, and hits Kessler.
He starts a fire to kill him and to cover his tracks. And
then realizes that he can't get the money back because he
is the only one who doesn't know the combination to the
safe.

It had to be right.

I finished my coffee and touched the back of my head.
There was a sticky, swelling lump where Steve Cowper
had clobbered me, but it wasn't bleeding much; he must
have used something soft, like a sock full of sand. Despite
the lack of a cut it was a pretty good blow. I wanted tea
and toast and to take to my own bed for several days, like
a faded Southern lady of nervous disposition. There wasn't
time for that. I would not find Susan again. Without her
testimony, I couldn't rely on the police to build a case
against Van Zandt. The last chance I had to prove Van
Zandt was guilty was to take a quick straight-ahead shot
and try to force him into giving something away.

I gathered up my wet clothes and doused the fire and
left. The night was very dark and I drove carefully on the
winding coastal road, not trusting my head or my eyes.
Just past Ocean City there was a gas station beside the
road. The station was closed but there was a lighted phone
booth beside the garage.

I stopped and went into the booth, pulling the door shut
behind me. I kept an eye on the highway as I rang up the

local operator and had her punch up Van Zandt's home telephone number. After a while his phone began ringing. I hoped like hell that Susan Haight hadn't gotten to him first.

When he answered he sounded tired and a bit woozy, as though he had dozed off while having a couple drinks in front of the television.

"Who is it?" he growled.

"It's Riordan, Greg. You and I need to talk."

"You're goddamn right we need to talk, Riordan. What the hell have you been trying to do to me? Suddenly I've got the SEC wanting to camp out in my offices, and my accountants and lawyers are running around making nervous noises about my books and looking as if they've just peed in their pants. And when I ask them what's wrong they all say something about you. I don't get it."

I laughed. "You will, babe, you will. I've been having a little talk with Susan Haight. Like a lot of people she wants to know where the money has been going, Greg. She's kind of worried about that. We had a nice, long talk."

"Where is Susan?" he asked, suddenly cautious. "I haven't seen her for two days."

"Just taking some overdue time off to think about things. And talk to people."

"Okay, Riordan," he said tiredly, "why don't you just cut the crap and tell me what you really want."

"I want you to be at the University of Washington Arboretum tomorrow morning," I said. "Say about five hundred yards north and east of the Japanese garden. There's a parking lot on the east side of Lake Washington Boulevard. I'll be up the hill from there. Come by yourself, at ten o'clock."

"I can't. I've got a meeting with my lawyers."

"Tough. Cancel it. You've got one chance to stay out of jail and keep the con going, Van Zandt. That's to see me tomorrow. Bring a present for me. Make it a nice one, because we're going to be talking about money. Don't think about getting cute. If you try anything the deal is off, and I'll be forced to go to the SEC with all my information."

There was silence. I heard only the clicks and chatter of county telephone line. Finally Van Zandt said, "I'll be here. At ten." He hung up.

If I had felt better I might have celebrated. As it was I ad twelve hours and much to do. I got going.

CHAPTER 27

The morning was bright with the cruel promise of false spring. In the night the last of the rain squalls had blown through to the east, and a warm onshore wind had drifted up from the south. The warm wind brought people out of their houses and cars and into the hilly, narrow streets of North Capitol Hill. Office workers left their musty raincoats at home and walked to their bus stops with their sleeves rolled up, suit jackets slung over one shoulder. The newspapers and books stayed folded under their arms as they sniffed happily at the warm new smells of sun and earth.

At a little after eight-thirty I parked on a side street off Interlaken Boulevard and began to walk through the densely treed neighborhood streets toward the University Arboretum. Unlike the office commuters I was wearing denim jeans made soft by a hundred washings, a blue work shirt, work boots, and a short jacket. At first glance, I probably looked like a gardener on my way to work in the affluent neighborhood of homes built in the 1920s and 1930s. A second look would reveal that the boots and jeans were too clean, the work shirt pressed with starch, and the neighbors would take me for a University instructor of sixties vintage and modest means who rented a spare room in one of the large old homes.

The walk was hilly and the morning was too warm for

the jacket. A trickle of sweat leaked down the center of my chest, soaking the wide band of cloth tape wrapped around my ribs. The wet tape had begun to chafe but I kept the jacket on anyway. It concealed the .32 automatic cradled in a woven leather shoulder holster. The tape held a remote microphone that fed the miniature wire recorder snuggled into the small of my back. I'd borrowed the equipment from Jerry McNair, a PI who specialized in electronic surveillance work. McNair had fitted me early that morning. He said that the equipment had never failed to work. I hoped it wouldn't fail this time.

The University Arboretum lies in a cleft between the northeast slope of Capitol Hill and the Broadmoor Golf Course. The Arboretum is a hilly garden, planted with trees and shrubs from a hundred countries. Nearly everything will grow on its sunny west slope, fed by the rich soil and the freshwater springs that bubble out of the hillside even in the driest summer.

It was still early spring. Some of the leaf trees had started to bud, but most were still winter-bare, naked against the soft blue-gray sky. There was plenty of ground cover, perennial bushes and head-high evergreens, so I tramped the paths that wound through the Arboretum grounds, trying to look like a casual hiker as I searched for anyone who might be setting up a position on me. The rolling woods were empty, though, as if the day was too fine even for the freaks and would-be rapists who sometimes hung out there.

When I was sure the area was clean I went to the designated meeting place, an open meadow beside a decorative pond about a third of a mile north of the Japanese garden.

I had chosen the spot from memory, but it looked like it would work. The meadow was about three hundred yards east of Lake Washington Boulevard, close enough to run for help but far enough to make it difficult for anyone in a passing car to see much. The meadow was on a slight rise, giving a view of the road and a nearby parking lot. The hill rose steeply behind the meadow. Part way up the hill a group of young sequoias had been planted. They were perhaps forty years old and already a hundred feet high. They formed a still, quiet gallery, like a small church. I walked up the hill to them, sometimes slipping on the dew-soaked grass. I sat down on the nearly dry ground beneath the trees and waited.

Van Zandt arrived at quarter after ten, about the fifteen minutes late that I had expected. He had left his Jaguar at home, stepping out of a plain brown sedan that he'd apparently rented. He casually slammed the car door shut and began to walk east from the parking lot, looking ahead expectantly but not looking back. He had come alone or was a damned good actor. I began to worry. The plain car and the decision to face me alone were both much smarter than I expected.

I moved out of the small copse of sequoias and walked toward Van Zandt to the open meadow. When I was there I stopped and waited for him.

I could see him clearly as he approached. He was dressed for business, in a blue vested suit and tan trench coat, wearing heavy black brogues that trampled the new grass of the park. His face looked drawn and weary, his skin sallow, dark smudges under his hard blue eyes. Despite his apparent exhaustion he walked easily and stood lightly, poised on the balls of his feet, his big hands and arms held loosely at his sides. Wherever he had come from, Van Zandt knew something about how to go into a confrontation. I began to worry a little more.

He stopped about ten feet in front of me and spoke first. "Riordan, what is this horseshit all about?" He asked tiredly. "Trading the currency markets every day is enough of a bitch. Now you come along with some crazy story and all of a sudden I've got my own damned lawyers and accountants crawling all over me, wanting to stick their noses into every fucking transaction I do."

"My heart bleeds, Greg," I said sarcastically. "I've found out a lot about you, things that ought to be worth plenty. If we don't do some business today you'll have a lot more trouble. Suppose we start out by me telling you about money laundering. Or the Ponzi racket you're running on your investors."

"I don't know what you're talking about," he said flatly.

"Sure you do, man. You're taking in washing for a rich criminal by the name of Henry Cruz. You know the money's dirty, even if you don't know who it's coming from. Otherwise you never would have broken it into little ten-thousand-dollar chunks."

He shrugged irritably. "I have an investor who wants to split his holdings into a bunch of accounts. I don't even know his name. So what." His face was scornful. "If we get caught we plead *nolo contendere* and maybe get hit with a fine, just like that big bank in Boston. If that's what you dragged me down here to tell me, you are wasting my time." He started to turn away.

"How long's the Ponzi scheme been running, Greg?" I called out after him. "Since you got wiped out in the dollar crash last December? Your much-vaunted genius go fishing the day that the finance ministers met? Or are you like the educated illiterates running Wall Street that don't know anything about politics or history, that can't read anything besides the columns in the stock and bond tables?"

He turned back and looked at me bleakly. "I don't have to listen to insults."

"Sure you do." I took a few steps closer to him. The microphone's range was supposed to be fifteen feet, but I didn't want to take any chances. "Since you don't want to answer any questions, Greg, why don't I just lay it out for you? You can nod or grunt or something when I get warm." He stayed where he was, standing in front of me, his feet rooted to the ground. "Let's start with last December," I said. "You took a bath in the foreign currency markets. When the finance ministers met the dollar went into free-fall. Everybody who failed to hedge got murdered. You weren't the only one. How much did the funds you manage lose? Five, maybe ten million? The papers say Couvert & Johnson lost over a hundred million. Anyway, you'd lost a big chunk of the capital in the funds. You had to cover. Fast.

"One of the first things you did is start to diddle the books. The Van Zandt funds began exchanging cash for assets they've never had much interest in, like Class B preferred stock in your own brokerage firm. The stock is really worth about a dollar ninety-eight but for accounting purposes you can temporarily assign it whatever value you want. It's an old trick, but it accounts for at least part of the trading losses, and it buys you some time.

"Next you had to raise enough new cash to keep going. That's how the Ponzi game really got going, wasn't it? You had to pay dividends in order to keep enough money flowing in so you could step back into the markets and try to make up your losses, like an old gambler going back one more time, needing a strike so bad his hands shake as he looks at the craps table.

"I've got to hand it to you, Greg. All through the holidays you were on the edge of the abyss and you stayed as calm as glacial ice, giving parties, making sales, bringing in new investors. That took real stones. God knows where you got them."

I stopped and looked at him. His face was blank, politely attentive but uninterested in what I was saying, as if we were two strangers who had met in the park and had stopped to talk about life or women or the ontological proof of the existence of God.

Finally he spoke. "How much of this," he said grimly, "did you get out of Susan?"

"Enough," I lied. "And don't start thinking that you're going to get back to her. She is in a nice, quiet place, waiting for me." It was a straight lie and a gamble. If Susan had talked to him since I had called him the night before he would laugh in my face and walk away. I waited and hoped.

"What do you want from me?" he asked. "You mentioned money. How much?"

"We'll get to that. First I want to know about the money laundering. You ran it through Hugh Prokop's safe, didn't you? You parked it there, off your own books, until it could be broken up into nice small lots and passed through the accounts. It would have been easy. Kessler still had the combination to Hugh's safe and access to the building since he was Prokop's accountant. Susan had a key, too, so either of you could go in there anytime you wanted."

He shrugged irritably. "So what. Prokop's dead and it's not going to matter to him."

"But it matters to me. I sat there at his trial with his life in my hands and I watched as he spiraled down to suicide, all because of that damned money he couldn't explain. That's going to cost you."

"That's not my fault. Just because he—"

I cut him off and went on. "Kessler was the bag man, moving the money back and forth. Sometime in late January or early February you got another installment of hot cash, a quarter-million dollars. Kessler put it in Prokop's safe. All business as usual. But Kessler's a man with problems. He's broke. His wife doesn't love him; she's messing around with half the guys in the neighborhood, including Prokop, probably including you. He's got visions of the Ponzi racket crashing down and being laid on him. That's bad. Months of trial, maybe years in prison. Kessler starts thinking that maybe he would like to grow old peacefully, down in the sunshine. He's got access to a quarter-million, in the kind of cash nobody can ever admit was stolen. So Kessler heads out to Prokop's warehouse and is going to lift the money when you find out about it. I'd bet Sandra Kessler told you about it, maybe directly, maybe she just said that Walter had gone out to Prokop's place. You trail him there and find him just as he's about to open the safe. You're not a man that likes being crossed, Greg. You bounce him around a little. Maybe you meant to kill him and maybe you didn't. The medical examiner thought he took a shot to the head that might have knocked him out. No matter. And there you are, with Kessler on the floor and the money in the safe, only you can't get to the money because you don't know the combination." I laughed. "That was pretty poor planning, don't you think? The best you can think of is to punch holes in a couple of tins of paint thinner and light a fire.

"Then you got lucky. The police and the arson squad finger Prokop for the fire. He owns the business, he needs money, and a fire would give him a lot of it. Things kept breaking your way when Prokop's alibi turned out to be weak. Prokop guessed the money in the safe was from you, but he bought the cover story you cooked up because he wanted to protect Susan. And once he did, he was stuck. Any other explanation about the source of the money was going to make it look more like Prokop had caught Kessler stealing from him, and killed him. He might have been okay if he had told the truth, but that would have put Susan in jail.

"Then the trial started and things looked better for Hugh. His alibi looked a lot stronger after the fire investigator let the videotapes be erased. You decided to help the prosecution out. You went out with Sandra Kessler. When she got drunk and came over to my office to demand money, you were just helpful as hell. And on the ride back to her place you persuaded her to testify. Did you give her money, or just help her figure out that if she sank Prokop in court she could collect a bunch of money from his estate in a later civil suit?"

Van Zandt smiled, an odd, bright smile, as bright as his harsh blue eyes. His hand came out of his trench coat pocket holding what I had expected, a little flat automatic so small it seemed to be swallowed up in his large fist. "I don't really think you can prove any of that," he said, still smiling, "but on the other hand, why take a chance?"

I smiled back at him. "I hope you don't think that gun is anything more than a bargaining chip, Greg. There are people who know why I'm here and who I'm meeting. Let's talk price. I figure you've got maybe two or three weeks left to run on the Ponzi game. If you get out now you probably could head south with three or four million. I think half that ought to be mine."

"No. Way too much. Suppose we say five hundred thousand, cash. That'd be the biggest money you've ever seen, Riordan. It's enough for a small time guy like you."

"A million," I said, and again stepped closer to him, wanting to be sure it got on tape. The more we haggled over the bribe, the more the words he had already said would take on a shape and color that no jury could mistake.

He shook his head. "It's not worth it. I'd rather just

walk you back into the woods and give you one round hole behind the ear. I had the same sort of choice with Kessler, you know. I popped him a couple of times and he just begged me to let him go. He was still begging when I killed him. Funny. It didn't bother me at all.'' His tone was conversational, his eyes the same blue, and with a sudden cold sweat I began to realize that he would have no last-minute indecision. I could see why he was the perfect trader in the perfect marketplace. He had no morals at all.

He began to gesture with the barrel of the small gun, pointing up the long, sloping footpath that wound into the heavier woods at the north end of the Arboretum. He had thought this out. He would kill me there or walk me a mile north, out along the waterside trail into the Union Bay marshes and shoot me down below the Highway 520 overpass, where the heavy traffic noise would drown out the explosion of the shot.

I was about to speak when I saw that two more cars had arrived, one parking in the lot near the garden, the other pulling up on the road and bouncing over the curb to stop on the flat grassy stretch at the base of the wide meadow. Three men got out of the cars and moved toward us at an easy loping pace that was deceptively fast. Two of the men were big and heavily muscled. The third was tall and slender, wearing his customary suit of funeral black. The third man was Henry Cruz.

Van Zandt saw them, too. His face took on a momentary look of confusion. He swung one way then the other, finally dodging behind me, hoping to use me as a shield. "Who are they?" he demanded, his voice suddenly high and breaking. "Did you call them? Who the hell are they?"

I laughed. "I think they're your customers, Greg. At least one of them is. He's been upset, probably had a tail on you. It looks like we've got a little self-help consumer protection going on."

Cruz and his men arrived and circled us. His two gunmen carried silenced automatics. One stepped forward and took the gun from Van Zandt. I opened my jacket and showed the other the gun in my shoulder holster. He took my gun and patted me down quickly. He was in too much of a hurry. He missed the wire.

Cruz walked slowly around us, surveying Van Zandt briefly, almost without interest. Then he came to a stop in front of me. His black eyes were swarming with anger. He slapped me just once, his heavy silver ring catching the flesh at the corner of my mouth and tearing it, loosing a small trickle of blood. The slap took my head back but wasn't hard enough to knock me down. I simply looked at Cruz as I dabbed at the blood with the sleeve of my jacket.

"You were supposed to tell me when my hypothesis had been confirmed," Cruz said tightly. "Not cut some deal of your own with this man."

I looked straight back at him. "I played along with you because I wanted Van Zandt for the arson fire and the murder of an accountant named Kessler. He's confessed to that. I'm satisfied. I don't give a good goddamn what you want."

"What about my money?"

"You and your damned money," I said nastily. "Your money is the driving force in your universe. Without it you're nothing but the small-time hood you've always been. Van Zandt has stolen your money, Cruz. Maybe he took your manhood with it. You're acting as if he had. Either way it is not my problem."

Cruz's face was set in hard dark lines, like obsidian. I thought he was going to haul off and hit me again, but he didn't. He stopped and thought, controlling his anger, considering his next move like a chess master. I decided to feed his sense of control.

"You've lost," I said calmly. "Treat it like any other investment. If you try to get your money out of Van Zandt now, you'll be caught up in this mess. He's been running a Ponzi racket, stealing from everybody, not just you. Within a day or two there will be IRS and SEC lawyers and accountants going over his books, trying to figure out what happened and how to distribute the amounts that are left. You show your face and you'll get swept up for tax evasion or worse. Give it up."

Cruz shook his head. "No. If there's no money, I'll

take him. No one steals from me." He started to turn away from me, preparing to take Van Zandt with him.

I grabbed him by the lapels of his coat and jerked him back to me. I held his face up close to mine. "Not this time," I hissed. "He goes with me. To the police. To court. You are not God and you don't have the right to declare life or death." I let him go and he stumbled back, the heels of his heavy dress shoes catching in the long grass. "We do it the right way, or everything you've said stays on this tape and goes straight to the U.S. Attorney." I jerked up my shirt and showed Cruz the wide band of surgical tape holding the remote wire microphone to my chest.

Cruz stared at the microphone for a stunned second. Then he shrugged. "You fool," he said calmly. He turned to one of the men holding Van Zandt. "Kill them. Kill both of them."

The gunman stepped away from Van Zandt and turned toward me. There was no emotion in his glance, only interest. As he turned I raised my left arm into the air.

The harsh flat *crack* of a high-powered rifle broke from the woods at the top of the slope. The gunman took the round in the hip, and it spun him around like a doll and knocked him to the ground. The second gunman turned, facing up the slope to return fire, when a second echoing shot dropped him flat on the wet grass. I picked up one of the silenced automatics that lay on the ground. I walked over to Henry Cruz. He was lying face down on the ground. I reached down and dragged him up into a kneeling position. I was so pumped up on adrenaline it seemed as though I were lifting a small child. I pressed the muzzle of the silencer into the hollow behind his right ear.

"You have no idea," I said breathing heavily, "how much pleasure it would give me to kill you here. Your goddamn money has cost a dozen lives that I know of. But there's been enough killing and I won't add to it. There will be no reprisals over this. If you attempt any action, the tape will go to the county prosecutor. Or I will try to kill you myself. If you leave, now, and forget this, your part will be left alone. Do we understand each other?"

He didn't answer. He began to stand up and I let him. When he was standing, with the leaves and twigs brushed from his suit, he answered. "Yes," was all he said.

I turned and looked up the hill. David Swenson, the angular fire investigator, was walking down carefully, his rifle poised in front of him, ready to shoot. When he got down the hill I took the rifle and stood aside and waited as he collected all the guns from Cruz's men. He brought them over to me and dumped them on the ground.

"You," I said when he was done, "are possibly the best shot I know. What was that, two hundred yards?"

"About that," he said with quiet satisfaction. "I didn't plan to be so far away, but I couldn't get good cover any closer." He looked at Van Zandt and Cruz, standing silently in the meadow. "How do we sort out the sheep from the goats?"

"The thin man and his hired help weren't involved in the fire. They wanted Van Zandt's head for another deal. It's not really related. I just used it to put pressure on Van Zandt. If Van Zandt could give enough testimony to hang something on them we could keep them. But he can't. I think we let them walk."

"Okay," Swenson said, shrugging. "What I want is Van Zandt. I don't really care about anything else."

I turned back to Cruz. He was waiting quietly. His unharmed man was tending to the one who'd been hit. Swenson's shot must have shattered his pelvis. He writhed on the ground, moaning.

"Get out of here," I said. "No reprisals." Cruz said nothing. He helped pick up the wounded man and carry him back to his car. Within minutes they were gone.

I caught Swenson looking at me a little strangely. "I appreciate your trusting me on that," I said, "after what we've been through. As much or more than your deciding to attend this little party. I wasn't sure you'd come."

He shrugged. "I've told you before, all I want is the guy who did the fire. You made your theory sound plausible when we talked last night. I'm not going to apologize for targeting Prokop. He had means, motive, opportunity. Now it looks like I was wrong. I just wish I could tell him that.'' His voice sounded dry and tight. "Look," he added, "how do you want to play this from here?"

"I think you should apprehend our friend here, shortly after the struggle in which I took away his gun. You didn't know I had a wire and you didn't know I was trying to set him up. You decided to put a loose tail on me for my own protection after I went to you with my continuing doubts about the fire.''

"Sounds good. When do I get the tape?"

"Soon. I think we should get going. Why don't you call for backup? I'm going to walk back to my car as soon as the uniforms arrive.''

We walked Van Zandt up the hill to Arboretum Drive, where Swenson had parked, and sat him down on a bench beside the road. When Swenson went off to call in, I sat down and talked to Van Zandt.

"I know what you're thinking, Greg," I began quietly. "You're thinking that you've got some money left, enough to pay a battalion of good lawyers, and maybe you can fight this for a long time, stay out of jail on bail, maybe split and start over someplace else. It won't work. Let me suggest a nice, quick plea of guilty, maybe to voluntary manslaughter. If you try to fight this thing, Cruz is going to have you killed. My deal covers me and mine, not you. Cruz will be able to find you and he'll do it, no matter where you go. He's done it before. If you testify, it won't convict Cruz and it won't get rid of him. Oh, the cops will try to help you. They'll give you protection, isolation, a special cell in another county, anything you want. They'll give it to you but it won't work. You'll be in the shower or in the infirmary or maybe in your own cell, and a guard is going to walk away and a door is going to get left open. When that happens you're going to be meat. Give it some thought.''

CHAPTER 28

The Mexican sunshine on the beach halfway down the coast from Zihuatanejo was boundlessly innocent, pure grace in its being. The morning was hot for mid-spring, and the heat was liquid. I felt as though I could rub it on my skin and it would work through to my bones, burn out the cold that had settled in through the long winter. I was wrong. Warm as it was, the light still did not reach the heart.

The final disposition of the case had gone quickly and well, as legal matters go. Gregory Van Zandt, his true name Robert Lee Bowman, had pleaded guilty to a single count of second degree murder in the death of Walter Kessler. In the story he told, he had killed Kessler during a fight, following Kessler's attempt to steal the money being laundered by Van Zandt & Company. The fire had been set in a panic-stricken attempt to cover Kessler's death.

Van Zandt never did confess to killing Tran Loc Minh, the arsonist that Hugh had talked to before the fire. He denied that Susan or Hugh had told him anything about Minh. I couldn't decide in my own mind whether he had done it or not. He would have had a motive to do it—the fear that Minh might identify him as the man leaving the building—but there wasn't any evidence to connect him to the actual killing. And Minh was in a very high-risk business. Vince Ahlberg thought it over and finally decided to leave the Minh file open.

Van Zandt was careful to say nothing about Henry Cruz. As a result, he was still alive to be sentenced to thirty years in prison, eligible for parole in thirteen years.

Van Zandt's confession had at least a casual relationship with what I had thought to be truth, and for my purposes it was enough. Confronted with the confession, the insurers quickly settled for the face value of the insurance policies, an even two million dollars plus a few thousand in attorney's fees. When the settlement was reached Mary Alice Thierrault had called to insist that I send a bill. After some thought I finally did. The check she sent was for twice the amount of the bill. It came with a note suggesting that if I didn't cash it I would be even a bigger fool than she thought I was. Unable to take that risk, I took the money instead.

The destruction of Van Zandt & Company was a bit more complicated. After the Ponzi fraud was disclosed, the accountants swarmed over the books and records of the company like ants, attempting to cover their previous lack of prudence with mind-numbing calculations and the usual dreary excuses. As expected, they found most of the investors' funds had been squandered away on mistaken currency trades, heavy overhead expenses, and the neurotic, massive spending of Van Zandt and Susan Haight. When the trading patterns were analyzed the SEC's investigators concluded that Van Zandt had resorted to the Ponzi scheme at about the time I had guessed, early December. Although he had major losses from the fall of the dollar, he had always overstated his results to attract investors. The inexorable mathematics of the fraud had eaten away at his trading funds, like a snake swallowing its own tail. In the last few days before I caught up with him, Van Zandt had been turning major assets to cash, planning to run. I guessed that it was only his greed, the desire for a few more days to shake loose more cash, that had brought Van Zandt out to meet me in the Arboretum.

When the SEC and the bankruptcy trustee had finished going over the assets, it appeared that the investors would get back about ten cents on the dollar. Eventually they would get a little more, since many investors, including

Henry Cruz, never stepped forward to make a claim. Van Zandt had collected more hot money than I thought.

Within three days after the public announcement of the fraud, a class-action lawsuit was filed against Van Zandt's lawyers and accountants, trying to pick up a piece of the investors' losses while earning a fat fee for the plaintiffs' lawyers. When I returned from Mexico I would be called as a witness and have my deposition taken for three or four days in a windowless room, trying to listen to each droning question, jabbing myself in the palm with untwisted paper-clip wire in a desperate attempt to stay awake. There would be five or ten lawyers present, most of them junior associates from big law firms who would read newspapers all day and shout "Objection!" whenever their client's name was mentioned. It would be expensive but it would keep them busy and more or less out of trouble, and life would go on.

On the long drive through the night from L.A. down to Mexico I began to ponder the complexity of connections in what had happened. The American bankers in New York decided to drive down the value of the dollar and got the government's help. Tokyo bankers reacted and began to sell dollars to the Swiss, who panicked and dumped their dollars for whatever they could get. The market crashed. The losses drove a small Seattle trader to the wall, to the point where he took dirty money and hid it in a friend's safe. The money drove one man to theft. The second to murder. The third to suicide.

Cause and effect.

I have learned a few things from all this. Daily life is an endless cycle of cause and effect, events set in motion by forces we can sometimes understand but seldom control. To do nothing is to concede both defeat and humanity. To fight each and every shove is as foolish as trying to hold back the tides with your hands. The middle way is to find things you hold true—and fight like hell for them.

In that sense Hugh Prokop had been right. He had come to love Susan Haight enough that he had willingly gone along with a lie to protect her. He had betrayed her once, but could not bring himself to do it again, even when he

egan to realize how things would end. Whether what he
elt was truly love or a kind of guilty hysteria over his
ffair with Sandra Kessler I would not judge. Hugh be-
ieved it was true, and he acted on his truth.

Susan Haight never returned to Seattle. Her bank ac-
ounts and other assets were eventually seized by the
ankruptcy trustee for the investors' benefit. If she had
ept anything at all, it was no more than the few thousand
ollars she had run with. I never looked for her, and
ecame very forgetful whenever her name was mentioned.
would not throw away what Hugh had done.

My morning walk had taken me a long way down the
oast. I padded back up the beach, my feet bare in the fine
ot sand. In three days the calluses had formed and I no
onger needed shoes.

Liz Kleinfeldt lay on a blanket in a hollow in the sand
elow the small stone house we had rented near the village
of Puerto Escondero. Her slender body retained its grace
even as she lay on her stomach, her sunglasses and book
ushed to one side, dozing gently in the sun. I dropped to
my knees beside her.

Her eyes were closed but she was not asleep. "Did you
get everything straightened out?" she asked. "You've
been thinking about it for a long time."

"Not completely. I don't think I ever will."

"Life's like that. Full of loose edges, unhappy endings,
unfinished business. It's something you are going to have
to accept."

"I know." I began to run a single finger down the
hollow of her back.

She sighed. "If you don't stop that," she said with
mock threat, "I'm going to have to drag you back inside.
And it's not even noon."

"Why do you think I started it?" I replied.

About the Author

Fredrick Huebner is also the author of THE JOSHUA SEQUENCE and THE BLACK ROSE. An attorney, he lives in Seattle, Washington.